P.C. Schneirla

Flawless

BLUE WHITE & D FLAWLESS

Flawless: Blue White & D Flawless

For information about this title or to order other books and/or electronic media, contact the publisher:

Big Gem Publishing LLC
www.schneirla.com
info@biggempublishing.com

ISBNs:
979-8-9866711-2-3 (hardcover)
979-8-9866711-0-9 (softcover)
979-8-9866711-1-6 (eBook)

Printed in the United States of America

Flawless: Blue White & D Flawless is a work of fiction. The names, characters, places, and incidents portrayed in the story are the product of the author's imagination or have been used fictitiously. Any resemblance to actual persons, living or dead, businesses, companies, events, or locales is entirely coincidental.

For Caroline
When we met, my life began.
You are my light.

Contents

CONTENTS

Part One

CHAPTER I

Wednesday Morning

Tom Strawbridge held the door to the mantrap as he said goodbye to Mrs. Nelson Wingate. The irony of the term was never lost on Tom. Especially when there was a stunning woman trapped in the rectangular entryway. A mantrap is a small space having two separate sets of interlocking doors. They typically include a door leading from a public hallway into a vestibule that leads to another door. The second inside door leads to a secured area. One door must be closed and locked before the other will open. Effectively "trapping" a person in the vestibule.

They finished their goodbyes, and Tom closed the inner door of the mantrap, electronically releasing the lock on the outer door, grudgingly granting Mrs. Wingate her freedom into the hallway of his office building.

She had been a referral from another customer's wife, Shirley Taylor. Tom always took time to acknowledge his good fortune in having a business that literally developed and expanded on its own. And Mrs. Wingate's mission held promise for great profit and new clients. Her situation is known in the jewelry trade as *glik* in Yiddish. *Mazal* in Hebrew. Luck or good fortune.

It was what every dealer who traded secondhand or estate jewelry was always looking for. "Goods." A client with a quality and valuable item they were looking to sell. With big room for profit. These opportunities were once common before the trade had become so competitive, and the auction houses so prominent as the default sales channel for high-end gemstones and jewelry to both the general public and collectors. But before proceeding with either purchasing or getting offers for Mrs. Wingate's brooch, Tom was going to have to address an all-too-familiar prickly ethical aspect of his circumstance.

He walked down the hall of his office, past his assistant's area, the private viewing rooms and the main showroom, the Salon, and into his private office, where he received most of his clients. And, invariably, all his attractive female guests. Whatever the reason for their visit. Walking around his desk, he noticed Mrs. Wingate's fragrance still hung faintly in the air. Sitting down, north light streaming in through the window behind him, he looked down on the extraordinary brooch she had brought in for him to evaluate.

Ignoring the urge to pick the piece up and examine it again, he took out a pad and began some calculations. While estimating and figuring various options on his pad, he ran through the ethical issue in his mind. If there actually was one. He wondered, as he had since entering the jewelry business, if any of his colleagues in the trade ever thought about the ethical or moral issues everyone invariably encountered. He was sure that they did not. And also, quite sure that, for some, like Moti

Kliener, the rewards were greater than simply making money when you screwed someone in the process. The bigger the screwing, the better.

Tom could not prevent himself from thinking about the old lawyer joke whenever faced with a similar decision: Two lawyers are having a drink at lunch, and one announces to the other that he was facing an ethical dilemma. An old lady had misread or simply made a mistake and paid him $5000 on an invoice he had sent her for $500. The second says, "Oh, I see. You're trying to decide whether to tell the old lady about her error." And the first one replies, "Hell no! I'm trying to decide whether or not to tell my partner."

The issue was a simple one. But the options on how to proceed were numerous, and they were anything but simple. Mrs. Wingate had inherited the circa early-1940s Van Cleef & Arpels brooch from a great-aunt in Milwaukee more than twenty years ago. They had seen each other only a handful of times, but Marla Wingate found her aunt intriguing and approachable, unlike much of the rest of her family. She had held on to the brooch out of sentimentality. In changing banks and cleaning out a safe-deposit box, she decided to see what it was worth. Her daughter was out of the house, in college. She had received a very large settlement from her ex-husband and found herself downsizing drastically. The brooch did not suit her lifestyle and would not be missed. Simply put, Mrs. Wingate had no idea and did not care what the brooch was worth. She had complete trust in Tom, based on his stellar reputation. Tom knew any reasonable offer would be acceptable to her and allow her to "move on."

As Tom turned his attention back to the brooch, he was struck all over again by the quality, scale, and execution. The overall design was very French, very Van Cleef & Arpels, and very typical. It represented a large flower. Obviously, an ambitious attempt at a rose, with a long stem, three leaves, and one immense blossom. The signature "VC&A," "France," and the French precious-metal fineness hallmarks for 18-karat yellow gold and platinum on discreet plaques on the back of the piece tied the bow. Truly breathtaking, it was only the subject that was typical. He told himself again the brooch was unprecedented, which was saying something, given his expertise and experience. Of course, his reaction upon seeing the brooch in front of Mrs. Wingate had been flat and expressionless.

The stem, which set the tone for the whole piece, was a masterwork in its own right. Held in place by nearly invisible, gossamer-like platinum wire was a collection of spectacular large Old Mine Cut and Emerald Cut diamonds. Very effectively imitating the elegance and randomness of the real thing. Including the suggestion of very subtle thorns. His initial examination of the diamonds had indicated top color and no eye-visible flaws or inclusions. The first of many issues jumped to the front of his mind. The piece pre-dated the ubiquitous gemological reports common for fine diamonds since the early 1980s. To accurately value the brooch, each gemstone, including those diamonds, would have to be examined by an independent gemological laboratory. Quality reports for the diamonds, and treatment and origin reports for the colored stones. And that meant at least some un-mounting of the stones, and that meant risk. The stones could be damaged, and the indisputable original and untouched condition of the piece could be compromised.

And Marla Wingate had no knowledge if the brooch had ever been evaluated for an insurance appraisal. Even if it *had* been appraised, Tom was certain none of the diamonds or colored stones had ever been removed and graded by modern gemological standards. In fact, it looked to Tom as though the brooch had never been worn. It was in new condition, with no signs of even normal wear. Only minor darkening of the gold around the clasp mechanisms, due to oxidation. The condition was rare, unusual, and a virtually impossible occurrence for pieces of this age and quality. Was it possible he had come upon a world-class jewel from one of the great Houses, of this caliber, that was completely unknown?

Sometimes important jewelry pieces purchased from the public were resold in the trade before complete analysis of the components and a proper evaluation were done. Reasons for this could be many, ranging from the desire for a quick but not maximum profit by a less than fully motivated dealer, to the desire to create "illusion." Secondhand dealers felt "illusion" was critical to achieving interest and maximum value. The better dealers also understood the importance of leaving something on the table for the next seller. Tom thought of the countless times he'd watched and listened to dealers in the many exchanges in the Diamond District wax poetic over the virtues of a piece simply because it had not been seen in the trade before. Or at least by every last dealer in the city. *Cretins*, he thought.

He'd take measurements eventually but quickly guesstimated that the diamonds ranged in size from just above two carats to more than five carats. Bingo! There were at least 35 carats of gleaming diamonds. And they were just the beginning. The three sets of leaves, two on the right of the stem and one on the left, were composed of top-grade and virtually flawless Colombian emeralds. Five Pear Shapes and three Ovals on each of the smaller leaves. Seven Pear Shapes and five Ovals on the single larger leaf. They were mounted in 18-karat yellow gold. The leaflets seamlessly transitioned away from the main platinum stem. The emeralds were so bright, well matched, and of such perfection that they could have come from the same rough crystal.

This fine material is known in the trade as "Old Mine." An Indian term that can confuse the novice as it suggests Indian origin. "Old Mine" emeralds are stones mined in Colombia before the 17th century. The Conquistadors, in 1538, tortured the local Indians to reveal the location of one of the mines. The Spaniards discovered the Muzo Mine in 1587 on their own, which produced the finest-quality emeralds of all time. After being "native cut," or cut *en cabochon*, the stones were exported in quantity to India and Persia. They are still regarded as the highest-quality emeralds. This material came from the best, and now mined-out, part of the legendary Colombian emerald mine at Muzo.

As staggering as the diamonds, the emeralds, the condition, and the execution of the brooch was, the *pièce de résistance* was the blossom. Barely visible from the front of the blossom itself was a mounting for the petals, which was unique in Tom's experience. The engineering and execution were extraordinary. But the thing truly distinguishing the entire piece, cut both *en cabochon* and faceted, were the large Burmese rubies that formed the petals. The most valuable of all colored gemstones. The last time Tom had seen more than one stone of such quality was early in his career, when he was working at Harry Winston. They had been in a piece known as the "Mazarin Necklace." The rubies supposedly came from a collection of the 17th-century Cardinal Mazarin himself. More illusion.

The interaction and modulation between the polished domes of the *cabochons* and the faceted stones were perfect. And the minute, 18-karat yellow gold prongs left discreetly exposed purposefully created depth and contrast. Tom conservatively estimated between 65 and 75 carats in 23 stones. The rarest and most sought-after colored stones, he did not let himself dwell for a second on the potential value of the rubies. Just one of these stones would be the "money piece," the featured lot, at any major sale at one of the large auction houses. Smiling broadly, he stared, fascinated at the quality and consistency of the rubies.

He had just put down his loupe and returned the brooch to its original mint-condition red box when his assistant, Heidi, appeared in his door, having returned from lunch.

"You didn't go out yet? You were supposed to be at Frank's 10 minutes ago."

Tom engaged her with a smile as he discreetly closed the top of the box, holding the push closure in so as not to cause an iota of wear to the metal catch. When she startled him back to Earth, he had been wondering if Claude or Jacques Arpels themselves had had a hand in designing the rose. Fully absorbed, he failed to hear Heidi let herself back into the office. He was sure one of the Arpels had been responsible for the unrivaled collection of colored stones. They had personally brought out of India many world-class gems. Including the famous 64-carat Rockefeller Sapphire. Tom had sold the sapphire to a Japanese trading company in the 1980s.

"Hi, Heidi. Would you call him and tell him I've just left?"

"Sure. Anything good?" she said, nodding at the box on Tom's desk.

"No. She's in no rush, so we'll work on it next week. Did you go to FedEx?" he said, trying to end their conversation and get her out of the doorway.

"Yes. Want me to put that in the safe?"

As he stood up, taking his copy of the receipt he'd given Marla Wingate, he stepped past her and headed for the back office and the safes. "Thank you. I got it. I want to look and see if we have an old ring mounting. I can ask Frank to clean it up for that carved amethyst I bought yesterday." She was so loyal and hardworking that he hated to mislead her. But no one, even his trusted right hand, was going to know about the brooch until he knew exactly how he would proceed.

He put the box containing the brooch and the memo in a soft felt bag and opened the main safe door. He put everything into the small inner safe, closed its door, and spun the tumbler. Heidi was the type who would not look at something if she felt Tom would be displeased. He put it in the only place she did not have a combination for anyway.

Heidi was opening mail when Tom stopped at her desk.

"Do I need to go anywhere else?"

"I'll call Koo and see if that Tanzanite has been re-cut and will call your cell if you can take a look at it."

"Great. I'll grab lunch on the way back. Can I bring you a coffee?"

"No, thanks," she said.

"Oh, and please call Sherry-Lehman and get a bottle of Taittinger, Extra Brut, up to Lily at Van Cleef." He anticipated the favor he would be asking their Jewelry Department Head.

Tom smiled, turned, and had his hand on the doorknob when Heidi said, "Quite a looker for an older gal." Heidi had received Marla Wingate before leaving for lunch.

Tom figured Marla Wingate to be 43–44-ish and enjoyed Heidi's teasing. He turned around to her and widened his eyes as he said, "Was she older? I didn't notice."

Smiling and out the door, he heard Heidi giggle. He wondered how far her obvious affection for him went.

CHAPTER 2

Wednesday Midday

TOM STEPPED FROM THE ELEVATOR into the lobby and nodded to the Hallman, who was gesticulating wildly as he chatted up a short, wide cleaning woman. He sized her up and made a mental note to finally check if Hemingway had actually used the phrase "beef to the heels." He liked Barney, but he was always more relieved than not when he didn't have to stop.

The raw cold tightened his face as he exited onto 46th Street and turned left for the short walk to Fifth Avenue. He took a right for the two-block walk to Frank Maranzani, one of his manufacturing jewelers.

Absorbed in fleeting disgust and not paying attention, always a liability in the Diamond District, he heard the familiar bellow of Henry Stacks, building and unavoidable. "*TaaaHHM!*" . . . in a Brooklynite's Brooklynese. Tom appreciated Henry and liked him. In a city he had lived in all his life, this was a character connoisseur's character. He reminded Tom of the double-talking comedian and former vaudevillian Professor Irwin Corey. In appearance, they could be brothers. Voice quality? The same.

As Henry Stacks bore down, Tom thought of the article he had seen recently in the paper, the first he had heard of Irwin Corey in years. Corey, now a very old man, had randomly said in the interview, “I always tell my son, ‘If you’re not in bed by 12:00 a.m., come home.’”

Tom was middle-aged, and there was an easy 30 years between them. During Tom’s stint at Tiffany’s in the early 1980s, he’d met Henry and his “designer” protégé, Dori Dunleavy. What a pair. Like certain kinds of divorced empty-nesters, Dori waded into the jewelry business. She met and immediately got involved with Henry. Prolifically creative, she, the Cold Spring Harbor WASP, did an admirable job cleaning up the streetwise, small-time jewelry-manufacturing Brooklyn Jew. Handsome, the Hermes ties and Barney’s suits still seemed a bit out of place. But they worked well enough to get the two of them past all of Tom’s buyers at Tiffany. None sure what to do with the forceful, odd couple.

Tom was smiling so broadly two minutes into that first meeting that he had to draw on all his creativity to answer their repeated inquiries about “What was so funny?” without coming clean and hurting feelings. He was amused by people who were funny, whatever the reason, and did not know it themselves. Apart from Dori’s ample, if raw, talent, her greatest feature were her legendary boobs. Truly enormous. It turned out later that, with the slightest prompt, she would straighten her back, adopting a toothy grin of the true psychotic, and, with an Ethel Merman-like delivery, declare them the “community chest.” You had to laugh. Every time. When you’d stopped, she’d acquire an intensity of expression that made one think of H.P. Lovecraft and follow it up with "Enough to go around for everybody!" As if one needed an explanation.

She designed in blue ballpoint pen on 3 x 5 white index cards. A refreshing relief from most independent jewelry designers. There was generally little to the dimensionless recycled themes flawlessly rendered, usually in watercolor and gouache, on museum-quality archival paper. Tom knew instantly these two could contribute. He also knew their maintenance manual would dwarf a helicopter's. *Vendor-management scenario 1-A*, he thought. *Short leash and fear.*

As they were about to leave that first meeting, Dori produced a small covered cardboard box. Henry, who had been rocking in his chair like Hitler at the 1939 Olympics, now looked as though he had seen a ghost. He must have been thinking, "Foot in the door, and now she's going to blow it." To that point, he had been mostly quiet, letting Dori handle the sale. Occasionally contributing astounding malapropisms as his eyes widened like a true myopic.

She smiled broadly and produced a green wax model, a few filaments of cotton from the box still attached. Jewelry manufactured by the casting process is first modeled in wax. Tom knew instantly she had come up with a winner. The design was so nauseating, success was guaranteed. There were Tiffany customers who would stop at nothing to own this *tour de force* of cutesy slop. Those were the pre-Internet days, and this was going to be a star in Tiffany's mail-order catalog. Tom held up the silhouette of a whimsical rabbit to judge its scale. It was formed by two very slightly squat open ovoids, one slightly smaller than the other. There were two ears. With one bent down and away.

Horrifying, but good, contained movement. As he looked up, Dori was reaching across to his hand, and in a voice that had no right to be so confident but had the energy of a moving train, she said, “Here’s the capper!”

She stuck a 7-millimeter cultured pearl at the base of the larger wax circle and screeched, “It’s the tail!” *No shit.* So revolting that Tom’s initial production-projection total increased twofold. Early on, Tom moved to the top of his “How to be a successful merchant” list that statement of H.L. Mencken’s, “Nobody ever went broke underestimating the taste of the American public.” The three of them would have their first success together with the “Bunny” and a long, strange friendship began in the process.

Henry and Tom shook hands, and, before Tom could speak, Henry demanded, “When’s lunch?” This was a Brooklynese Tom loved and missed as native New Yorkers continued to disappear. “Your *cherce*, Tom.”

“Henry.” As Tom started to speak, Henry’s eyes narrowed, and he leaned in close with a seriousness of expression that could only mean he was about to learn the location of the fountain of youth. “Let’s talk this afternoon and pick a day. It’s cold as a witch’s earlobe out here, and I’m late to my jeweler.”

“Sure thing, Tom. When should I call?”

Walking up Fifth, Tom turned and said, “Anytime after 3:30.”

As they waved, Henry yelled after him, “Any *woik* for me?” The emphasis on the *me*.

Tom smiled and turned away. He really liked Henry, even after all the troubles. They had been caught representing themselves as agents for Tiffany at a trade show. He almost felt badly and wondered if he would be in the mood to take Henry’s call later.

Usually he was not, but Henry never took offense. Rottweilers usually don't. They genuinely liked and respected each other. And they liked the idea of each other as well. At the same time as different and as similar to each other as two native New Yorkers could be.

Standing at the light on 47th Street, Tom thought back to his Linguistics professor in college, Dr. Ashcott. He had put together a dictionary of slang specific to Tom's university. While accurate, some of the definitions had a way of neutralizing the meaning. "Roach: The remaining remnant of a smoked marijuana cigarette. Generally small. A roach clip may be employed to facilitate smoking. See Roach Clip."

One day in class, they were discussing American dialects. Dr. Ashcott was a recognized expert, with a sharp ear. He explained to the class that, after Edward R. Morrow had started to report on World War II, New Yorkers were exposed to different American dialects. Morrow was from Washington State and was responsible for hiring other smooth-toned reporters like Eric Sevareid. Then, in the '40s and '50s, after radio, television began to have a broader impact, and it was only the upper and lower classes that had New York accents. The largely nonnative middle class in New Yok's five boroughs lacked native elocution and diction. Gradually as the radio voices and television talking heads became more a part of everyday life, native children effectively learned to speak from the milder tones of native Midwestern media people. Not their parents. The beginning of the end.

Getting to the corner of 48th Street, Tom turned left and cursed as a tourist stepped backwards directly into his path. He swore he was going to write a list of pedestrian foot-traffic rules for tourists. The large woman stared up at him with a mix of confusion and self-entitlement. Her "man" appeared to have fewer teeth than brains, which placed him in the same phylum as the chipmunk. Based on the color palette and quality of their clothing, Tom snarled, "West Virginia" as he stormed past.

Ironically, the woman was trying to decide between two counterfeit Burberry scarves from a street vendor. She had stepped back to see herself in a small hand mirror wired to the vendor's cart. Either color palette would have been acceptable only to nocturnal insects. Heading west and almost out of earshot, Tom heard the male say, "How'd *he* know?" Dr. Ashcott would be proud. Even if Tom's guess was pure luck. The question dissipated any residual irritation, and a smile came to his face even before he saw Jan, Frank's Greek office manager. Already smiling when their eyes finally met, Jan said, "Fancy meeting you here."

They stepped to the curb together. "Jan, you're the best-looking woman in New York. Why would you never go out with me?"

Rolling her eyes, but smiling, she said, "Because you never asked."

"Was that it?"

"You know it was."

Tom considered his next statement carefully. He couldn't recall where Jan was on *The List*. "Well, I'm going to change that. Frank still up there?"

"Yes, he is." Turning from each other, Jan looked back and said, "He who snoozes loses, Handsome."

Tom smiled and got caught watching her walk away as she looked back at him, her thick, black mane bouncing.

Tom walked past the expressionless Indian man at the candy-and-newspaper stand in the lobby and waited for the elevator in Frank's grimy building. One of the second-level buildings in the Jewelry and Diamond District, the range of activities related to the highly fragmented jewelry trade was almost unimaginable.

Every nationality doing every imaginable task in the industry, in one non-homogeneous beehive. There was one of the largest casting houses left in New York City that serviced everybody from large luxury retail chains to small independent wholesale manufacturers. The nasty byproducts from some procedures and necessary chemicals like cyanide used in manufacturing precious metals made it tough to meet environmental laws, as such, in the city. Understanding landlords are well rewarded. At the other extreme, there was even one mineral specimen dealer, Luke Connor. Another native, he was an eccentric, and Tom wished he could spend more time visiting. Tom had contributed the Foreword to one of Luke's books on the pioneering 19th-century gemologist George F. Kunz. Among other things in an astounding and prolific career, Kunz, as a young man in the late 19th century, had supervised the cutting of the Tiffany Diamond. Later, he convinced J.P. Morgan to fund the first mineral collection at a museum in the country, still housed at The American Museum of Natural History. Upon its discovery, Kunz had named the gemstone "Morganite" in his honor.

In between, there were diamond cutters, dealers in all species of colored stones, people who treated gemstones, lapidaries, box vendors, and finding houses. *Findings* are all the countless little bits used to finish off jewelry pieces from clasps to clutches.

Tom was well positioned when the middle elevator finally arrived. As the elevator drained, Tom swept his head one final time to be sure no ladies were waiting to get on. Before he could step in, and, for no reason, a short, middle-aged Hasidic diamond broker elbowed past Tom. He pressed a button, turned, and stood in the doorway. His elbow had been hit hard enough to push his arm. Never expecting manners or common courtesy, Tom rarely rankled at these daily Fun City annoyances. But, probably primed by the incest twins from West Virginia, he steamed at the unnecessary nature of this move.

As the crowd around Tom tightened and moved forward, he stepped in and turned sharply, elbow out for rebounding, striking the broker in the chest, dispatching him to the back wall. Pressing the button for Frank's floor, he turned and glared down at the broker as they were both jostled by other passengers. He had seen this guy around for more than 20 years. Predictably, the man stared straight ahead, as if what had occurred was a normal greeting. Tom wanted to believe the man did not know better but knew differently. He tried to justify his lack of anger management with that knowledge. Note to self: return the favor the next time you see this weasel. The elevator stopped on the 14th floor. Arriving at Frank's door, Tom buzzed and was let into the tiny mantrap. Exiting the inside door and greeting, but looking past the brassy Italian bookkeeper from New Jersey, Tom looked to Jan's seat, hoping she would magically be there.

"Where's Boy Wonder?"

"On the phone, yelling at somebody," said the bookkeeper, motioning Tom with her hand to go.

Tom could hear Frank on the phone and walked past the glass window into the shop, where the jewelers were working. He stood in Frank's door.

Frank, seated and red-faced, waved him in with classic Italian histrionics and handed Tom a half-finished necklace mounting set in shellac as he sat down.

Pretending to pay attention, he took his loupe from his jacket pocket and examined the piece out of respect. Like most of Frank's more ambitious work, the necklace just did not hang together. Rough around the edges and no modulation.

They had met right after Tom started his own business. And despite the fact the first job he had Frank do was an annoyance, they became friends and had done a great deal of business together. Tom had won Frank's respect on that first job. A 20-plus-carat fancy yellow Emerald Cut diamond ring remount. When he first picked up the completed ring, the stone was slightly off center in the newly built mounting. Tom's eye had always been impeccable, and Frank denied the asymmetry. Finally, Frank realized his setter had mounted the stone 180 degrees backwards in the handmade platinum and gold mounting. The pavilion, the bottom half of the diamond, had variations in angles from one end to the other. A big stone like that can only fit properly into the mounting in one direction. Tom liked to remind Frank about the incident with every remount.

Frank slammed down the phone. "Son of a bitch."

"I guess so."

"My gold guy upped the vigorish on my 'special orders,'" making air quotes while saying *special orders.*

"How much?"

"Ten percent total now. Unbelievable."

Frank, like a lot of people in the trade, "bought" gold from certain people and never took possession. They would take an invoice for $100,000 and, instead of gold, get cash. $90,000. The commission was worth it. In Frank's case, he paid his jewelers' monthly overtime in cash. Good for them, less payroll tax for him.

"What do you think?" Frank said, nodding down at the necklace as he hung up the phone.

"Perfect."

"How's Heidi?"

"Living for you. Saw Jan downstairs."

Before they could start talking about women, Tom blurted out, "You will not believe what walked into my office today."

CHAPTER 3

Wednesday Evening

TOM HAD JUST SAID GOODNIGHT to Heidi and the office building's cleaning lady and buzzed them out. He was resisting the urge to take a last look at the brooch when the phone rang. He had not yet turned on the answering system, so he picked up. "Tom Strawbridge."

"Tom, Mark Keesling. Glad I caught you. Any chance you can swing by the office for a minute?"

Keesling was a highly successful LA-based dealer with an office in New York. He was a rarity in the trade, in that he tried to help people. And when selling, he always left something on the table. His casual partnerships were numerous and effectively involved him in deals he would not have otherwise seen. Tom and Mark had discussed a collaboration of their own years ago.

"Hi, Mark. You're in town?"

"Yeah. . . . came in today for the Christie's sale preview. You see that blue?" Keesling was referring to an 8-carat blue Pear-Shaped diamond. Tom had been traveling the week before and had missed the dealer-appointment period. These are private, where one can more fully examine the goods without the public present. Fancy-colored diamond prices, anything other than stones within the colorless range, had skyrocketed in recent years. They were in tremendous demand by the trade, private buyers, and collectors alike.

The best bet to gain a reasonable margin when buying fancy-colored diamonds at auction was to trust one's eyes. If one was skilled and had the experience and courage. Relying solely on the color grade on the gemological report, was a recipe for disaster. This was because the preeminent laboratory's grading standards had softened in the last two decades, and many dealers, especially the newer ones, relied predominantly on two things: The laboratory grade and recent public sales results for fancy-colored diamonds of the same grade. Anything but fungible, this sector was the trickiest area in the industry, and fortunes were made and lost overnight based on extreme subtleties of body color. The capital requirements to play in this arena are immense.

"No. I'll get over there before the sale. I was out last week. What do you think?"

Mark hesitated, trying not to give away his opinion or honest level of interest and said, "Funny stone. The color will improve with re-cutting I think, but there is a lot of gray in it. No one seems to know if it is a new or old stone, but the cutting is strange. If you ask me, I say it's new material, and the cutter did this on purpose to create illusion."

Tom rolled his eyes so hard they hurt. "What's up?"

"I've got an important Alexandrite here, and I'd like to offer tonight. I need your opinion."

Tom was flattered. While it was true that Mark never bought a diamond or a diamond piece without additional opinion and consensus, he was legendary for his decisive and solitary action regarding colored gemstones. In addition to which, they had not seen each other in more than two years and had not done a deal in a longer time than that.

"How big?"

"19 carats plus. Yes or no, right now?" Mark sounded agitated and annoyed, and Tom was not sure why, beyond the need for an immediate offer.

Mostly out of professional curiosity but also because 19 carats was large for a gem Alexandrite, Tom said, "On my way. 818 right?" referring to the suite Mark leased in the 608 Fifth Avenue building. If Mark were considering offering, it would be worth a look and the trip. Mark allowed a New York dealer who had worked for Tom at the Gemological Institute of America to operate in that space, as Mark spent most of his time in California.

"That's it. Tom, I know I don't need to say this, but say nothing to no one," Mark said and hung up.

Tom had wanted a night off at home and thought it would now be only slightly delayed as he finished putting goods away, locking up the safes, and alarming his office. The trick would be not stopping for a drink after looking at the stone.

As Tom rode the elevator to the lobby, he readied himself for full-on darkness, as daylight saving time had ended just two weeks before. He hated the early darkness. It was the worst in late January and February in the city. Dark when he left the apartment, and dark when he left the office.

He nodded to the janitor in the lobby and followed a UPS woman into the revolving door. Taking the same route as earlier in the day, he began his walk to meet Mark. The stream of people heading down Fifth to Grand Central Station seemed lighter than normal, until he realized it was already 6:45 p.m.

Tom again tried to put the brooch out of his mind and started to wonder if he should take somebody into his confidence. Did he need to? *Decide tomorrow*, he thought. He then started to think about Mark. They were both unusual in their industry because they were not Jewish, yet had achieved. Mark's father started the business, in the predominantly Jewish jewelry world. Tom and Mark both had established relationships to a degree that would indicate they were almost accepted. Tom knew better. He also knew that as close and trusted as the closest relationships were, if you weren't Jewish, when push came to shove, you were an outsider. He had long ago abandoned concern for what his image might be. The trade knew he was successful and good, and that was that. Like everyone, he had fans and enemies in the business. But, unlike most, he had no real friends in the business, though you would never know it to see him operate.

Behind the little desk in the art deco lobby of 608 Fifth Avenue sat the usual droopy-eyed security guard. Tom made a "Want me to sign the book?" gesture, and the guard waved him by with an open, yellow smile. 608 had one of the lowest levels of security in any building in the District. As everyone knows, security is little more than the attempt to create a secure image and ultimately, secure feelings.

Tom always admired the art deco bronze and aluminum work in the elevator cars. On the eighth floor, he turned left down the corridor. Coming around all sides of an office door was the raised voice of a dealer loudly berating someone over the phone. Tom stopped in front of Mark's door and pressed the buzzer. Muffled talk from inside stopped, and the door lock was released a few seconds later. Tom looked up at the camera in the corner of the mantrap and noticed the venetian blind was down behind the bulletproof pass-through security window. He heard, in a strong but hushed tone, the word *"No!"* Female. Mark had company. The inside door lock released, and he pushed the door and entered the office.

As Mark headed over, smiling and hand extended, Tom saw three other people in the small two-room office. A woman seated at the table, a man beside her, and another man leaning against the radiator by the window.

"Thanks for coming, Tom. You know everybody."

Tom not only didn't know everybody, he'd never seen any of them before.

Tom was instantly uneasy, annoyed, and double-looked each face as he won a grip contest with Mark. Tom stared Mark flatly in the eyes and said, "Nobody. They in the trade?" None of them had moved or changed expression. The woman dropped a half-smoked cigarette into a coffee cup with a hiss.

"Well, not exactly. This is Sheila, and Mr. Provst, and Yuri Propakov," he said, waving at the man by the window. "I thought you might have met them at one of the shows in Palm Beach, or in Basel or Maastricht. They know your reputation," Mark said, smiling.

Then why didn't you know we'd not met? thought Tom.

Russian Jews, thought Tom. He guessed the couple at the table was the money, and the other guy bird-dogged deals.

"The Provsts and I have friends in common, and Yuri is an art collector with a passion for fine gems and jewelry."

Bingo. Tom slowly panned his head at the motionless trio and thought, *If he's an art collector, I'm a ballerina.*

"Want a drink?"

"No, thanks. I am in a rush, Mark. Let's see the stone."

"Have a seat, Tom." Mark pointed to the table. Tom stared at Mark, trying to convey his sense of unease and annoyance. If Tom had not known Mark for more than 20 years, he would have been seriously irritated.

Mark walked to the safe in the corner, opened it, and handed Tom a gemstone parcel paper. Tom walked past the couple at the table to a built-in desk under some bookshelves, sat down, and switched on the ubiquitous fluorescent diamond and gemstone grading lamp. Variants can be found in every dealer and every gem merchant's office in all corners of the world.

He noticed "Gem Alexandrite" written in pencil in the center of the parcel paper and that "21.65 carats" had been erased from the lower left corner of the parcel paper. As he opened it, he said, "Your friends don't say much, Mark, do they?"

"Everyone's tired, Tom. We've all come in today. Me from California, and everyone else from Geneva."

Tom picked up a gem-cleaning chamois cloth, put it over the Alexandrite, and removed it from the parcel paper. These are used by the better and more knowledgeable dealers, but they are not good for diamonds, which are always a challenge to clean. Tom wanted to ask who owned the stone but knew better.

He rubbed the stone firmly but gently inside the chamois and put it down on the grading pad before him. It was a staggering example of Alexandrite. The color-change variety of the gem mineral species, Chrysoberyl. Perfectly cut, polished, and eye-clean. And the layout! Layout, a trade term reflecting how a stone shows in terms of balance and proportion, relative to its weight, was also perfect.

Then there was the color! Alexandrite belongs to a class of gemstones known as "phenomenal." Phenomenal gemstones exhibit an additional visual effect beyond their basic body color. Moonstone, opal, star sapphires, and the other variety of Chrysoberyl known as cat's-eye are examples. A fine quality cat's-eye displays a sharp luminous line down the apex of a stone cut *en cabochon*, a polished dome without facets. Phenomenal gems are most highly prized in the Far East.

Good Alexandrite changes color from green in daylight, to red in incandescent light. The theoretical ideal is from "emerald green to ruby red." And while examples of that extreme, pure color change are rare, if near non-existent, the purity of the color is also important and very dependent on the geographical source. Regardless of the specific hue, the strength of the "color change" is a major factor in determining value. And an Emerald Cut on top of it, the rarest shape for most of the important colored stones, with the exception of emerald itself. Because Emerald Cuts have a very open faceting arrangement, any inclusions or flaws are easy to see. Emeralds, due to their formation process, are generally included. "Eye-clean" emeralds are rare, so if one does not like inclusions, emeralds are generally not the right choice. This beauty looked like a top-quality, eye-clean Emerald Cut Alexandrite.

In fact, Tom had never seen a large Alexandrite of this quality before. He was about to ask Mark for a penlight, the artificial or incandescent light source, when he saw one extended into his field of vision from where Mark was standing. Both men's eyes met as Tom took the light and turned it on.

Tom placed the stone in a V-shaped white paper grading tray and directed the beam of light on the stone. As he enjoyed the burning ruby-red color, he recalled how Alexandrite was named. Legend holds that the discovery in the Ural Mountains was made the day Prince Nicholas Alexander II was born. Other sources include Sri Lanka. Alexandrites from a new Brazilian source in the 1980s are a listless bluish green in daylight and appear a brownish violet in incandescent light. The purity of the hue and resting body color from these other sources cannot compare to Russian material.

Quickly moving the penlight away and back a few times, noting the strength of the change, Tom reached for his loupe and quickly checked the stone. Only two very small natural inclusions at one end of the stone. Alexandrite had never been successfully synthesized like other colored stones. But, even if it had, the crystals in the stone proved its natural origin.

"Well?" Mark demanded.

Tom had nearly forgotten the others in the room.

He cleaned the stone with the cloth and placed it back into the parcel paper and, re-folding it, stood up, handing it back to Mark.

Tempted to quickly end the meeting by corroborating the quality and leveling his opinion, he decided to see if he could find out anything else. After all, it was entirely possible that this would be his only experience with this stone. Like most world-class gemstones, it would soon disappear, unlikely to surface again. And, since he was not in on the deal, there was no risk in poking them in the eye.

"Do you have a candle, Mark?"

The slob at the window shifted his position and, in a thick Northern Russian accent, balked, "Jesus Christ."

Mark smiled, acknowledging that Tom was one of the only men in the trade who knew Alexandrite's red was best seen under the glow of a candle.

"No, we don't."

Tom was staring flatly at "Yuri" when he said, "Well, that is something I'd like to see. You know what you've got there, Mark."

"Have you ever seen another like it?"

"Over the years, two or three of the same change and quality but none of them over 6 carats."

"How much per carat, Tom?"

Tom would not let the familiar game of "I'll show you mine if you show me yours" begin. Mark knew this was not proper protocol, especially with an unknown audience. Tom always reacted the same way in these situations.

Abandoning the need to demonstrate his experience and expertise, Tom said, "If I saw the stone from one of my Alexandrite guys, he would ask me at least $28,000, $29,000. A carat." A stupendous lowball.

Yuri Propakov hit the radiator with his heel as he stood, and the couple began to shift as Lady Provst lit a cigarette.

Subscribing to the theory of "The best defense is a good offense," before Mark could say anything, Tom demanded, "What gives, Mark? What do you want to know?"

CHAPTER 4

Wednesday Night

As Tom grabbed his hand, Mark Kessling's expression was part "Of course, I know that I shouldn't have put you in this position" and part, "I wish you'd helped me anyway." Tom released his hand and entered the mantrap without acknowledging or looking back at the Russians.

Once Tom was in the hall, he pressed his ear to the door, which proved unnecessary, as at least three of the four people inside the office, including the woman, began to talk at once. A door opened further down the hall from Tom, and he started to walk toward the elevator.

As he pressed the button for the elevator, a short Persian man appeared next to Tom as an office door swung shut across the hall. The man was impeccably dressed and had a miraculous comb-over. The elevator arrived, and, when the doors opened, Tom gestured for the man to enter first. In a theatrical arabesque, the dapper little man slid to the right, lowered his head, and extended his arm into the open doorway. Tom obliged and stepped deep into the back corner of the car.

The Persian man followed him in, pressed the button for the lobby, and turned to face Tom. "You're Mr. Tom," he said, with a reserved smile. Tom had met countless dealers from every part of the globe over the years, so this was not an uncommon experience.

He was about to respond when the elevator stopped on the third floor, and two very agitated, dark-complexioned men literally leapt into the elevator, stabbing at the lobby button. Almost simultaneously, the report of a gunshot and a frantic scream from the hall, "STOP!" filled Tom's head. The bullet intended for the men stuck in the jamb of the elevator with a metallic thud as the doors closed.

The car started down as everyone's eyes met in an amalgam of desperation, shared terror, and fear. The man closest to Tom produced a large-caliber revolver. He backhanded the Persian in the right side of the jaw with the barrel of the gun. The man then leveled the gun at Tom's throat, as the second man said in a heavy eastern European accent, "One move, one word, you both die." The Persian man was on his knees, with blood cascading between the fingers covering his mouth. Tom stared down into the corner of the car, fighting the urge to look up. Fear rose in him like pain from a severe injury. The two men screamed whispers at each other in something resembling Hungarian or Romanian.

As the elevator opened to the lobby and the man closest to the door broke out and to the right, the second man pointed his gun to the top of the Persian's head. A voice from the Fifth Avenue end of the lobby boomed, "FREEZE IT UP!"

A single handgun shot was instantly obliterated by two shocking blasts from a shotgun, as blood, the handgun, and part of a hand rained down on the terrazzo in front of the elevator.

Simultaneously, as the elevator's door began to close, the second gunman snapped his head to the left. With no conscious thought, Tom buried the toe of his shoe in the man's genitals as he grabbed the man's forearm, holding the gun with both hands, and, with every ounce of strength in him, drove the man's arm into the corner of the button panel closer to the wrist than the elbow. The Persian whimpered, and, as Tom bent the arm around broken bones, the pistol dropped to the floor. The man's hair smelled foul. The elevator doors bounced open as shotguns filled the car like a cluster of crystals.

"FREEZE IT UP!"

The first armor-clad cop got the picture and grabbed the gunman by the back of his neck, pressing the barrel of his shotgun into the small of the man's back. Incredibly, the gunman reached for his weapon with his left hand but was already being pulled down to his back as other officers subdued him.

Tom felt his knees weakening as a huge cop demanded, "What the hell happened here!?"

The Persian was crying, coughing, and spurting blood in syncopated time. Instinctively, Tom raised his hands over his head as his eyes focused on the gore on the floor visible beyond the sea of navy Kevlar.

Apparently a very well-known and highly discreet Swiss dealer, Robbie Tabah, had been set up over the course of a few weeks by a very tony, middle-aged foreign couple posing as wealthy jewelry buyers. They had made a final selection the day before and arranged to send a man, supposedly in their employ, with payment and to collect the goods. Two men showed up, and, once in the office, they had pistol-whipped Tabah. The safe was open. His clerk managed to hit the concealed alarm button and locked himself in an inner back office. Upon seeing the men leave on the security monitor, the clerk stepped into the hall and fired a shot from Tabah's licensed handgun.

The man who lay opened up and dead on the lobby floor had a notebook-computer bag containing vintage jewels and gemstones worth roughly $8,000,000. Wholesale. Tom had seen the bag lying under the legs of the body as he and the Persian man were escorted to the building Superintendent's offices in the back of the lobby.

The two men were separated and interviewed by detectives for close to 40 minutes. Based on his experience with police, Tom was surprised he did not feel like he was guilty or under suspicion during the process. After the facts were checked and their stories compared, another plainclothes man knocked as he entered the office where Tom was sitting. Tom was sitting in silence with one of the officers who had interviewed him. Tom crossed his legs and noticed dried blood on his shoe as the uniformed officer stood to leave. As the plainclothes man entered and closed the door, Tom got a flash of the Persian being pushed into the hall in a wheelchair. It looked as though the lone pistol smack had done serious and complicated damage.

"Detective Steve Napoli, Mr. Strawbridge. Manhattan Homicide North. I'm assisting the crime scene unit. How do you feel?"

"Lucky. And rattled shitless. What's the story?"

Napoli explained the set-up and the robbery. They had picked up a third man, the driver, waiting around the corner near Rockefeller Center. Once sirens could be heard, a beat cop had seen him leave the double-parked car, walking quickly toward Sixth Avenue. Other officers appeared, and they picked him up.

He went on to say they had Interpol intelligence on a highly organized eastern European gang, The Pink Panthers, which had been successful in London, Paris, and The Middle East over the last two years. Apparently, they were setting up a string of jobs in New York and Beverly Hills. And that these men were possibly part of that group.

Napoli handed Tom his card and asked him not to leave town, even for the weekend, without speaking to him. They were not sure if they would need to talk to him again. He then asked if Tom wanted to see a counselor.

"I know you've been asked this already tonight, but are you sure you never saw either of those two men before?" Napoli was educated and, Tom guessed, born in Queens.

"Four," said Tom.

"Come again?"

"Been asked four times. Honestly, Detective Napoli, I'm not sure I could pick the two of them out of a group of three right now. With that said, I have no recollection of ever having seen them before. You know, people in my trade run on "orange alert all the time." As smooth and cool as Napoli appeared, Tom wondered what his "issue" was. The thing every cop he had ever met had. He believed the personality elements that attracted people to law enforcement were closer to the traits that drove people to crime, rather than at opposite ends of a straight continuum. The good/evil version of the horseshoe theory in politics.

Napoli then said, "One final question. What made you do what you did? You're a City boy, and experienced professionals like you would know what to do in those situations. And, what not to do."

Tom had been wondering the same thing. He exhaled and said, "To me, they looked and acted like serious pros who'd been unexpectedly interrupted. And their heist wasn't clean. And I thought the one with the gun was going to execute the short guy. And probably me. What's his name?"

"Pourat. Says he met and worked with you in Geneva six, eight years ago. Respects you."

"I don't know. And I was scared."

"Scared? The men are calling you *Rambo*."

"Not quite. How is Tabah?" Tom knew Tabah and had known his father. Both gentlemen.

"He'll be OK. His employee is very shaken."

Tom stood, they shook hands, and detective Napoli opened the door into the hallway of 608's maintenance office. In the lobby, an N.Y.P.D. photographer passed Tom as a crew cleaned the floor and walls. The few tenants and visitors who had been in the building during the shooting were just beginning to be escorted out the back entrance of the building after questioning.

As Tom walked toward the entrance, one of the responding officers smiled and nodded to him. Tom returned the gesture and made his way to the street. He was led to the perimeter of the yellow plastic crime-scene tape, and Detective Napoli held it up as Tom ducked under. He ignored the lone reporter and the few onlookers, hoping no one present was from the trade who would recognize him.

He walked to the corner and crossed Fifth Avenue. Stopping on the opposite corner, he looked back at the front of the building. Tom felt detached from himself. And from the balance of humanity for that matter. It was almost 8:30 p.m.

CHAPTER 5

Wednesday Night

WITH ANY PROSPECT of a quiet solitary night at home long gone, Tom headed for The Melrose, his favorite bar and steakhouse. He needed a drink. Badly.

He continued up Fifth Avenue, and in deconstructing the events of the last few hours, began to wonder. What would have happened to him and Pourat if he had not acted? Why did he react? Was he a strong, confident ex-jock or a coward? Would there be repercussions? And, if so, what and from whom? Damn lucky, he thought.

He crossed 59th Street as a hansom cab clopped past behind him. A clear, dry, cold November night. And despite being in the heart of New York City, many stars were visible. Tom thought the blackness of Central Park across the Avenue probably contributed to the visibility and sharpness of the winter night sky. Shrugging his shoulders against the cold, he filled his lungs with sharp air as he passed under the heat lamps in the canopy of The Pierre Hotel.

Turning right at The Knickerbocker Club on 62nd Street, the wind off the Park pushed him along east. Who should he tell about this? Why tell anyone? John, his ex-brother-in-law and close friend? His "connected" acquaintances? Should he have spoken to the cops about protection? Was it a time to step back and take a break for a while?

All of a sudden, Tom realized his underarms and lower back were soaked, even though he was cold. He crossed Madison Avenue against the light, stopping halfway across to let an uptown bus rattle north. The few passengers were well lit, pallid, and expressionless. A mobile *Nighthawks.* Continuing across the Avenue and down the block, he hoped he would feel better once he got to the bar.

As he entered The Melrose, he saw a few seats at the bar, noticing it wasn't busy for a Wednesday. He also saw Jack, his favorite bartender and friend, at the far end of the bar. He stopped at the coat check, even though he wasn't wearing a topcoat, to give Ginny, the ancient Chinese coat lady, a $20 bill. "Thank you, Tom," she chirped.

Taking the stool closest to the near end of the bar, Tom realized he'd badly bruised the fingers of his left hand when it hit the elevator panel. Sitting, Tom looked straight ahead, not wanting to make eye contact with other patrons. There was a good person-to-noise ratio, so Tom hoped he could avoid any unnecessary small talk. Jack materialized, hand extended, displaying his broad, angular smile.

"Hiya, Tom."

"Hi, Jack. How are you?"

"Everything is copasetic." Tom had heard the phrase, Jack's standard rejoinder, for most of the 20 years they had known each other. And he was never more glad to hear it. Tom realized and, for the first time, admitted to himself he was seriously rattled. He stood to go to the restroom. He didn't know why.

"The usual?"

"Please," said Tom.

Jack began to prepare one of his legendary Dagwood Bumstead-sized martinis as Tom left the bar. When he got to the men's room, he realized he just wanted to look in the mirror. He felt nothing like himself and wanted to make sure he was still him. Running cold water over his fingers, Tom recalled that from a young age he had always reacted with great calm during a crisis. He remembered, at eight years old, listening from a hospital bed to the family pediatrician speak to his mother while he waited for a vicious compound fracture of his arm to be set. Dr. Koota went on and on about Tom's composure and calm reaction to the injury. Tom always felt, whether it was true or not, that was when he learned the benefits of the "art of under-reacting."

But now, standing in the men's room with sweat flooding out of him, he could not help but think of his mother's theory of the "delayed reaction." If there ever was a classic example, this was it.

He took a deep breath, and, while clammy, his face felt hot as he splashed water on his cheeks and forehead. He half considered going straight home without even returning to the bar. As he was adjusting his tie, two young Wall Street types burst in, loudly laughing over each other. Tom did not flinch as he eyed them in the mirror. He smoothed his thick hair, turned, and stared down into the eyes of the closest man. The man stepped aside, and Tom walked past them, feeling a bit more like himself.

Jack produced a glass cocktail mixer full of ice from behind the bar, into which he poured a considerable amount of vodka. He always stirred martinis unless his client requested otherwise. This was so he would avoid "bruising" the vodka. While Tom had never been fully satisfied with what *bruising* actually meant, he and Jack often re-opened a now decade-old legendary debate that had begun years before on a wintry December evening. They had bantered to the great fascination and delight of three Rockettes at the bar. It began by Tom asking at exactly the right moment if Jack knew if gin bruised in the same way vodka did.

Tom watched Jack, standing in front of him, slowly stirring the ice and vodka, slowly smile and say, "Long day?"

"Well, it was going pretty well until two guys robbed a dealer in the building I was in. They got on the elevator with me and another dealer."

Not knowing the reality of the situation but fully aware of Tom's personality, Jack said, "Really?"

Jack dumped the ice from the fish-bowl-sized martini glass and set it down on the napkin in front of Tom. He poured the chilled contents of the shaker through a strainer. Tom said, "Look, I don't want anyone else to know about this right now, but the cops showed, and one of the thugs ended up in both parts of the lobby."

"Are you serious?" Jack's eyes widened in a way Tom had never seen.

"Dead serious. Me and the other guy were already on the elevator as these goons were leaving the job, and we got caught in the middle. Not pretty."

"Holy shit."

A waiter appeared at the service station at the far end of the bar and barked over the din, "Jack, two Johnny Blacks on ice, bourbon Manhattan up." Jack looked at Tom with genuine concern and, pointing, said, "I need to hear it all," and turned to make the drinks.

Tom drained the glass of ice water Jack always provided and moved it to the far edge of the bar, signaling a refill. He slid the martini closer to him and watched the roiled appearance of the vodka surrounding a few tiny ice shards near the twist. He lifted the glass; he was not shaking; he took a sip. Before he could return the glass to the bar, he felt a hand on his shoulder.

His nerves made him watch the glass back to the bar, and, as he turned, the fragrance, pheromones, and face hit him all at once. Standing to his left, almost at eye level, was Marla Wingate. Scrambling to contextualize as he rose, extending his hand, he realized there was another woman by her side.

"Mrs. Wingate, what a wonderful surprise."

"Marla, please. This, Ann, is the gentleman I was telling you about. Tom, I'd like you to meet Ann Ross. We went to school together."

"How do you do?" Tom said, and, looking back at Marla Wingate, he added, "May I offer you two a drink?"

Ann Ross was well packaged, moneyed, and very attractive but without the elegance and sexiness of Marla Wingate.

"That is most kind, Tom, but we've finished dinner, and, unfortunately, to be paid for tomorrow, two bottles of wine." *Lightweights*, thought Tom.

Tom re-extended his hand to Ann Ross and said, smiling, "Well, perhaps another time. Did you enjoy your food?"

As he shook Marla Wingate's hand, she said, "Goodnight, and enjoy your dinner, Tom."

He said goodnight and remained standing until they rounded the corner to the checkroom. The place was filling up and had started to get loud.

Looking back over the bar as Tom seated himself, Jack smiled, shook his head, and said, "I've said it before, and I'll say it again. I wish I had what you had."

"Come on, Jack—she's a client," Tom said and smiled.

Another bartender, Jimmy, came through the bar for the nine o'clock spot and shook Tom's hand, saying in an almost unintelligible Irish brogue, "Up to no good as *useyal,* I *spose*?"

"Hi, Jimmy."

As Jimmy walked past, Jack's expression leveled, and he leaned in, putting his hand on the bar, saying, "Let's have it, Tom."

CHAPTER 6

Wednesday Night

Tom arrived home close to 10:30 p.m. He should have been crawling but found his mind bouncing from various events of the day, thoughts for the day to come, and then the gut-grabbing recollection of the robbery and shooting. And, that brooch.

Standing in his foyer, he jumped when his house phone buzzed. Tom threw his jacket on a chair, walked to the phone, and said, "Yes."

It was one of the evening doormen, John. "Mr. Strawbridge, we've got a package delivery for you. Should we send it up?"

"Please, John."

A thought of food crossed Tom's mind as entered his kitchen. He filled a large tumbler with ice. He filled that with vodka, leaving enough room for a splash of cranberry juice.

He ordered chicken marsala from Vico's around the corner and sat down on a couch, the day's mail in front of him. He took a sip and sat back, turning on the television for company. Almost as if he had been robbed, he remembered, "My phone!"

Standing, he realized he'd shut the ringer off on the elevator going to Mark Kessling's office and never unmuted. He realized, save for international flights, this hiatus must be a record. As he felt for it in his suit-jacket pocket, he was anticipating the routine voicemails and emails that would hopefully be grounding, as well as experiencing some uneasiness about any possible surprise.

Twelve emails and five voicemails. About what he would have guessed. But there were also five incoming calls from "unknown number" with no voicemails. As he switched screens to check his emails first, in case one of his business relationships in Asia or Europe needed something, the phone screen came on and rang. "Unknown number" appeared.

It was closing in on 11:00 p.m., and he had not given his number out to anyone during the day. Except for Marla Wingate. Knowing that she would be calling him was unlikely, he was nevertheless hopeful as he said, "Tom Strawbridge" into the device.

"Mr. Strawbridge, Detective Napoli. I was calling to check in on you."

Tom was livid—and anxious. "That's very maternal of you, Detective. Did you know it is 11 o'clock? What could be the problem that would cause you to call and leave no message . . . five times?"

The service phone buzzed again, and, before Napoli could answer, Tom excused himself and set the phone down. His food had arrived and was on its way up to Tom's apartment. Tom reminded himself he was well lit and to take the edge off. He was also anxious all over again.

"Yes, Detective."

"Mr. Strawbridge, in the kinder, gentler N.Y.P.D., some of our client-relationship counselors have studied the benefits of regular follow-up calls to eyewitnesses of violent crimes. In an effort to be supportive and provide help, if necessary. We've also learned to listen for additional and overlooked facts that may have escaped the witness due to stress from the experience."

Client-relationship counselors! Is he kidding?

Tom was not buying it. The doorbell rang. Tom excused himself again, took his meal directly from the Porter, and took the shopping bag left earlier on his hall table by the Hallman. He tipped the porter a $5, put the shopping bag on his foyer table, and put the bag from Vico in the oven.

Taking his phone from his shirt pocket, he said, "Yes, Detective."

"Do you have company, Mr. Strawbridge?"

Fighting the urge to crack *way* wise, Tom said, "That was my dinner. What is this about?"

"Well, we'll talk more about it, but it appears those men are serious professionals and are well supported. That was not their first job in the States. And the group is made up of some rough customers. We don't have anything on where to start to look for the couple that set up Mr. . . ."

"Tabah. No shit?" He couldn't filter much longer. "And this call is about what again?"

"Routine follow-up. We are going to want to ask you a few more questions."

Tom drew hard on his vodka to push down the anxiousness in his gut.

"Tonight? Should I employ an attorney, Detective?"

"No, not tonight. It's up to you on the attorney. But we will need to talk at some point. Soon."

As cool as possible, "Anything else Sergeant . . . , Detective?"

As anxious as Tom was, he not only knew he was innocent but also that there were no skeletons to be unearthed from anywhere in his past. The call seemed odd and unnecessary. Until demonstrated otherwise, while not one of contentiousness, Tom's relationship with the Detective would be distant and fully filtered. Like hospitals, any contact with the law was anxiety provoking and held the prospect of nothing turning into something.

Tom knew it would be best to stay on the right side of Detective Napoli. But the guy reminded Tom of someone he knew at school, forced to interact, as they were on several athletic teams together. He made a good initial impression that quickly fell away. The young man had convinced a coach to address the team before an important game on the merits of sportsmanship. One of Tom's pals had referred to him as "a louche-eyed bumbler and a half gene away from a Down syndrome case." Napoli's manner reminded Tom of his former teammate in some ways. And coupled with all the standard, accepted stereotypes about the psychic profile of law-enforcement professionals, Tom moved him to another, lower phylum. Apparently, the man did not run deep.

Besides, law-enforcement people, like most attorneys, generally must create purpose and work.

"Have your dinner, Mr. Strawbridge. Goodnight."

Tom clicked off the phone.

Draining his drink, Tom glanced at a very crisply wrapped box inside the bag on the foyer table as he walked to his kitchen.

As he made a refill, he tried again to process what he had witnessed. Mostly he tried to imagine what Napoli really wanted. He told himself his dinner would still be warm after this drink as he sat down.

He looked at his emails and listened to his voice mails, and made a note on a follow-up item for tomorrow. He then crafted a return email. An apology to a woman he'd promised to call and never did. He hoped she meant what she called him in her scathing email and would hold true to her threat never to speak to him again. *So why are you emailing me?* he thought.

Maybe Napoli's call was routine. Survey the obviously legitimate and uninvolved lightly the first time and then drill down later. *Could I be a suspect? Of what?* he answered in his head. Maybe Napoli wanted to tell him that, as a witness, he might be in danger. Did something Pourat said conflict with Tom's recollection?

Was this about some merchandise Tom may have sold at one time that either ended up with Tabah or was found with the thugs? Highly unlikely. What, then?

He rattled the ice in his glass as he headed in to serve himself dinner.

Tom watched the end of the 11 o'clock news as he ate. A man of fastidious nature and flawless hygiene, Tom, uncharacteristically, decided to take a shower before bed. Errant and unseen gore? Wash off whatever he may have picked up from the gun? A paltry attempt at absolution? He had no idea. But he did know there was another small bloodstain on his cuff he'd found while taking off his shoes.

A Wednesday, Tom's cleaning lady had been at his apartment. He sorted the dress shirts on his bed she had picked up from the Chinese laundry—the only thing he did not allow her to launder herself—and put them away.

He showered with a mostly blank and decidedly fuzzy mind and prepared for bed. His suit and tie selected for the coming day, he saw it was somehow 12:45 a.m.

He climbed into bed and noticed a very dim light shining in the hallway outside his bedroom. "Dammit." The last thing he wanted to do was get up again, as he now felt bone-tired.

Walking down the hall and turning into the main part of the apartment, he noticed it was the foyer light he had missed. *Of course*, he thought. *The complete opposite end of the place.*

Just then, he stopped at the package that had been delivered. Tom, in highly disciplined fashion, never opened a gift before reading the note. He was no fan of gifts. *What the hell?* he thought. Tough day. Lifting the box from the bag, he tore into the distinctive wrapping paper and was happy and pleased to see an old friend. Dom Perignon.

Taking the card from the bag, he opened the envelope and removed the note card. First-order stationery in a light lavender stock with a thin white double border. MWJ was engraved in darker lavender at the top.

"Dear Tom,

It was a pleasure to meet you today. I must say your reputation is well-deserved.

Please know you have my complete confidence, and I am sure your decision and recommendation regarding my property will be the most appropriate and in my best interest."

Bingo!

"Also, I look forward to a time when I may take you to a celebratory dinner at the conclusion of our business.

Fondly, Marla"

Tom lay down and focused his pre-sleep thoughts on the brooch, and on the very thick, dark eyebrows of Marla Wingate.

Part Two

CHAPTER 7

Thursday Morning

TOM ANGLED HIS NECK AND HEAD toward the clock on his bedside table. It was 6:00 a.m. 30 minutes later than his usual wake-up time. He swung his legs over the side of the bed to bury any chance of going back to sleep. Assessing the damage, it appeared his cottonmouth was edging out his headache as the early leader in the second heat of the week's hangover contest.

As he showered and shaved, he prepared himself, as best he could, to move beyond the events of yesterday evening. Even if Napoli were done with him, the possibility existed that people would learn of Tom's involvement in a major crime. A reality he didn't need. But the fact he would have another encounter with the police would be a lingering annoyance until it had passed. He wondered if one ever completely gets beyond this kind of experience.

At 6:45 a.m., he was dressed, having coffee, and listening to *The Business Report.* He snapped off the television before the urge to turn to *The Today Show,* the morning TV equivalent of a gossip column for the light-minded, solidified. It was possible there would be a report on the attempted robbery. Had it made the late news last night? Jewel thieves and armed robbery were sexy news subjects. *His mind raced with different possibilities on how he might, if at all, be mentioned. Well-known gem dealer Tom Strawbridge subdued one of the perpetrators, most likely saving his life and that of another man. Police are still questioning a tall, well-dressed man as a person of interest seen leaving the crime scene.* Dammit. But maybe there'd be nothing.

Stepping out of his apartment and into the hall, he was greeted by his neighbor. Tom was the sort of man who never discussed anything with people not directly involved with the matter at hand. Yet he fought the urge to ask Jane if she had heard anything about the crime.

"Be good, Tom," as she closed her apartment door, her yapping cur in tow.

On the elevator bench, stacks of newspapers waited to be delivered. Some people, like Tom, had the Hallman leave their papers with the Doorman to be picked up on the way to their office. Looking from left to right at the headlines of *The Financial Times*, *The Wall Street Journal*, and *The New York Times*, his eyes zoomed in on the *New York Post*. One of their classics. *"Armed Jewel Thief Iced During Diamond District Heist Gone Bad."* Great. He was considering pinching a neighbor's copy of *The Post* when the elevator stopped.

As the door opened to the lobby, the immediate space in front of the elevator was filled with an enormous housekeeper. Tom thought he detected a smile in the mass of olive flesh as she stepped aside.

As Tom strode across the lobby, George, the Doorman, picked up *The Wall Street Journal.* He greeted Tom as he had for nearly fourteen years. "Good morning, Handsome." Familiarity of this kind is the exception, not the rule in pre-war luxury Park Avenue Co-Ops. One of Tom's credos, though, was "I look up to no man and down to no man." Tom treated everyone with respect, in addition to which Tom and George were friends.

"You hear about the action in the District?"

"Yeah." So nonchalant Tom thought maybe George either really hadn't heard or didn't read it was Tom who was involved.

"Unbelievable." Tom left it alone.

Tom took *The Journal* from George. He would worry about getting *The Post* later. They walked together under the awning and into the street. The day was gray and raw.

"How's Michael doing, George?" Any mention of George's son put a pin in anything else being talked about and changed the subject. Worked like a charm, every time.

George hailed a cab and opened and held the door for Tom.

"Thank you, George."

"Yes, Sir."

Tom cursed as his knee smashed into the ridiculous TV monitor on the back of the front seat of the taxi. The cab smelled like a tack room.

"45th and Fifth, please."

The driver snorted and accelerated like he was on a highway, only to then apply the brakes so heavily Tom had to brace himself with his hands against the plexiglass partition. Apparently, this was the only person in the neighborhood who had not seen the stoplight on the corner change to yellow.

Tom glared at the driver in the cab's rearview mirror and said, "First day on the job, huh?" The New York Tom grew up in was long gone. The current cross section of the cab-driver population was a constant reminder.

The driver looked up and muttered. Tom resisted the urge to torture this pig. He needed an outlet for the anxiety and frustration he was feeling, but this guy wasn't a good solution.

Staring out the window for the ride down Fifth Avenue, Tom, as usual, kept his mind off work. This day, he was thinking about his plans for that evening. He had accepted an invitation from one of his clients to meet a couple recently moved to New York. He wished to Hell he hadn't. But social activity greased the skids of his business and obviated the need for formal marketing. And even though he didn't know the client that well socially, it might not be too painful. How bad could a cocktail party be at the hostess's new penthouse?

Tom gave the driver the exact amount on the meter and got out on the Southeast corner of 45th Street. It was just before 7 a.m.

Tom walked to his building and entered. The night security officer greeted Tom on his way to the elevator. He rode the elevator to the 19th floor.

He heard his office phone before he had the key in the door. He unlocked the outside door and stepped into the mantrap. Unlocking the inside door, he walked quickly to the first security box and punched in the code. He punched in the second code after the "Premises Disarmed" signal. Moving to the inner office, he repeated the procedure for the second alarmed zone. Finally, he moved to the back inside office to disarm the two safes. He chose not to unlock the safes immediately, as he wanted some time to think.

The phone had stopped ringing when the answering machine picked up, but the message light was not lit. Detective Napoli?

All his life, the early morning was when he was most productive and creative. As a Senior Officer at both Harry Winston and Tiffany, he was invariably the first one in because, once the phones started, sustained periods for work were impossible. The phone started again as he was taking off his coat and suit jacket.

He routinely ignored early calls unless something had been arranged. The circumstances made the phone impossible to ignore. The phone stopped, and, again, no message was left.

Tom sat down at his desk and began to review his options. Do nothing. Call his attorney for advice and possible retention. Reach out to Napoli. He started to email Heidi to ask her to call Eddy Poinarski, the gossip know-it-all of 608 Fifth, and to get the contact information for Pourat and send flowers, $200 worth, to his home. The phone.

Tom's jaw clenched, but he answered slow and cool, "Tom Strawbridge."

"Tom!" *Of course, Henry Stacks.* "Bad time, Tom?"

"I *am* a little busy, Henry. Did you want to set lunch?" Henry was notorious for the early-morning call and left messages only if his need of Tom was urgent. For once, Tom was thrilled to hear Henry at this hour. Henry loved Heidi and would stop at nothing to try to get information about Tom.

"Sure, lunch, yeah. But first I want to know if you're okay."

"What do you mean?" somehow not making the connection.

"Well, that was a hell of a thing. I mean, you remember when those *bastids* got to me and Dori . . . in the morning, they just tied us up. We was scared shitless but no shooting, you know."

"Wait, Henry. You heard what happened already?"

"Of course. Didn't you see the paper?"

"Just *The Post's* headline."

"Well, it's all in there. I'm bringing it over."

"No, Henry. *Stop!* What's it say?"

Tom got up and held the receiver to his ear with his shoulder while putting on his overcoat. Henry told him the gist of *The Post* article.

Apparently Pourat started singing to anyone who would listen the second he was done being interviewed by the police and giving his statement. From the ambulance staff to the ER crew. *Note to self: Scratch the flowers.*

A *New York Post* reporter got him as he was being released from St. Luke's Roosevelt around 11:00 p.m. and had the scoop. Mostly, Pourat whined on about his experience, but Tom and his role were more or less correctly reported. A second phone line started to flash as they were talking. Pourat's last quote was "God Bless Mr. Tom Strawbridge. My wife and I owe him my life. He saved my life." *Fucking-A.*

As Tom was telling Henry they would talk later, a message light came on the phone. He desperately wanted to get downstairs and get the paper before he would have to talk to anyone who had seen the story. He hung up with Henry and punched the "Message" button.

"Good morning. This is Jim Sherman of *The Post.* I can be reached at 2 . . ." Tom hit the "Erase" button, turned on his computer, and headed to the door. The phone rang again.

Tom picked up the closest phone and said, "T.C. Strawbridge, good morning."

"Mr. Strawbridge?" It was Sherman again.

"Who's calling, please?"

"Jim Sherman."

"Mr. Sherman, Mr. Strawbridge isn't expected in until later this morning. May I take a message?"

"No, just ask him to call me. 212 646 1800. Got it?"

"Yes. Are you a client?"

"No. Who are you?"

"I'm one of Mr. Strawbridge's assistants. Excuse me, Mr. Sherman, there goes another line."

Tom hung up without listening for a response. On his way out, Tom remembered the likelihood of reaching his attorney, David Mitchell, this early was good. It was 7:40 a.m.

Hurrying through the lobby and out onto the street, Tom took a right to Madison Avenue. The closest newsstand was across the street. Tom bought the paper and returned to his building without any unwanted encounters.

At this point, he just wanted the next big story as soon as possible. He now realized that no matter what happened, he could be hearing about this for years.

Back at his desk, Tom's computer displayed a reminder that today was Heidi's birthday. He would put the gift he got her on her desk when she was out to lunch.

He then noticed there were four messages, but he read the article in *The Post* and then dialed David Mitchell. Tom got little more from the article beyond Henry's description, save for the mention of most of the big luxury brands where he had worked.

David had become a good friend during a contract dispute regarding his equity position when Tom resigned from Harry Winston. One of the good lawyers, David was a problem-solver, not a work-creator. David's answering system picked up, and it was one of those that records your name. Virtual screening. Tom wished he had one. Enough time having gone by, Tom expected he would have to leave a message.

Just then, David Mitchell came on the line. "Good morning, Rambo."

"God dammit, David!"

"You know, Tom, I was going to bust your balls for not calling me back last week but now, I'm afraid."

"You'd better be, you bastard."

CHAPTER 8

Thursday Morning

TOM SAT IN HIS CHAIR, not sure what to do first. His conversation with his attorney had been somewhat calming. It was also largely undefined and vague in terms of how to proceed. They agreed to talk again Friday morning after Mitchell had talked to Napoli.

He was instructed by David Mitchell to refer Sherman and any other press directly to one of Mitchell's partners. He would tell this to Heidi when she got in. He would also tell her not to bother logging in any non-business voicemails from anyone they did not know.

He wanted a coffee and something to eat and was about to get up from his desk when the phone rang.

Tom grabbed the phone angrily with a wave of tension, expecting the reporter from *The Post* and said, "T.C. Strawbridge."

"Mr. Strawbridge, good morning. Detective Napoli. How are you today? We would like to have a few words. Is now a good time to meet?"

"Detective, as you can imagine, things have gone very hectic, very quickly. I have every intention of continuing to cooperate and have just had an initial consultation with my attorney. I have a busy morning ahead of me."

"Mr. Strawbridge, I need just a few minutes of your time, and as soon as possible."

Was this guy going to be an unrelenting pain in the wrist? Tom decided to get it over with as quickly as possible. He hoped the meeting would somehow help put the whole episode behind him and help normalize things. "When were you thinking of meeting, Detective?"

"Well, as it turns out, Mr. Strawbridge, I had other business in the neighborhood this morning. I am right around the corner. You mind if I stop up?"

Baloney. Tom felt a mix of emotions. On the one hand, he would be relieved to put any further dealings with the police behind him, but, on the other, he was anxious and annoyed. He wondered if there was more to the detective's intent than he was saying.

It became apparent he would not be having anything close to a normal morning. He was struck again with the realization that significant time would have to pass before the failed robbery was not front of mind. At one point in his time at Tiffany, a fellow senior officer had been accused of severe wrongdoing, and his actions had sullied the reputations of much of management. It was a long time before people stopped asking about the event.

"Okay, Detective. Come over now." Deciding in this case that the best defense was a good offense, Tom asked, "Business in the neighborhood . . . delivering newspapers? I'm assuming I don't need to tell you where my office is."

"No, Mr. Strawbridge. I'll be there in five to ten minutes."

Tom hung up the phone without waiting to see if Detective Napoli had anything else to say. He went into the kitchen and started the coffee maker. It was just before 8:00 a.m. Heidi would be in any minute. He had gotten her an Hermes scarf for her birthday. She was a very sexy, cultured young woman, and Tom was looking forward to seeing her wearing the scarf. There was no question the color palette he had chosen would complement her natural beauty.

Tom returned from the kitchen with his coffee, sat down in his chair, and spun around, looking out at the modern office building on the north side of 46th Street. Directly across from him sat a man who had worked in the same office for several years. Always in before 8:00 a.m. and out by 5:00 p.m., he seemed to do little save for staring blankly at a computer screen on his desk.

This morning he was vigorously ratcheting his nose when a colleague strode into the office, interrupting him. Startled, he stood up and approached the woman who had entered. Apparently disgusted, she abruptly turned and exited the office.

Tom's doorbell rang. And the phone started again. He turned to look at the security monitor built into his bookshelf and saw Detective Napoli standing in the hall. Tom pressed the buzzer under the edge of his desk, releasing the detective into the man-trap. Once the door closed behind Napoli, Tom hit the second buzzer, allowing the detective to walk into the office reception area. Tom got up and walked to meet him.

As Tom turned into the main hallway, he saw Napoli staring at the neatly arranged documents on the reception desk. Tom thought to himself, *A-hole.*

"Good morning, Detective. Please come with me."

They shook hands, and Tom motioned down the hall. He stepped aside, and Napoli walked ahead. "In there, Detective." Once in his office, Tom said, "Let me have your coat. May I get you some coffee?"

The phone. The detective looked at the phone and then at Tom.

"No, thank you."

Tom took the coat and laid it across a chair in the corner. Both seated, Detective Napoli chose the chair that allowed him to see the door to Tom's office.

His eyes moved to an extraordinary specimen of the mineral fluorite that Tom kept on the corner of his desk. A novice would think it the work of man, not a naturally occurring mineral specimen. A perfectly formed cluster of bright, sharp crystals and spectacularly colorful. A brilliant indigo.

Tom's uncle, a world-renowned sociobiologist, had been the curator of the American Museum of Natural History. And ever since Tom's first behind-the-scenes visit as a small boy to his uncle's laboratory, minerals had fascinated Tom. Like every other little boy, Tom left the museum that day with a dinosaur in one hand. He had a smoky quartz crystal in the other. He was struck by the incredible nature of minerals. Mineralogy became a hobby, and, years later, when he'd had his moment and decided his life's work, the relationship between gem minerals and gemstones would figure heavily into his education, passion, and success.

Tom felt better on his own turf, and rather than try to educate or interest his guest, he said, "So, Detective, what's on with the case?"

Detective Napoli redirected his eyes and carefully explained what had happened since the events of last evening. Pourat was out of the hospital, with a broken jaw, broken teeth, and thirty-some stitches. The driver was still in custody. But unless he and the surviving gunman started talking, they wouldn't be able to hold the driver. The car was a rental from Newark, and the only thing definitively connecting him to the failed robbery were the personal possessions, including wallets, of the two thieves. They were found in the trunk. The driver claimed he had no idea what his friends were doing.

This was slightly more than the other suspect had offered. He had admitted only his name, Dragan Milankovic, a Serbian national. He'd apparently used his phone call for an attorney, who had not shown as of this morning. The preliminary search of international criminal databases, including Interpol, quickly revealed Milankovic was ex-military. He had a violent and substantial record. Napoli would have more within hours. They still strongly suspected these men were part of or related to the notorious gang of Eastern European jewel thieves, the "Pink Panthers."

No I.D. on the corpse.

Tom had forgotten, or not thought to ask the night before how the police came to be in the lobby of a robbery in process? Apparently, they were tipped off, because the clerk at the rental agency at Newark Airport detected a discrepancy between the credit card used to rent the car and the I.D. presented.

Intimidated, he proceeded with the rental and called the New Jersey State Police as the car was leaving the lot. The car and the three men were made at the Turnpike toll plaza. The State Police alerted the N.Y.P.D. when the would-be thieves headed to the Lincoln Tunnel. The cops then tailed them from the New York side of the tunnel. The detective said good luck often played a role in successful police work.

As the detective continued talking, Tom saw Heidi at the front door in the closed-circuit monitors built into his bookshelves. They were designed and installed not to be visible unless one was on Tom's side of the desk. This was not for any particular security reason. The setup was so private clients would not be distracted or reminded of the high value and possible associated risks of fine gemstones and jewelry. Tom believed some of his great success in getting people to separate themselves from enormous amounts of money was, in part, due to projecting an air of "Of course, everybody does this."

Tom's eyes were focused on the detective's as Napoli heard keys in the lock and instinctively looked in the direction of the sound. He stopped talking and turned back to Tom, clearly expecting an explanation.

"Please go on, Detective."

Napoli, clearly annoyed, continued on to say they were still looking for people who may have seen something. They were re-interviewing some of the people who had been in or around the building at the time. The various security-camera footages were being edited into chronological order from the rental to the shooting. The police had also interviewed Tabah in the E.R. of New York Presbyterian.

Heidi appeared at the door, looking stunning on her birthday. But her expression was one of deep concern. Later, Tom would find out she'd learned of the attempted robbery just fifteen minutes earlier after seeing *The Post's* headline on the Fifth Avenue bus.

"Good morning," Tom said as Napoli turned to investigate. In that instant, Tom widened his eyes and motioned with his chin for Heidi to leave them. Tom introduced them.

"Are you sure we can't offer you something, Detective?"

Turning back to Tom, Napoli said, "No."

As Heidi smiled and turned from the doorway Tom said, "Detective, is there anything else?"

"On the robbery, not at this time. There is an unrelated question I have for you."

Tom was tempted to ask if it would be a 6.00 or 7.00 carat diamond for his wife's Christmas gift.

"Before we get to that, I have two questions, if you don't mind. What will be required of me going forward, and do you feel I'm in any danger?"

"We'll need you to sign a release once the formal statement you gave last night has been prepared and we have finished interviewing. Some of my associates do want to speak to you. And depending on how things play out, you could be required to serve as a witness. Of course, we expect you to inform us if you hear anything on the street. We don't think they were working with any of the local industry."

Knowing the trade, Tom knew it would not be long before fact and fiction were inexorably amalgamated. And subsequent rumormongering would become sport.

"We believe you are in no danger, currently. But don't hesitate to contact me at any time if you are uneasy about anything or feel like you'd want to talk to someone."

Tom imagined any shrink associated with the N.Y.P.D. would be a real prize.

"I'm speaking with my attorney again in the morning, Detective. He wants to talk to you, and I assume you'd be willing to speak to him directly."

Napoli said, "We're required to speak to witnesses' attorneys, Mr. Strawbridge."

"I will give him your information and ask him to call you. What's your question, Detective?"

"Do you know Yuri Propakov, Mr. Strawbridge?"

CHAPTER 9

Thursday Morning

TAKEN ABACK, Tom somehow remained expressionless.

The detective told Tom he had no knowledge of Propakov's and Tom's introductory meeting just prior to last night's robbery and did not seem moved by the coincidence. Napoli explained that Propakov was a person of interest related to a series of "situations." Specifically, there had been several leads tying him to known fences in New York, Geneva, and Milan. One thief had been picked up on 47th Street trying to move a freshly stolen ring. In bargaining, he went as far as to suggest that Propakov planned heists, and third parties subsequently executed them. Professionals working closely with known fences.

There were also other rumors indicating his involvement with known international criminals. The N.Y.P.D. were investigating aggressively. At this point, there was no clear connection or any apparent involvement between Propakov and the Pink Panthers.

The detective wanted Tom to nose around in the trade and see if he could come up with anything on Propakov. In an apparent attempt to curry favor with Tom, he recounted, with surprising accuracy, virtually all of Tom's involvement with the police or the F.B.I. over the course of his career. The detective was also aware of the several occasions when Tom had acted as a special or expert witness in court. There were not many occasions, but he knew Tom had acted as the F.B.I.'s special witness in the recovery of the largest jewel heist up to that time in northern Europe. The "challenged" son of a wealthy Middle Eastern family had stolen a suite of very important emerald pieces during a Harry Winston sales presentation in Milan.

He also knew about Tom's "swinging the case" in favor of Christie's and two defendants in the trade because of his expert testimony. This was after the contested sale of a $40,000,000 Vivid Orange diamond. Napoli acknowledged that Tom's record was spotless, and, so, he was somewhat sensitive to the fact any inquiries regarding Propakov would have to be positioned delicately. Tom laughed to himself at the detective's naiveté.

Even as a retail buyer working for large corporations during the time when "gifts" to buyers were the norm, Tom never accepted anything. And once promoted to management, he instituted policies limiting gifts and created guidelines for the kind of things suitable for gifts. He established a procedure that documented disclosure. Tom's actions were not popular with colleagues or within the trade. He told the detective that, at one point early in his career, several "favored vendors" tried to ruin his reputation. They were afraid that, without preferential treatment from buyers, they might have to compete on a level playing field. Of course, material gifts were only one form of influence used by vendors.

Tom's first experience with the then-common type of endemic malfeasance came when he was asked to appraise the picked-over inventory of the then-desiccated Tiffany & Company. A group of inside investors purchased the firm in the 1980s from Avon, the cosmetic company. As a junior officer, Tom had just joined the firm. He had started his career at the Gemological Institute of America, the trade side of the business. He knew, had worked with, and was well known by most of the important colored-stone and diamond dealers. He was put in a very awkward position as a result.

Tom was tasked with trying to "sell back" some of the gemstone inventories to vendors who had taken advantage of the firm. Tom quickly learned of the relationship that existed between certain vendors and the former head merchant, who had been forced out prior to the leveraged buyout. The vendors resented and resisted Tom's attempts to get them to take back goods. They quickly rolled over on the head merchant. And the arrangement was remarkably simple. The vendors were to pay 10% off the top of any purchase back to the merchant. Regardless of the quality of the gemstones.

In his own business, Tom followed the letter of the law regarding sales to retail brands. The purchase of secondhand goods from the public was tedious as well. A licensed secondhand dealer had to document the identity of the seller. And there was the two-week holding period in case a theft was reported, and so on. Selling or buying, Tom never cut a corner.

Tom asked Napoli if he was aware that certain "brokers" dealt regularly in stolen goods. For the most part, these were office-less flunkies. Not really part of the trade, they would act as middlemen between thieves and buyers. The detective said he assumed as much but knew of no particulars. Tom told the detective it took several years after opening his own office for these openly crooked brokers to stop soliciting him.

They discussed the relationship that had flourished since the late 1940s between the jewelry trade and organized crime, and compared notes. The wise guys would take stolen goods to the Jewelry Districts on Canal Street and to 47th Street. They would sell for cents on the dollar and expected a cut of the profit later. Tom and Napoli shared a smile when each speculated on which group would generally take the bigger screwing.

Tom then related a conversation he'd had early on in his career with a now-deceased secondhand dealer. He had been the first tenant of the then-new Empire State Building. This very prominent and prescient man was the first to reap the benefits of the then-novel power of radio advertising, long before television.

Old at the time, the man had told Tom all the big-name dealers on 47th Street had fenced goods for organized crime, until they became successful enough to go legit. Or go legit most of the time. Tom stopped short of naming names but explained that many of the most important and prominent dealers today were the sons and grandchildren of these men. Tom said, "A good example of that old saying, 'A dead wolf is already half a lamb,' isn't it, Detective?" Detective Napoli took out his notebook and copied down the phrase.

Unlike most art, stolen jewelry was small and portable, and could easily be remounted or re-cut. Tom quickly explained The Hope Diamond, the most famous gemstone in the world, was originally part of a larger diamond. The "French Blue" had been re-cut to its current shape and weight to conceal its theft from the French Crown Jewels. Tom glanced at a photograph on the wall of him holding The Hope Diamond at the Smithsonian Institute.

It was 8:40 a.m., and Heidi called Tom to tell him his first appointment had arrived early. Tom, feeling more relaxed than he had all morning, had a rush of excitement when he realized the lady who had just arrived would be all over Marla Wingate's brooch. That brooch.

"I'll let you know anything I might find out or hear, Detective. And I'll call my attorney later, and he'll be in touch. His name is David Mitchell." Accelerating the process somehow made Tom feel better.

Standing and turning for his coat, Napoli said, "Have Mitchell call me at his convenience. Thank you for your time. I'm sorry about last night, but all things considered, it could have been much worse."

That sobered Tom right up. *No shit*, he thought.

Tom stepped on the button under the carpet that flashed a discreet light across from Heidi's desk.

Heidi, on cue, appeared at the door to walk the detective out. As they left, Tom sat down and watched them in the monitors. Heidi watched as Detective Napoli let himself out. She turned, smiling at the lady in the waiting area, and made a beeline back toward Tom's office.

She was on the verge of tears as she stood in Tom's doorway. He smiled broadly, "Happy Birthday!"

"I'll tell you everything after we're done with Mrs. Goldfaden. Opera-length Tahitian pearl re-stringing and a replacement

Lightning Ridge black opal for her ring, yes? Please put her in the big room, and I'll be right along."

Heidi glanced at the unopened safe. She looked as radiant as a movie star and, while confident, had no idea how striking she was.

"Look, between Henry Stacks, *The Post* reporter, and that cop, I haven't had a moment. Let's go."

CHAPTER 10

Thursday Midmorning

IT TOOK TOM FORTY-FIVE MINUTES to finish with Mrs. Goldfaden. It should have taken ten. Clearly too much money and time on her hands, Mrs. Goldfaden was not only tedious but also needy. One of those joyless spirits who found that the best was not good enough.

Tom had asked Heidi to screen all calls and take messages, and had been back working at his desk when she phoned him on the intercom. "Sorry, Tom. It's Mark Kessling. He says it's important, has to do with last night, and that he won't take a lot of your time. You want to take it?"

"Tell him to hold a minute."

Kessling opened with concerned curiosity about the incident and Tom's well-being. Tom explained there was really nothing more to it than Kessling already knew from the news and his own interview with the police. Kessling asked Tom if he was aware that the entire street was talking about nothing else.

To move off the subject of the robbery, Tom asked about the Alexandrite. Kessling immediately apologized and said he was sorry to have put Tom in such an awkward position. He said that the Provsts were acquaintances of some of his philanthropic friends in California. They had called him and offered to put him in touch with Propakov. They claimed he was one of the newly coined Russian billionaires who was buying art, jewels, and real estate very aggressively. Last night was their first meeting, as everybody was in town for the upcoming sales next week. Tom held off asking what was going on in terms of who was potentially buying and who was potentially selling.

Tom asked if Mark had any substantive information on Propakov's background, or if he had even bothered to google him. Kessling said he hadn't bothered looking into it until yesterday, since the people referring the Provsts were very well known to him. And when he did google Propakov, while his name came up, it was only in reference to nebulous associations with various Russian oil and energy companies.

"Anybody on the street know him?"

"You know me, Tom. I like to keep it close to the vest, especially when I'm buying. I assume the Provsts are real; they claim to have access to many fine jewels and gemstones, and are apparently strong buyers. I haven't asked word one about them."

Tom asked, "What about the Alexandrite?"

"I made him an offer, and he told me he'd get back to me."

Tom assumed that Propakov was selling the Alexandrite and that the Provsts were using Kessling as an expert. Tom speculated what Kessling may have offered, but he knew however much it was, Mark would have offered strong.

Tom didn't appreciate and was very surprised that Kessling had misrepresented the weight of the stone. A magnificent stone like that was extremely rare, and, therefore, very valuable at any weight. But there was a big difference in an Alexandrite at 19 carats "plus" and, all things being equal, one at more than 20 carats. In general, with pricing gemstones, especially diamonds, there are increments known as "critical weights." Simply stated, a .96 ct. diamond is less valuable, beyond the weight difference, than the identical quality diamond at 1.02 carats. 1.00 carats being a critical weight.

In most cases, diamond cutters will do everything they can to keep a diamond at or above each critical weight, including sacrificing cutting proportions. Which, while ending up with a heavier diamond, its beauty could be impacted negatively. To be cut properly, a 1.00 carat piece of diamond rough will lose half its weight in polishing. But since they are valued at a per-carat price, many cutters will sacrifice beauty for a heavier stone.

With colored stones, it is more about the rarity of any given species, as larger gemstones are simply less common. Over a given carat weight, a gemstone will be more valuable than a comparable stone that is close but below that weight. Of course, without the benefit of a universal language, such as the Four Cs in the diamond world, a heavier colored stone affords the seller more leverage on pricing.

"I'm surprised at you Mark—I really am. I would never have thought you would ask me for a price like that. But I have to say, that was the most incredible Alexandrite I've ever seen. Any chance you think we'll see it again?"

"Let's write it off to age-related bad judgment, Tom. And I give you my word, if I see the stone again and have a shot, you'll be my partner."

Again, Mark Kessling apologized to Tom for putting him in an awkward position and misrepresenting his relationship with the Russians.

Tom hung up and made a note about the actual relationship between Mark Kessling and his previous evening's guests. Earlier, Detective Napoli had asked Tom if Kessling was legitimate and honest. Tom explained Mark was as good as it gets in the jewelry business, and, up until now, that spoke well for the Provsts and Mr. Propakov.

Intrigued, Tom was trying to determine whom to ask first about Propakov when Heidi came to his door. She sat down and explained that the volume of calls had been so great she would have to type everything up for him by the end of the day.

They reviewed the schedule for that afternoon, for Friday, and for the following week. Mercifully, there was only one more appointment coming to see him. Tom asked Heidi to cancel his preview appointment with Christie's and all of his other outside appointments. He was planning on coming in Saturday morning to do the full figuring, as is said in the trade, on Marla Wingate's brooch. He would then go to Christie's, although that meant crowds and dealing with the public. He asked her to call Christie's and see if they could make a special accommodation for him with a private room and someone to shuttle the goods back and forth from the preview gallery. He'd even come before they opened, if they wanted.

He then took ten minutes and explained to Heidi what had happened the night before. Almost immediately, she became visibly tense and upset. By the time he had reached the end of his explanation, there were tears in her eyes. He told her to sit tight and relax, as he passed a box of Kleenex across his desk. When she regained composure, he stood up, walked around the desk, and put his hand on her shoulder.

"Now, it's your birthday, so we're not to have any more tears today. What say you go get us Cuban?" When possible, their Thursday Cuban lunches were a winter routine.

The door buzzer rang, and Tom turned to look at the monitors. "That's UPS. Don't forget the shipment of rough sapphire to the cutter in California, and stop back before you head out to get lunch. I'm sorry about this, Heidi. We'll talk more about it later."

She tried to smile and nodded her head up and down. As soon as Heidi left the office for her errands, Tom retrieved her birthday gift and put it on her desk. As generous as his gesture was, he reminded himself it was not really possible to adequately compensate employees like Heidi. He leaned over her desk and filled out the card he had purchased the week before.

Tom took the next half hour to make an outline of everything that had transpired since he'd met Pourat in the hallway of 608 Fifth Avenue the night before. Satisfied with its accuracy, he emailed it to David Mitchell, copying Detective Napoli. There was no way to escape what had happened. The phones had barely stopped once all day, but by proactively documenting the event, Tom felt he'd done all he could do to get some control on the situation.

Beyond what Kessling had offered, he would call three people in the trade to ask about Propakov. Two of them were longtime associates he had known for years. The third was more specialized, as independent as Tom, and was shunned by much of the trade because he "really wasn't from the business." The reality was, the trade was jealous, as this man's business was the envy of anyone who knew anything about it. He was one of two or maybe three who could get an audience with The Sultan of Brunei instantly. Everyone knew this, so the best goods were brought to him, and he acted much like an exclusive broker.

Tom was on the phone with his sister and looking at his email when Heidi returned with lunch. Tom saw her smile on the monitor when she looked at the package on her desk. He watched her leave the mail in the administration area and take their lunch into the small dealer room in the back of the office. He hung up the phone and walked out to the front of the office.

Tom went to the restroom, washed his hands, surveyed himself in the mirror, and returned to Heidi's area. "How bad is it?" Heidi was looking at the list of phone calls.

"Bad. But it's mostly turned into repeats. It must be a slow news day, because that guy from *The Post* has called five more times."

"I know. We really need a blizzard to keep all the intellectuals occupied. Let's have lunch. Did you get us anything to drink? Oh, my sister asked after you and said, 'Happy Birthday.'"

"How is she? Did she know about last night?"

"No less crazy. No, and I didn't tell her."

"Tom, really?"

It was approaching 2:00 p.m. when they finished their lunch and the second round of talk. Heidi asked Tom if she should open her gift now, and he said maybe after the dealer, who was due any time, had left. He hated to open gifts in front of others, and he hated to have gifts he had given opened in front of him.

When Uli Bank arrived, Tom apologized and said there was no way he could look at colored stones that afternoon. Tom had dealt with Uli's father, and they were one of the old and most venerable families from the Idar-Oberstein area of Germany. They specialized in tanzanite and aquamarine, but had one of the deepest selections of unmounted, polished gemstones of almost every species. Their family controlled several mines in Africa, and one of their aquamarine mines produced spectacular material. The traditional source for aqua had been Brazil, discovered by the Germans once local quartz and agate deposits began to dry up in Germany. But the African material was almost like a separate species, it could be so spectacular. A very unusual blue.

Tom and Uli talked for a few minutes about the robbery and other robberies they had both known about. Uli left with a promise to return mid-next week after the sales at Christie's and Sotheby's, but before he returned to Europe.

CHAPTER 11

Thursday Afternoon

TOM HAD SAID GOODBYE TO ULI BANK on the street, gone to the polisher to pick up a ring mounting, and was back at his desk. It was almost 4:00 p.m. He rang Heidi, asking her to update his call list and calendar through the coming week, including the upcoming Magnificent Jewels auction at Christie's on Tuesday. The complementary New York November sale at Sotheby's would be held on Wednesday. She declined his offer to take Friday off as a birthday bonus.

As he prepared a few questions for the next conversation with his lawyer, Tom tried to assess any potential impact from the robbery on his business . . . and himself. The way things stood, the likelihood of potential threats to him as retribution seemed low. He hoped. The publicity would pass and may, in the end, not be all bad. He reminded himself that less than twenty-four hours had passed. He would try to organize his thinking to put it all behind him and move on. *Control what you can control, and forget the rest.* He began crafting an email to Heidi outlining a gentle set of instructions on how to neutralize phone inquiries regarding the robbery, based on the caller's relationship with Tom.

He felt no emotion, of any kind, about the thief with the broken arm or the one who was opened up in the lobby. No reaction to the scene.

His call to Benjamin Kosuk about Yuri Propakov was almost as useless as it was predictable. "A lot of money. What you got?" An old-timer worth millions, Kosuk had been around forever and operated in the shadows of several of the major international dealers. He was not someone you noticed on the street. And the enthusiasm regarding an inquiry would be equally important to him if it were a gold-filled earring or a 30 carat gem emerald. Tom told him he would have something for him soon. The trade's standard delay tactic. This was his baseline reference, suggesting Propakov probably had not operated significantly in certain large segments of the trade. Kosuk ended the call with, "Lucky you didn't get shot."

Dennis Mangini was a well-respected "upstairs" dealer like Tom, with an excellent reputation. He was older now and spent less time than ever, which had never been much, in the office. Considered successful, he had worked at Sotheby's early in his career. His big break came when, in the sales room before an auction, he met the woman who would become his wife. A moneyed, Swiss ex-ski champion, she was the key to his social station and his business success outside the trade. They wintered in Hobe Sound, Florida, which not only helped with finding clients but also allowed Dennis to run in elevated circles relative to the trade.

They briefly discussed the robbery and shooting. Mangini's office was in 608, but he had left for the day following lunch on Wednesday.

"Never met him, Tom. Saw him at a distance at the Basel Fair in the spring. He was pointed out to me by Sonny Yang. You know Sonny. Supposedly he is a private, or a private's representative who invests in important stones. What's up?"

Tom told Dennis he'd been introduced to him by a client. Almost the truth. Dennis felt Propakov operated primarily in Northern Europe. While he was not certain, he felt sure his interest and dealings in the gemstone and jewelry world were relatively recent. No one in his immediate circle had actually worked with Propakov. Dennis said that it was rumored that his actual buying was done through an Israeli or Chinese broker. If true, this information limited Propakov's actual footprint and involvement in the trade even further.

"So, Tom, any action?" Nothing if not selfish, Dennis always made one feel like you were leaving him out of something. He was, however, one of the few who might have a creative idea on how to handle the Wingate brooch if it came to that. But Tom could never include him, as he was not capable of being a "good" partner. The rules always changed during the game.

To cover the entire range of dealers in the trade, Tom had left a message with the assistant of Serge Wienkoff. Everyone criticized Serge. That was because they were so envious. When Tom was starting out as a young salesman at Harry Winston, Wienkoff ran the Geneva office before leaving and going out on his own. Once Tom became aware of Wienkoff, he tried to learn everything he could about the man, thinking anything he picked up might be valuable and was probably worth emulating.

Tom assisted him once at a sales event in Gstaad, and they bonded. He hoped, at the time, it was the beginning of a relationship that could be fruitful in the future. They knew and respected each other, and often sought each other out at the Christie's and Sotheby's dinners held for important trade partners prior to big sales in Geneva. And on other occasions, they gravitated to each other at similar events because they felt insulated from the rest of the trade. They did little business directly. Given the nature of the high-end jewel business, each man had bought from and sold some magnificent items to the other without knowing it at the time, only to find out later. It was as if they each felt knowing too much about the other would somehow be giving up an advantage.

In addition to being a world-class salesman during the Golden Age of 20th-century society, Wienkoff had turned every private business he had been associated with into gold. Now in his 80s, Tom figured he spent 30% to 50% of his efforts in the trade and pursued any other opportunity that came along if the numbers were right. It was public knowledge that Wienkoff had pocketed close to € 60,000,000 on a deal taking a Swiss hospital-bed company public. The trade, with the confidence only pure ignorance can bring, dismissed this as a "lucky deal" that was "handed to him."

Heidi buzzed. Wienkoff was on the phone. "Serge, how are you?"

"My dear friend. All is well. We can only hope for more."

Men with Wienkoff's breeding and education were rare in the jewelry industry, and Tom got a boost whenever they talked.

"Tell me, Tom. How bad was it?"

"About like you can imagine. Between us, Serge, I did what I felt I had to do at that moment. Just reacted. Turned very ugly, very quickly."

"Thank God."

"Is there anything I can do for you, Tom?"

"Thank you, no."

"To what do I owe the pleasure of your call?"

"Very between us, Serge, I have been introduced to someone, and I need information. Yuri Propakov."

"Of course. He was a crude Russian thug working for their government before the end of the Cold War. And now, thanks to his connections, timing, and being in the right place at the right time, he is an extraordinarily rich crude Russian thug."

Tom chuckled, politely.

"As far as I know, his dealings in our business have been straight. Meaning simply, he has paid his obligations. I understand he buys very strong, what he thinks is the best, and re-sells mostly to rich acquaintances. Then there are the stories."

"Yes?"

"Well, Tom, he apparently did some work for, or at least had an association with, Igor Yatkin. The arms broker. It is said Yatkin got started in gold, gemstones, and art to clean his commissions. Beyond that, I know nothing. However, I did buy a Faberge piece from *"a la Russe Brat'ya,"* which they had on consignment from Propakov. It was obviously an original. And in untouched, mint condition. I demanded to know the origin and provenance before purchasing. They produced documentation that was acceptable, but who knows? My client was happy. Never met or saw Propakov and will never receive him directly. You know how it is, Tom."

"Serge, very interesting. Thank you very much. All between us, of course."

"Of course. Shall we lunch soon?"

"Wonderful. I will be in touch after the sales, Serge. Do you like the blue?"

"No. The color might improve in re-cutting, but just too gray. And the cut is less than delicate. Your opinion, Tom?"

"I'll see it tomorrow. I have been away. I did get to Sotheby's to preview their sale before I left, but nothing special."

"Agree. A thin offering."

"Thank you again, Serge. *Ciao*."

"*Ciao*."

All their infrequent conversations ended the same way. There would be no lunch.

It was 5:15 p.m., and Tom wanted to go to his club for a steam.

Heidi alerted him. "Detective Napoli." Tom told her to put him through.

"Mr. Strawbridge, we've positively confirmed the identities of the driver and the deceased perpetrator. The initial I.D. on Milankovic held up. Both Serbian nationals, ex-military, and tied directly to several Pink Panther jobs. We believe the third one can be seen on YouTube in a mall-robbery video from 2007. In Dubai, where they drove their cars into the mall and then into the façade of the Graff boutique. These two aren't going anywhere and will be extradited."

"I know about the Harry Winston robberies in Paris and the Graff incident in London. Are you talking about the cars in the Wafi Mall in Dubai story? Did that really happen the way I've heard?"

"Oh, it happened. Take a look. That one was in 2007, but they have been active for well over a decade, and at least three of the principals have been arrested, tried, and sentenced to prison. And then escaped. With a lot of help, mostly while being moved.

"Two. The Provsts, who we interviewed last night, are legit. All the way. There was a tax issue at one time, but it was settled. Kessling, which will be no surprise to you, checks out. Very charitable. How he met the Provsts? Says they wanted an important item, and he was helping them. They concurred. That apparently means he was acting as a broker, expert, or go-between.

"And three, our friend, Propakov. Kessling didn't know much. And the Provsts say Propakov approached them at the Basil Fair."

Tom interjected, "Basel."

"Right. He looks to be what we might call semi-legit. Too early to know. Shady past, well-heeled, but almost certainly has fenced . . . knowingly or unknowingly. Not to mention buying and selling stolen property. My gut is he's more crooked than not. Have you had a chance to ask around?"

"Just starting, Detective. A little information but nothing of interest yet."

Tom knew he would have to say whatever he was going to say about Propakov soon but held back.

"Here's the good part, Mr. Strawbridge. Interpol and others have had him in their sights for more than a year. They suspect there was some relationship with Igor Yatkin. Ever hear of him?"

"No."

"He's wanted in several countries for, among other things, a series of illegal arms deals. And I mean very major. Bad guy.

How Propakov fits in with him, if he does, we don't know." There was a pause. "Will you be available all day tomorrow?"

"Yes, Detective."

"How you doing, anyway?"

"Thank you, Detective."

"Right."

CHAPTER 12

Thursday Evening

On his way out, Tom stopped at Heidi's desk and took a look at his messages. "Marla Wingate, 3:15 p.m." popped out. Message: "To let you know how sorry she is about what happened."

"Anything I need to do tonight?"

"No. Get going."

"Thanks. The safes are alarmed."

"Tom, go."

"Enjoy your birthday."

Cocktails were at 7:00 p.m. He would have time for a steam and to pick up some champagne, his signature client gift of Veuve Clicquot, on his way to the Russos'.

Walking through the lobby of the New York Athletic Club, Frankie, the Locker Floor Manager, came up to him. Tom had known Frankie since the 1980s. He'd started at the A.C. as a Shower Attendant. A former Gold Glove finalist, Frankie's eye sockets were a little rounded.

"Mr. S. I heard about everything and . . ."

Tom put up one hand and slipped Frankie a $20 with the other, saying, "Thanks, Frankie. All OK now. In a rush. We'll talk later, OK?"

"Sure, Mr. S. Just let me know if you need me." Frankie meant it, and Tom knew it. Some of Tom's casual relationships were his most open. And even though he had been a member of the club for more than 25 years, most of his interactions involved no more than a nod or, at most, a casual, "How are you?"

Tom managed to avoid anyone he might have had to acknowledge as he undressed and headed to the steam room. While he enjoyed the Tap Room and the restaurants on occasion, he never thought of the Club as a social spot. Most members did.

He did entertain there when he needed an impressive venue. The Club was also his default location for presentations to targeted "lunch and learn" type events. Alumni Clubs, big bank Senior Relationship Managers learning about alternative hard-asset investments for their H.N.W. clients, and targeted "ladies who lunch" events organized by one of Tom's bird dogs. The A.C. did a good job with the catering, and the various banquet rooms were magnificent; most had spectacular views of Central Park.

The relative isolation and steamy, hot mist of the steam room was liberating. He spent 20 minutes there, drained three cups of ice water, showered, and dressed.

Miraculously he got a cab right outside at Seventh Avenue and 59th Street, and then had the driver wait outside Sherry-Lehmann on Park Avenue. Gift-wrapped bottles secured, they drove uptown. The Russos were at Park and 83rd. A quick, sharp, hammer of a visual of the carnage on the lobby floor from last night, post the shooting, surprised Tom.

Rather than dwell on and ruminate about the details of the robbery, Tom interrupted his thoughts by revisiting the image of the brooch and possible next steps. He would spend Saturday morning in his office before the Christie's viewing fully analyzing the brooch. And, via Lili on the inside, check the Van Cleef & Arpels archives just in case it hadn't, for some reason, gotten into the definitive Van Cleef book. If it had gotten into the book, he felt sure he would have remembered it. Funny enough, through the confusion of all that had happened and the stellar magnificence of the Wingate pin, the mental image of the Alexandrite would not go away. Especially the red change.

Tom got out of the cab on the corner and walked into the lobby of 1080 Park Avenue saying, "Russo." The Doorman said, "Nineteen, Sir," as he picked up the house phone. Jeff Russo was a good, if infrequent client. Whenever he was in trouble, he'd call Tom, blather a watered-down confession, as if Tom had a price list, and ask, "How much is it going to cost me to get out of this one?" Tom knew what Mrs. Russo liked and always treated them well. About Tom's age, the Russos both had their own money. He did not really know them well, but they were relatively easy to take. They liked Tom and invited him to everything. The price of doing business.

When Jennifer Russo called to confirm Tom's acceptance, she was running down the guest list, mentioned a name, described a friend from Fort Worth, and said, "She's single, Tom."

Tom recoiled at the idea. He felt tired, and his thoughts continued to bounce all over. He noticed that the elevator operator's uniform clearly belonged on a much larger man. The shirt collar fit his neck like a tire would fit a broomstick. The man opened the elevator door on Nineteen, and Tom stepped out and into the hall. The Russos had the only apartment on the floor, and Tom was enveloped in the cocktail chatter spilling into the foyer. It was 7:00 p.m.

Jennifer Russo spied him immediately and waved, signaling him to come her way. Tom ordered a double vodka on the rocks from a spikey-haired waiter as he headed in her direction.

He reached her quickly and, before she could talk, kissed her on both cheeks. "Jennifer, you look stunning, as always," handing her one of the gift bags holding the champagne. She was in heaven. Tom knew he'd made an impression, and, while he didn't enjoy leveraging his appearance, success, or station, he took it very seriously. Tom had been an occasional minor celebrity before the robbery, mostly due to interviews and P.R. work. He'd been on the *Charlie Rose Show* several times while working at Tiffany, and people still remembered. Poor Charlie. And, Tom was a master at knowing when to break character.

"Tom, Darling, I'd like you to meet Lisa and Rich Johnson, from Santa Barbara." Perfect. The guests of honor, straight away. He would be virtually free to leave after ten more minutes, including a quick hello to Jeff Russo.

"Of course. How wonderful. Welcome to New York." Tom seamlessly handed the other gift bag to Mrs. Johnson as he shook Rich Johnson's hand. "I hope you like the wine." They were doing their best to appear cool and were almost dressed appropriately. Clearly, they had researched the protocol. She was moved and impressed, and Mr. Johnson seemed like he had "arrived."

"Thank you, Tom. How nice. Some of our friends are your good clients." Her jewelry was expensive but, at best, uninspired.

"And we were sorry to hear about last night." Awkwardly coughed up, apparently unable to control herself. That look of knowing one had erred overtook her expression.

Tom's drink arrived. "Just another day in Fun City. Jennifer, where is Jeff?" He took a solid drink and stared down over the edge of the glass at Lisa Johnson.

"Last time I saw him, on the front terrace." He nodded and smiled weakly to the Johnsons, but before he got away, Jennifer Russo got his arm. "Please don't disappear too quickly, Tom. There is someone else you need to meet." Tom looked at her with an expression that could only be interpreted as, "Weren't these two enough for one night?"

"Of course. Wonderful to meet you both, and good luck here in town." He didn't have the energy for passive selling or the interest to make the effort to ask where they were living, what brought them to New York, or anything else, for that matter.

Tom moved through the crowd and past the small quintet covering the American Songbook to the French doors leading to the terrace. In surveying the largely familiar group, he noticed there were an unusual number of smokers. There were already between 40 and 50 guests, all told, and while he'd seen many of them for years all over New York, he could recall very little about any of them. As a young boy, his father had told him that New York City was really like a small village. It was true. At this point in his life and career, unless it was a client, someone known to be well read or be interesting, he was on the move.

Jeff Russo stood in the corner of the terrace, silhouetted by the darkening sky to the west and the lights of Park Avenue. He was holding court for two men, one wearing a tuxedo. Waving a baseball bat-sized cigar, Jeff Russo called, "Tom, over here."

Shaking hands, Russo said, "You've met Al, my partner, and do you know Ted Jones?"

"Thank you for having me, Jeff. Hello, Al," shaking hands. "And, no, I don't think we've met."

"Sure, we have. At Old Oaks, last Spring."

"Of course. Been a long day. Forgive me." Tom had no idea if he had ever seen Ted Jones before.

"Tom's my fixer, gentlemen. Right, Tom?"

"We do what we can. Gentlemen, I'm going to get a refill." Tom stepped back, readying to go.

Jeff Russo called to Tom's back, "Call me next week, Tom. Something or other is coming up." Tom put a hand up to acknowledge he had heard.

He was now free to leave. The only trick would be avoiding his hostess. Stepping back into the apartment, Tom saw a group of four or five people looking at him. He assumed they had noticed him and had been discussing the robbery. He also noticed a very tall, attractive brunette woman in a bright-blue dress off to their left. He moved to the closer of two bar stations to plan his escape. Ordering, he wondered if the men on the terrace had not mentioned the robbery because they hadn't heard or because they were trying to be polite. Again, realizing he wasn't himself, he took his drink and took a deep breath.

There was a classic escape set-up. A textbook Irish goodbye. Slow crawl. More or less along the long front wall, engage a few people on the way, and, by the time his drink was done, he'd be at the front door. *Voila*.

He turned, refill in hand, right into the smiling face of Jennifer Russo. At her side was the woman in the blue dress. She was at least six feet tall, naturally radiant, and exuded confidence. In her mid- to upper 30s.

"Almost made it, Tom. This is Ashley Prescott. From Fort Worth, originally from Pelham. Buck Prescott is her father."

"Well, how do you do? And how is your father? We used to shoot trap together at Winged Foot, out over Lower Bay, before they decided that the lead in the shotgun shells was worse than what the G.E. was releasing into the water." Caught. This meant fifteen more minutes, but the woman was easy on the eyes, and there was a chance she would have a brain. At least Jennifer shot high.

"Thank you. Dad is well. We'll be having dinner at Paola's later. Perhaps you'll join us? He's such a sucker for a good shoot-'em-up story."

Not bad. Tom wanted to smile but said, "Not tonight, unfortunately. But thank you for the invitation."

Jennifer said, smiling, "Good luck, Ashley. He's really very sweet. Aren't you, Tom?" and turned back into her guests.

A waiter stopped, and Ashley took a red wine from the tray. The waiter smelled of pot.

"That is a stunning blue," careful not to compliment her actual taste.

"Thank you."

"What brings you to town? Family visit?"

"I started a business after graduate school, and we've been lucky, so I am moving the head office here. Oil brokerage. We have a good team in Texas, and I travel a lot, anyway, so I prefer to be home and near to my father at this point."

"Very exciting. Congratulations. Do you have office space?"

"Downtown. It'll be done by Christmas, soft opening. We'll be official in January. We will have about nine people here eventually. I'll see you get an invitation to the party."

"That's wonderful. I wish you all the continued good luck."

Tom was drinking when she said, "It's also time to get serious about a husband." He liked her, and he had to smile.

"Well, will that pose a problem?"

"Rumor has it the only men in New York are married or gay. Save for the occasional man-child."

Tom did like her—not bad. "Well, those adult-boy types—"failed boys," according to Updike—right?—are mostly urban legend, aren't they? I always aspired to be one myself. Lacked the maturity. And control."

She smiled broadly. "Actually, I believe Updike admitted he stole the line from Cheever." Tom was bested and was impressed, and he was thinking it was unusual knowledge for someone her age.

"Dad made me read all the Cheever stuff once he discovered it."

As they bantered, Tom relaxed and told this woman more about the robbery than he'd actually thought about since his initial interview by the police. She was very bright. He told her he'd been married and had no children. She assured him she knew that, indicating she knew a lot more than that about him, and asked if he'd reconsider her dinner invitation.

"Look at the time." He handed her his card and then wondered why. "Sorry about all that blather," waving his drink hand. "New territory. See you again."

He waved to Jennifer, who blew him a kiss. There were two couples waiting for the elevator, and they all rode down together.

Outside, he started uptown and decided to stop for a bite on the way home. He turned east toward Lexington Avenue. It was just 8 p.m.

CHAPTER 13

Thursday Night

MAI FUN NOODLE SOUP, thin noodles, from Pick Up Stix, was as authentic as it gets anywhere in the city. Uptown or Chinatown. Tom ate in the back of the small, bare-bones restaurant. He left and was waiting for the light on Park and 86th when he heard his name being called from across the Avenue. Females . . . giggles.

Looking downtown, back across Park Avenue, he saw a group of women, pulsating and waving on the opposite corner. . . . a lot of legs and hair, with Heidi out front. Post-birthday cocktail gaggle. He waved, walking west with the light across Park Avenue, waiting to determine if he could avoid a meet-up. When he got to the corner, he waited for the light and crossed 86th Street, knowing he would have to say hello. The talent looked good.

As the light changed, a cab pulled up to the group, but they waved the driver on. There were about eleven of them, and, as he crossed the street, he could see Heidi clearly. She looked beautiful and was wearing her new scarf. Standing next to Heidi was Max, her roommate. Tom was now glad they had crossed paths.

Max was one of those women one runs across only occasionally. Stunning, sexy, powerful. To-the-manner born and a force to be reckoned with. Best friends with Heidi since Sacred Heart. Born to wealth and breeding, she had turned her background to her full advantage. The only question was how long the inevitable souring to be anticipated in these types could be delayed. At 38, she was an accomplished hedge-fund principal, sat on all the right Boards, friend to business moguls and celebrities, with enough interest in sport to show all the signs of a classic man-eater. In a city of formidable women, Max had no equal.

Air-kissing Heidi and Max, Tom politely waited out the introductions of the other women. "We're so sorry!" "Oh, my God, I would have died!" "My boyfriend says he'd have done the same thing," and similar comments glazing onto one another every few seconds. Max stared hard and silently at Tom.

Tom leveled a blank stare at Heidi, and, cutting everyone off, he said, "Well, ladies. You know what they say. In this town, believe nothing you hear and half of what you see." Good, solid, unanimous laugh. A slight smile from Max.

Standing at some distance in a loose semi-circle were three young men, patiently waiting to separate the weak or sick from the herd. The ladies made an impression and created a target-rich environment. Tom imagined sheer numbers must have made any effective approach impossible at The Carlyle.

All the young women were feeling no pain, especially Heidi. Tom got them all in cabs and on their way, graciously accepting compliments on the scarf. The young men began to drift back toward Madison Avenue. Heidi, Max, and their Indian friend Sureka were left standing on the curb.

Heidi demanded Tom come to the apartment for a nightcap. Tom had never been. They lived just two blocks south of Tom. He agreed, saying, "Why not? A special occasion," partly because of the way Max was looking at him. He would make it quick and have only a few blocks' walk home.

Heidi chirped, "Terrific!" with equal amounts of surprise and excitement. They waited for the light and then headed north, four abreast, with Tom on the outside, closest to the curb.

"One condition, ladies. No discussion of last night."

A gust of wind came up, and Heidi said, "I'm always trying to get Tom to wear a coat." She and Sureka were arm in arm.

Tom had never been in this building. There was a semi-circular driveway outside, which was not common on the Upper East Side, especially on a side street. They got off the elevator on the twelfth floor of Heidi's and Max's luxury co-op. Rather than feeling hesitant and regretting his decision, Tom was up. He would try to hold court, a challenge with Max, ask about the birthday celebration, and leave after a quick two drinks or an hour. Whichever came first.

As Sureka and Heidi disappeared into the apartment, Max asked, "What are you having?"

"Vodka, rocks."

"Ketel or Stoli?"

"Ketel, thanks."

"I'll have the same."

Tom walked around the reasonably spacious main room that looked south with an open view, but not too far before it was interrupted by the back of another building. *Surprising*, thought Tom, expecting the best of the best. There was a good-sized dining area at one end and a long, narrow kitchen off to one side.

Max appeared, and she and Tom were studying each other as they touched glasses. They'd had only one conversation of any length, and that was for ten minutes during a break at an investment seminar Tom had been obligated to attend at the request of a client. Occasionally, one of Tom's clients used his profession and expertise to introduce an alternative instrument, diamonds, into their asset-management worlds.

Sexual tension between the two was as considerable and undeniable as it was predictable. Max was magnificent. The high-estrogen type. Raw, fundamental appeal that can't be bought or truly ruined with bad taste. As appealing as Tom found her, he knew it would not be a good idea to move forward, but he didn't break the moment, either. Her danger-potential was significant, and who knew what she might view as sport? He could not afford problems with Heidi. Or risk collateral damage to her. She was not of Max's ilk and did not have her constitution.

"So. How's business for the master jewel designer and world's greatest gemologist and gem man?"

He took a sip. "Nothing to complain about except the lack of important goods, especially fine colored stones. As always. Last time I looked, your fund's performance was what, in the top 10% last quarter?"

"Good for you. Not quite that good, right now. We have been hurt recently by institutional redemptions, like a lot of funds. Don't like the noise the government is making."

They sat on the couch and talked easily for a few minutes when Heidi and Sureka reappeared. Heidi looked a little pale and sat down on a chair facing Max and Tom. Sureka left for the kitchen. "I'll fix us something. You two OK?"

Heidi made an effort, but all the cosmos, coupled with a young lady professional's diet, proved too much. She fell off shortly after she managed, "So, what have you two been talking about?"

Sureka returned with glasses as Max stood and asked her for help getting Heidi into bed. They led her out. Tom was nursing his drink and was just about to get up to leave when Sureka and Max returned.

"Be gentle tomorrow, Tom. She was so excited to have you here, and her disappointment in herself will be what she remembers. She gets like this only about twice a year."

"Well, I'm off," and before Tom could offer to put Sureka in a cab, Max said, "We'll see you Saturday. Thanks for everything."

Sureka took Tom's hand in the open doorway, told him it was nice to see him again, and left. Tom suddenly remembered he had sold Sureka's husband their engagement ring. He drained his drink.

Max looked back at her empty glass on the coffee table, turned, and smiled at Tom. "Refill?"

They walked to the kitchen, and Tom tossed ice cubes into the sink, handing Max his glass. He knew he would have to leave soon to avoid any issue. Priding himself on a staid, yet knowing, discipline, he was challenged. Her smell alone, and apparently her pheromones, were getting at him.

She handed Tom his glass and took a big sip of hers. "Heidi thinks she loves you, you know."

"Really. In the divine or carnal way?"

"Come on, Tom. You understand perfectly well."

"Ah, the protective roommate. Unusual role for you, I think. And I know you can understand I've done nothing to encourage her, and as a matter of fact, made it my mission to develop her as responsibly as possible."

"I didn't say you'd done anything, Tom."

Max was leaning against the counter opposite Tom, more or less mirroring his stance. He had to go, now. He was trying to recall what her man situation was when she put her drink down and stepped to him. She stopped inches from him and, looking up, asked, "What's it been like having every girl after you?"

"Ha."

"You know they are, and you know they all talk. And this. This is something Heidi and I have talked about, too."

She got a firm hold on him and smiled. "Of course. As expected."

If he was going, he had to move, now. One of her breasts touched his arm through her turtleneck. She was looking into his eyes, tightening and relaxing her hand. In one motion, she hiked up her short skirt and lowered herself in front of him while she opened his zipper.

A gifted woman. Tom would have happily ended things right there, having failed to leave. Max stood up, stepped back, and, pulling him toward her by his tie, hopped up on the counter. She took his hand and put it under her skirt and licked his neck. She led him back to the living room, her drink in one hand and his tie in the other. He adjusted himself on the way in case it was time to leave.

She put her drink down and, facing away from him, pulled off her turtleneck. Tom took his jacket off and tossed it on a chair as she reached behind her and unhooked her skirt, which fell with a soft whoosh to the floor. Moving it aside with her foot, she undid her bra, dropped it on the growing pile, and turned around.

Tom, very impressed, auto scanned an historical review and confidently placed her in his top five all-time-best-bodies grouping.

"Heidi?"

"No worries."

"That's it?" he kiddingly asked as he waved his hand at her pantyhose.

She smiled and began to pull them down, removing each of her spikey red Manolo's at the last moment. Her panties were gray lace. A goddess. Made more attractive by the extreme confidence she exuded. Tom went to her and, lifting her into his arms, aggressively put his tongue deep into her mouth. A swell of feminine energy and lust engulfed him.

He looked at his watch, 3:10 a.m. Max was curled up next to him on the couch. She was wearing his Paul Stuart shirt. What a stunner. He dressed, put his suit coat on over his undershirt, and folded his tie into his breast pocket. He checked for his wallet and keys, and gently put the back of his hand on her forehead, not wanting Heidi to find her, and his shirt, like that. She cooed awake.

And, without missing a beat, she said, "Waited years for that. So well worth it . . ."

"I'm letting myself out. Goodbye."

"Bye, Tom."

On the walk home, Tom enjoyed how guiltless and liberated he felt. Surprised, he guessed that was just what he needed. He wondered briefly about Max's personal life but knew this had to be left alone. For good.

Part Three

CHAPTER 14

Friday Morning

TOM WOKE BEFORE THE ALARM. He was alert. His pillow smelled like Max.

He put out his clothes before showering, and shaved. He arrived at his office at 7:45 a.m. with coffee from a street vendor. He had not been to Hasan's cart since the robbery. There were always a few copies of *The Post* for sale, and he wondered if he picked up a bit of the stink-eye as he took his coffee.

Tom came to his office, and the door lock tripped as Tom took out his keys. Heidi had seen him on the security monitor. She was never in before him unless there was an early meeting or presentation. She was at her desk and looked rested. She had been in for a while.

"Thanks for the drink last night. Nice place."

"Tom, I am so sorry. I'm afraid I wasn't the best hostess, and . . ."

"Please. A good birthday in a tough week. And I am glad you liked your gift. Have you eaten?"

He went to his office and took a quick look at *The Post*. Unbelievably, he found nothing. He asked Heidi to look at all the papers and see what she could find.

Settling in, he spent a good thirty minutes on the internet reading about the Pink Panthers. The YouTube video of the Wafi Mall robbery in 2007 was the stuff of a 007 film. All the information available online suggested the crew was loosely organized, but there seemed to be structure and a definite chain of command. They were violent, ruthless, and, when caught, tight lipped. Those who had been picked up over the years and could be held offered little to authorities, patiently serving their sentences.

Tom remembered hearing via friends at Harry Winston about the unbelievable—and awful—coincidence when the Paris Salon was hit for the second time. One of the Sales Assistants had been so traumatized by the first robbery, she spent close to a year on medical leave for counseling and treatment. It turned out to be an inside job, and the thieves had threatened violence at gunpoint. Within a week of her return to work, a little over a year later, in 2008, she was face to face with one of the men from the first robbery. He was disguised as a woman when they entered the Salon. The employee broke down and collapsed as the man removed his wig and dark glasses, and produced an automatic weapon from beneath the dress he was wearing.

One of Tom's great creations had been stolen in that second robbery. It was a magnificent 35.01 carat Ascher Cut, D Flawless, nicknamed "The Dude." It was almost two years later that, on a tip, it was recovered with other stolen pieces from a Paris rooftop. They were hidden in a drainpipe. Tom was still working at Harry Winston when he originally bought the 113 carat piece of rough at a diamond tender in Antwerp, outbidding Graff by a little more than $3,000. At $3,366,000. Bids on very important rough were never that close, so the buy was particularly gratifying.

Diamond rough from independent producers, those outside the DeBeers network of site holders, is generally sold in open tenders, where the goods can be examined, and sealed bids are submitted. Not an exact science, it was easy to lose big and hard to win big because of the skill of the *diamantaires* analyzing the rough. Rough-grading technology had evolved to the point where much of the guesswork had been taken out of the process due to the Sarine machines, which effectively analyze and plan rough diamonds. The machines are not permitted in tenders.

Tom and his colleagues figured that, before the advent of the planning technology, they lost a minimum of 10% of the weight of any given rough. The machine also shows whether to make one or two stones, and how to position the rough for cutting. And they accurately project the finished quality, clarity, color, and cut.

His cellphone rang. Napoli.

"Detective."

"Hello. All OK?"

"Never better."

"Your lawyer, nice guy. Well-connected, too. We'll want to see you both Monday. Downtown. Mr. Mitchell can make 10:00 a.m. Is that convenient?"

"I'll be there."

"Good. It's One Police Plaza, which you know well from your handgun permits." Tom couldn't help mouthing *Asshole.*

"I'll email information on what to tell the officer at the second desk after security screening."

"Anything new, Detective?"

"On the robbery, not really. Save for the fact the two perps from Wednesday are going back to Europe on Sunday. And before you ask me, I don't know any more, but the word in the precinct is that Interpol is coming. There is another subject we want to talk to you about."

"And I need a lawyer?"

"Relax, Mr. Strawbridge. We'll see you Monday. Oh, are you planning to be in town all next week?"

"Yes."

"Thank you. Have a good weekend."

Tom hung up and thought that Napoli may have had an audience. Before he could dial David Mitchell, his office phone rang. It was Mitchell.

"Did Napoli already get to you?"

"Yes. What's on?"

"Not sure, but it's unrelated to what happened Wednesday. By the way, we are preparing a release to go with their statement that you will be signing. Our talk went well, and I don't think I got his back up, but it's hard to tell sometimes with the lower primates."

Tom chuckled.

"My guess is, they want your help. He said someone from the F.B.I. would be in the meeting."

"I'm not the helpful type, David."

Mitchell chuckled. "Look, it may be beneficial. Oh, he mentioned a name I've heard. More on that in a minute."

"Beneficial to whom? But I should have no concern?"

Mitchell continued on to say his firm had done some research on the Pink Panthers and looked at the Provsts, Propakov, and even Mark Kessling. His findings jibed, for the most part, with the information Napoli had shared with Tom. For some reason, this made Tom feel better.

"We're still looking into Propakov, Tom. He may be dirty. Very dirty. Our partners in Milan tell us he was suspected of fencing a piece of stolen Nazi art from that discovered cache in Salzburg last year. When the buyer got picked up, he did the Italian version of copping a plea and never had to name names. Paid a steep fine and was out."

"Interesting. Does he have a record beyond that?"

"Not that we've been able to find. Still looking. But there is an enormous amount of information on the guy in the press because of his associations. Ever hear of Igor Yatkin?"

"Funny. I think Napoli mentioned him."

"What a character. I assume you know or have heard of Benny Friman."

"Who hasn't? I've met him. Lunch once."

Friman, through shrewd and ruthless means, had worked himself into position as one of the largest and most important *diamantaires* in the world. That was for starters. He had a lot of important friends in high places because of government connections made while he was a member of the Shayetet 13, the Israeli Special Forces. While his unit was on a mission in the African country of Guinea, he developed relationships that eventually led to him securing exclusive control of the world's largest-known deposits of iron ore. A stunning turn of events, as the licenses had been in exclusive control of Anglo American. The world's largest mining producer of many minerals, including iron ore and diamonds. One of the most lightly populated and underdeveloped countries in Africa, Guinea was virtually without infrastructure. The inland ore source needed a railway system for transport, but there was none. That, no mining capacity, and the lack of a necessary deepwater port made the rumors about bribery all the more plausible.

"Well one of his sometime business associates is Igor Yatkin. And Yatkin is a major buyer and seller of stolen art, antiquities, and jewels. Most importantly, he is the world's largest arms broker. The worst kind. One of our people in Geneva found out through a connection at Barclays that there was a meeting six weeks ago in Monte Carlo, where Friman is forced to remain. Ongoing tax investigations that began last year. Main residence is Monaco. Among others, besides the bankers, Friman, Yatkin, and Propakov were all in attendance. It may be nothing, but forewarned is forearmed. I asked Napoli to get you information on the Pink Panthers and Yatkin."

"Are you telling me everything you learned from Napoli, David?"

"Seriously? Look, because he said you could be helpful to them, and because of his probing on Propakov, they may want to use you to get access to someone or something. I don't know."

"Annoying. Do I need to do anything more before Monday?"

"No."

"What can we do about the press calls? There are still a lot."

"Don't say anything to anybody, and don't, above all else, comment on the case to anyone, either. Press or not. Have Heidi direct everyone to our offices, and ask for Mike Kaiser. He'll handle it."

"OK. Thanks. Good weekend."

"See you Monday. Bye."

Tom opened and read a thank-you note from Heidi and quickly wrote one to Marla Wingate. He looked over his appointments for the day and planned his calendar for Saturday and Monday.

Heidi came in and produced a clipping from the second Section of the *New York Times* entitled "Eastern European Jewel Thieves Strike in New York's Diamond District." No mention of Tom Strawbridge, only "a New York dealer" who "intervened."

She then reminded Tom that he had to complete a layout of diamonds and emeralds for a bracelet that needed to get into the shop by the end of the following week.

He got the necessary gemstones out of the safe and went to the small office where he did his technical work. When the sky was clear, the room was flooded with natural north light. Indirect north sunlight is the best light to view gemstones, particularly diamonds, and this little office was what had sold Tom on the space.

He sat down and picked up a pair of gem tweezers with rubber-coated tips used for handling emeralds. A phone rang at the front of the office. Tom realized it had been ringing almost nonstop since he got in.

Pleased with and relieved the layout was done, Tom returned the unused goods to the safe and sat down in his office. He prepared the wax sheet, which now held the emeralds and diamonds in a pattern reflecting the design to be used for the bracelet. He placed the wax in a plastic box and put it, along with a copy of the original rendering, into an envelope. Unless it was urgent, Heidi never disturbed Tom during what he called "stonework."

He called for Heidi. She told him he was set for Christie's tomorrow. They would accommodate him with a private room even though it was a public viewing day—if he got there just before they opened at 10:00 a.m. They suggested he be ready for extra attention because of all the industry buzz, based on his involvement with the attempted robbery. They were also good enough to offer him use of the employee entrance to the viewing gallery if he wanted. Heidi had taken his sale catalog and made a list of the fourteen lots he wanted to examine, and she emailed a copy to the assistant to the department head, so they'd be ready for Tom. She put the catalog on his desk with the list of lots on top.

It was no secret that Heidi loved jewelry, and she'd already been to the upcoming Christie's and Sotheby's sale previews on her own time. He would ask her opinion on Monday on the lots he was interested in to find out what she noticed. He was going to have to give her more responsibility, as it was time for her to take the next step. And that meant selling. She had already taken the necessary coursework for a Graduate Gemologist degree and was just waiting for her 20 Stone Identification final to be scheduled. Successful completion would lead to her G.G. degree. Maybe he would let her try to finish the California sapphire client, who was new and a bit prickly. Tom's business demanded more expertise now, and that meant a new hire. He'd had up to five full-time employees in the past. He really liked the current set-up with

Heidi and the bookkeeper, plus the part-time Japanese designer at two days a week.

She handed him a list of phone messages from the morning. Sherman from *The Post* had called again. Tom asked Heidi to call Sherman back with Mitchell's instructions. He also told her to fully downplay any questions, even from friends, and to say nothing to anyone. She looked stressed.

He asked her to take the bracelet layout and design to their top jeweler, Arvin French, when she went out for lunch.

Heidi left the office and returned a short time later to pick up the emerald bracelet layout. She told Tom that she was leaving, and she offered to bring him lunch; he declined.

"Tom, between Wednesday and my performance last night, I need a reality check." She looked like she might be on the verge of tears.

He took a deep breath and patiently reviewed the events of the last two days. He told her it was particularly important that she remain cool and collected, and ended by complimenting how well she had comported herself under difficult circumstances.

CHAPTER 15

Friday Morning

TOM WAS ALONE IN THE OFFICE, and the phone was not ringing. He started to read the messages on the call list and prepared to return calls he felt were necessary to acknowledge. His patience was already thin, and he knew the number of calls he would be able to make in one sitting would be limited.

He noticed Robbie Tabah had called to thank Tom for what he did and offered to help in any way he could. Tom would see him when he saw him—and probably at next week's sale. And Marla Wingate had called. The message log said, "With an invitation."

Tom started to return calls, including one from his brother, who had just heard the news in California. His younger brother was too serious and jumpy, for a psychiatrist, for his own good, in Tom's mind. He was uncharacteristically emotional once he heard some of the details and was also annoyed that Tom had not called him. Tom promised he would consider a visit over Christmas. A fleeting mental image of his sister-in-law put that possibility to bed.

"Mrs. Wingate. Tom Strawbridge. Am I catching you at a bad moment?"

"*Marla*, please. And no. Thank you for getting back so promptly. Are you all right?"

"Yes, thank you. Unsettling, to be sure."

"I can't imagine. Ann Ross, from Wednesday evening, and a small group are coming for cocktails tomorrow. I would love for you to join us, assuming you have no plans, with dinner for the two of us the minute the guests leave. Sorry for the short notice. I have one or two things I want to tell you about the brooch, so I am hopeful you can make it. It is a good group, and it will be painless. I promise."

Tom, anxious about the brooch opportunity evaporating and sensing a strong new-client potential, accepted, apologizing, "You know, I was quite rattled Wednesday evening, as you can imagine. Your thoughtful gift was the high point of my day, by the way. I was about to drop you a note, as a matter of fact."

"That is not necessary, and you are most welcome. Please join me. Cocktails are at 6:30 to 8:00 p.m., 835 Fifth. I'm afraid you'll be most comfortable in a tie."

Tom double-checked his calendar. "Thank you for the invitation. What may I bring?"

"Not a thing. Is there something special you would like to eat? Maria is a fabulous cook."

"Anything will be fine."

"Good. Goodbye, Tom."

"Goodbye."

Something could have changed regarding the brooch, or Marla Wingate could have changed her mind, but Tom didn't think so. He hated business events on the weekend but had no choice.

Hopefully, the cocktails and dinner would help his frame of mind. Tom knew that, after analyzing the extraordinary brooch and viewing the lots at Christie's tomorrow, he would be primed for the always-welcome potential of new clients.

The office line rang as Tom was about to leave, and he saw the caller I.D. at Heidi's desk. "Van Cleef & Arpels."

"Lily, Darling!" taking a chance. It was thankfully her, not her assistant.

Lily giggled. She had been at Van Cleef & Arpels almost thirty years, through two family feuds, and the acquisition by Richemont. The Paris office still ran the show, but Lily was the Head Expert and invaluable. Lily hated the institutionalized lethargy of what had happened to the old jewelry Houses, and much of the luxury retailing world and all that went with it. The general lack of creativity, as well as the veiled contempt for expertise and process from the sterile corporate types was particularly frustrating. Tom and she had known each other for years and saw eye to eye. And Van Cleef was also a good customer.

"Lily, I need your help. And I need you to keep my confidence. I've come across an extraordinary piece I can't figure. Or find out anything about. And, unless there are designs or finished pieces not included in Meylan's book, this one may be unknown." Meylan's book on Van Cleef reportedly contained photographs of nearly every finished piece from 1906 through 2012, as well as the entire rendering archive of designs that were never manufactured. Leaving no wiggle room, Tom said, "If you are working tomorrow, please stop by. I'll be here all day except for 90 minutes or so at Christie's. It is worth your time." Saturdays in the fall were a necessary evil for most luxury retailers.

"Van Cleef?"

"Of course. House number, maker's mark, and fineness marks, all there"

"Well. This must be something. Any chance I can come by later today?"

"Perfect. What time?"

"I have to be on 47th at 4:00 p.m., so say. . . . 3:30 p.m.?"

"Perfect. See you then."

"Bye, Tom. And, I can't wait to have my champagne!"

Tom finally headed out to 10 West 47th Street to do a favor. Some of the same street hawkers, a few still wearing modern-day sandwich boards, that he'd seen for 20 years—and, in some cases, longer—still asked him if he was looking for a diamond or had gold to sell.

Most major cities have jewelry districts where many of the trades that support retail businesses are clustered. The Diamond District, as New York City's jewelry area is known, is centered on 47th Street between Fifth and Sixth Avenues and overflows into the surrounding area. In the 1800s, the City's best jewelers were located in Maiden Lane, now in the city's Financial District.

The district moved north during the 1920s, as the large banks and insurance companies grew, and rents rose downtown. The jewelry trade was then centered on the corner of Canal Street and Bowery, and there are still many businesses there today. But by midcentury, the modern Diamond District had moved to 47th Street.

World War II triggered rapid growth in the district, as thousands of Orthodox Jews crossed the Atlantic to escape Nazi oppression in the early 1940s. The emigrants included jewelers and diamond merchants previously based in cities like Amsterdam and Antwerp.

The arrival of these jewelers was key to the transformation of this small part of Manhattan into New York City's Diamond District. Some of these immigrants returned to Europe after the War, but many stayed, permanently shaping the District's community and culture.

The street-level exchanges in the Diamond District are the closet thing in the United States to an Arab bazaar. Just more crooked. The ethnic shift on the street since Tom started in the trade was profound. Once decidedly American, with some Israelis, Indians, Belgians, Persians, and Afghanis, the arrival of Russians, Eastern Europeans, and a few Bucharesters had changed the entire tone, complexion, and atmosphere. Regardless of era, a common denominator remained. Many of the people working on 47th Street shuttling between the various buildings and standing about could have easily been cast into the cantina scene from *Star Wars*.

Tom did not like to spend too much time in the exchanges, under the best of circumstances. And today could bring unwanted attention and conversation. He entered one of the two doors to 10 West on the south side of 47th Street.

Like most exchanges, 10 West is a series of businesses fronted by display cases. The individual businesses were separated by an entranceway to the inside, behind the display cases. There were two aisles separating two sets of facing businesses. The first booth on the left had display windows to the street. It was owned and operated by Isi Cohen. An individual particularly committed to expertise aversion. Tom felt that, in general, the two predominant traits best characterizing members of the trade were ignorance and arrogance. Isi could be the poster child. None of that had prevented him from having made millions.

Tom stood at the counter while the elderly saleswoman faked a smile. Isi looked up, "You, Strawbridge. . . . still in the jewelry business?"

Choking back an insult, Tom asked, "Where's the ring?"

Isi Cohen produced a box from the safe under the counter and handed it to Tom. "Some rough stuff. Gives the street a bad name."

Tom wondered if Cohen actually thought "the street" had a good name. He opened a box and removed a ring set with an oval pink diamond. Tom produced his loupe, eyed the piece, and quickly put it back in the box. "That's not the diamond."

"Irwin says you sold that ring. He remembers seeing it in your office."

"That is my mounting from Harry Winston. But that is not the pink from Brazil I set it with. And the original diamond was 5.38 carats. That stone might not even weigh 4.00 carats. The 5.38 carater was graded Intense Pink back then. Today it would be Vivid Pink, and this diamond would be lucky to get Fancy Light Pink." Referencing the Gemological Institute of America's fancy-colored diamond-grading scale. The G.I.A.'s grading standards had eroded and softened over the years.

Cohen began a rapid-fire series of questions suggesting Tom was wrong, trying to save face. But he knew Tom could not be wrong in this case. The ring went back more than ten years, and Cohen had just bought it at The Miami Antique Show. Someone had taken out the original diamond and replaced it with a smaller, inferior stone but used the original gemological report and original mounting to sell it to Isi Cohen. A rookie mistake. No one bought important fancy-colored diamonds any more without unmounting the stone and getting a new gemological report, to confirm that the diamond matched the associated report.

Tom asked for the report, and Cohen produced a copy that was for the original 5.38 carat diamond.

Everyone knew the ring because it had been created by Tom at Harry Winston and given to the singer Patsy Grimes as an engagement ring by Ben Jackson, the actor. Tom and the ring had even ended up in *People Magazine* before the engagement collapsed. Harry Winston took the ring back, and Tom later sold it to a couple at the Palm Beach Art & Antique Fair. Tom remembered the husband had clearly made a serious misstep and was furious making the purchase, but quiet.

Tom sensed the three other people in the booth backing away, and, looking up from the report, he noticed Cohen was bright red. Someone put his hand on Tom's arm and said, "Thank God" quietly as they walked by and out to the street. Tom never moved his eyes from Cohen, as there was nothing more to be said. Looking to leave, Tom did the exact opposite of what any other trade member would have done in a similar situation—humiliate Isi Cohen. He said, "I'm sure you paid the right price" and left the exchange.

He ate lunch alone at a quiet Brazilian place on 46th Street where he knew he could sit alone in the back. He took his time and had two glasses of heavy red wine.

On the way back to his office, he ran into to Ernie Splinto, one of his oldest acquaintances. Ernie and Tom often joked about the general character of people in the trade. He told Tom that the reactions he'd heard to the attempted robbery and Tom's involvement were the usual mix of ignorance and apathy. Ernie said he hadn't called because he couldn't do anything to help.

Tom rang the bell, and Heidi buzzed him through the mantrap. He was surprised to see Max sitting on the settee across from the reception desk. He remembered Heidi saying earlier in the week that today was Max's birthday. The roommates had gone to lunch to celebrate both of their days. She was stunning. He had not thought about the night before since he had woken up that morning.

He wished Max a happy birthday, and she thanked him, stood up, and thrust her left hand out toward Tom. He was looking at an 8.00 or 9.00 carat, very gemmy, Emerald Cut diamond ring when Heidi said, "Tom. Max is engaged! We're so excited!"

"Well, how wonderful, and good luck. Who is the lucky guy?"

"In-house counsel for one of our prime brokers. Very persistent."

"And, very lucky," Tom said, resisting the urge to wink at Max with his right eye, away from Heidi. "Well, ladies, enjoy your visit. Heidi, I'm expecting Lily around 3:30 p.m. I'll be making some more calls until then. Did the bracelet layout meet Kendal's approval?"

"Yes, and just to confirm, the emerald boxes are to be 18 karat yellow gold, and the diamonds are to be set in platinum?"

"Correct."

"Oh, I put a Paul Stuart bag on your side table that was delivered while I was out."

"Thank you. Bye, Max. And good luck again." Thinking, *and especially to the poor sucker who is walking into that.*

"Goodbye, Tom, and thank you. And I hope to see you again soon." Her expression, while complicated, was unreadable.

Tom closed the door to his office behind him and adjusted the blinds, as the low winter light was harsh at that hour. He removed his coat, hung it up, and resumed making calls. What was Max thinking? Or doing?

At 3:15 p.m., Tom went into the safe room, opened the main door to the safe, and started the combination for the inner compartment. Once the safe was opened, he went to the hall to see who had rung the bell. Heidi was on the phone and taking a FedEx package through the reception window. He took the brooch back to his office and put the box in his lower drawer, resisting the urge to take a quick look, as though that might somehow diminish Lily's reaction.

He went to the Paul Stuart bag and removed the box and the ribbon. On top of the tissue paper was a note. "Dear Tom, I hope you like this one. When and where is next time? And, there *is* going to be a next time. XXX, Max." Her cell number was at the bottom. Her personal stationery was pistachio with cream engraving. Tom put the top back on the box without looking at the contents, put the box in the bag, and the bag in a lower cabinet, shutting the door. Tom wondered if she was unstable, bipolar, or if her extreme behavioral contradictions were just—well, *her.*

Tom was staring out the window and down to Fifth Avenue when Heidi knocked quietly on the doorframe and showed Lily into Tom's office. As Heidi left, Tom closed the door behind her. Lily made the most of her limited gifts but was dressed very smartly. Excellent taste. They hugged, and, even with her heels, the top of her head barely reached Tom's chest. She was carrying her overcoat on her arm, and she put it down with her purse on one of the chairs in front of Tom's desk. She sat in the other as Tom returned to his chair.

"What really happened?"

Tom gave her the overview, including some of the information on the robbers. He watched her expression flatten. In the 1980s, there had been a horrible error on the part of the police during a daylong hostage standoff at the Van Cleef's on Rodeo Drive in Beverly Hills. It had ended in gunfire. Three store employees slain. The man who held five hostages at gunpoint was eventually captured, but not before he fled the store shielded by three of the hostages tied together. All four of them had been covered by a blanket. One of the hostages was accidentally killed by a police sniper, wrongly thinking it was the thief. The entire event shook Van Cleef, and Lily, to the core. Tom made no mention.

"Well, you are very lucky."

"Yes, indeed."

Tom took the brooch from the drawer, placed the box on his desk, and opened it. He raised his eyes to meet Lily's. He turned the open side to her as he gently pushed the box closer across the velvet pad.

She looked down and covered her mouth with her hand, her eyes widening. She pointed to the window, and Tom waved his hand in permission. She carried the box to Tom's side of the desk. The ceiling of the office erupted in colored flashes as the sunlight hit the jewel.

Lily returned to her seat and put the box back on the desk. They were both grinning as their eyes met.

"Tom, I have seen the design for this piece!"

CHAPTER 16

Friday Evening

LILY SPENT THE NEXT FIFTEEN MINUTES thinking out loud, literally, as she tried to remember how and under what circumstances she had seen the design for the brooch. Tom said nothing in an effort to let her concentrate. At one point, she appeared to confuse the brooch with another piece from a Van Cleef & Arpels anniversary show at the Paris headquarters on the Place Vendome in the '80s. At another point, she questioned if she had seen the design of the brooch at all. Given that her career at Van Cleef had spanned so many years, Tom was telling himself it might take her some time to recall. But he was inwardly irritated by her high-pitched prattling, nonetheless.

When it was time for her go, Tom helped her with her coat and walked her to the door. She produced an envelope for Heidi, apologizing for the card being a day late. Tom was impressed that she knew about the birthday at all. Apparently, they were closer than he knew.

He walked her to the elevator and said nothing more about the brooch. It was clear that Lily was consumed with trying to remember anything she could about the brooch design. Tom sensed that her anxiety was a mixture of professional interest, pride, and the desire to get to the bottom of such a magnificent mystery. She assured him she would be in touch as soon as something occurred to her. He had declined her request for a picture, citing professional courtesy for his client. He did reassure Lily she would see the brooch again. Whatever happened. And she told Tom that Van Cleef would like first refusal if it was to be sold.

Tom stopped at Heidi's desk on his way back to his office, and they talked about next week's appointments. Heidi would send him an updated calendar that he would review to make sure they were on the same page.

Back in his office, Tom took the time again to return the calls of several friends and business relationships he felt were genuine in their concern. Or that he felt he must do, so as not to be rude. And, as is often the case with major life events, he was more surprised by whom he did not hear from than by those who had reached out.

Although there were surprises there as well. Particularly a call from Ira Mabin. Mabin was a Salesman for one of the stronger trade dealers in secondhand jewelry and important diamonds, Elliot Finkel. Mabin had angered Tom early in Tom's career by not extending a minor discount during Tom's and the new Management Team's first Christmas season. They had just completed the leveraged buyout of Tiffany from Avon, and every margin point counted.

Tom had sold four pieces to a new customer and admitted as much upfront to Mabin. This approach contrasted with the routine practice in the trade when something is on consignment and is sold. The owner would get a call from the seller, who would ask something like "Do you have any room?" or "Can you do something for me?" without disclosing the sale. Tom felt being upfront would be good for future dealings. He asked for a small discount on one piece from Mabin to improve the profitability of the overall transaction. The gross-margin equivalent of cost averaging. Mabin had the authority, but, apparently, as he was paid commission on profit, he declined to help. Elliot Finkel missed a career's worth of business over the course of Tom's time at Tiffany & Co. as a result.

Tom decided to return the brooch to the safe for a break, and to stretch his legs. As he removed the box containing the brooch from a lower desk drawer, a wave of memory from what he assumed was Wednesday evening, rose in him. A very bad memory. He recalled part of a dream that mirrored the robbery closely but not exactly. In the dream, he was in the elevator with the crooks and sensing it would not end well for him. He was straining for recall when Heidi's "Tom?" caused him to jump and sit down in one motion. He held onto the box firmly.

"Tom! What's wrong? I've never seen you like this."

Suppressing the urge to snap, he looked at her calmly. "I guess Wednesday evening paid a visit. I am more tired than anything. Would you get me a Pellegrino?"

Tom put the brooch box on his desk as Heidi returned with the water and his appointment schedule for next week. She asked Tom if she could talk to him, and he motioned to a chair.

"Tom, I have been trying really hard, but what happened Wednesday has definitely shaken me. You have spent a lot of time schooling me on security, but I never suspected anything like that could ever happen. And I can't stop thinking about what could have happened." He let her go on. "My father keeps asking me if we are now in danger here and thinks I should consider doing something else." Tom had had several conversations with Heidi's father, and by Tom's estimation, he had done exactly one thing right in his entire life. Marrying Heidi's mother. He drained his Pellegrino.

"I haven't let anything interfere with my responsibilities, but it's, I don't know, it won't go away." Tom waited her out. She went on for a few more minutes and finally stopped after she realized she had started repeating herself.

"This has been a real shock, Heidi, and you have been fantastic. And I can't thank you enough. I want you to know that I would not have been able to process anything *or* keep the work going without your help." Her shoulders relaxed a bit. "The police keep offering me counseling. Is that something you think might be for you?"

She admitted she had seen a psychologist, the same one, more or less steadily, since her sophomore year in school. Her next appointment was a 5 p.m. later that day. While not surprised, Tom asked himself if there was anyone he knew in New York City who was not in counseling, on tranquilizers, or both.

His expression remained flat. "Good. Look, this may be bad timing, but I was about to add to your role around here. Starting with making you fully responsible for our new sapphire client. We need you to start selling and handling clients on your own. And I would like you to start looking for someone to manage the office. And take over a lot of your responsibilities. Also, if

I decide to go for any of the items at this Christie's sale, I want you to do the bidding. It's time you develop your own style. Having said that, I understand if this environment, atmosphere, whatever, has become too difficult for you. You should ask the shrink, but maybe it would be a good idea to take some time off to think about it."

He thought again about the Harry Winston employee who came face to face with the same thief during the second robbery, just after returning from a long time off. People handle things and react differently, and maybe Heidi was just not going to be comfortable again.

"Thank you for considering the additional responsibilities. I love what I do, and I still plan on making this my career. I just . . ." She broke down. Tom wanted a steam and took a look at his watch as he slid a box of tissues to Heidi.

She excused herself and went to the ladies room. Tom looked at next week's schedule and continued to get organized to leave for the day.

He remembered Max's gift and thought he ought to get it out of the office to avoid it, or the note, ever seeing the light of day. He took the Paul Stuart bag out of the cabinet and took out the tie box. He put the note in his inside breast pocket and looked at the tie. Not one he would ever buy for himself, but tasteful and serviceable. As he went to put the box back in the bag, something shifted in the box. He discovered a pair of mink-lined handcuffs under the tissue paper.

Heidi reappeared, and, as if their conversation had never happened, asked him if he needed her to come in tomorrow. He told her he did not and said again to ask her doctor about some time off. They could talk about her potential new responsibilities again when she was ready.

He had put a lot of time into training her and did not want to have to think about replacing her. But if she wanted to leave or could not cope going forward, he would have no choice. He told her to enjoy the weekend and that he would lock up. It was almost 5 p.m.

He secured the safes, armed the office, walked to Sixth Avenue, and caught a cab to the New York Athletic Club. After his steam, he lay down on a chaise in the salon and quickly fell asleep but woke to two young men shouting somewhere in another room. He had been out for about twenty minutes and couldn't quite understand why he felt so awful. The shower helped with his fogginess, and he was soon dressed and looking for a cab on 59th Street.

The bar at the Melrose was quiet as it usually was early Friday evenings, when a large percentage of Jewish customers observed the Sabbath. Or at least wanted to give that impression. Jack and Tom exchanged their customary greeting, with Jack reaching for a pitcher to mix a martini. "Everything is copasetic, Tom."

Tom told Jack that the two thieves were going to be extradited to France by Interpol to face prior charges. And that Tom would find out Monday what, if anything, his further involvement would be with the investigation.

As Tom enjoyed his drink, he began to wonder again if Detective Napoli wanted something beyond asking Tom to check out Propakov. He reminded himself that he had to decide what he would say about his three phone calls before

Monday. He took out his phone and emailed David Mitchell, asking if it would be a good idea to meet before their meeting with Napoli Monday.

Tom got to his apartment before 8:00, looked at his mail, and was asleep before 9:30 p.m.

Part Four

CHAPTER 17

Saturday Morning

IT WAS 7:00 A.M. WHEN TOM GOT TO THE OFFICE. The morning was unseasonally brisk even with a cloudless sky and bright sun. He wished he had worn a topcoat. Early-winter weekend mornings in the City were quiet and pleasant. The German anecdote *Die morgenstund hat gold im mund* came to mind. "The morning hours have gold in their mouths." Always his maxim.

He disarmed the security system, opened the safes, and made a coffee. He was at his desk, jacket off, by 7:20 a.m. with the Van Cleef & Arpels box containing the brooch in front of him.

Opening the box, he marveled at the scale, execution, quality, and visual impact of the brooch. He put on white cotton gloves, used for preventing fingerprints on fine gemstones and jewelry. In his long career, he had never come across something of this importance that was, for all intents and purposes, unknown. Or, at least unseen for a long time. Tom lifted the brooch from the box and began the process of counting and measuring each gemstone in the piece. He would note other details of manufacture as he went along. First diamond, then emerald, and lastly, ruby.

Taken alone, the stem appeared too stout for the ruby flower. But because of the scale and positioning of the emerald leaves, the entire piece was a study in harmonious balance. There were seven Emerald Cut diamonds graduating very slightly in size from the top of the stem to the bottom. The first Emerald Cut diamond appeared just below the ruby flower. Above that diamond, the stem mounting transitioned to a set of four platinum wires that continued up to the center-back of the blossom, securing the stem to the mounting.

There were six Old Mine Cut diamonds in between each Emerald Cut, so the stem began and ended with an Emerald Cut. He put on his magnifying visor and began to carefully measure each Emerald Cut with a digital caliper. He calculated that the length and width difference between each diamond was consistently between 2% and 3%. Astounding. And the same held true for the cushion-shaped Old Miners. The Old Mine Cut was a precursor to the modern Round Brilliant Cut. While they both have the same number and general type of facets, their proportioning and shape outline are quite different.

There was a single "spine" of platinum wire, to which each setting for the Emerald Cuts and Old Miners were secured. The platinum spine extended ever so slightly beyond the last Emerald Cut, giving a slight angled appearance to the bottom tip of the stem. *Brilliant.* The prongs holding each diamond in its setting were discreet and struck the perfect balance between size and security. The cutting excellence and the superlative platinum work contributed to the subtle yet perceptible modulation of the stem. At the top of every third mounting, alternating sides, each Emerald Cut setting had a second, slightly larger, purely decorative prong. A highly effective suggestion of thorns. And, somehow, while the stem had a slight but perceptible curve from right to left, there was virtually no difference in the spacing between one diamond and the next.

Tom calculated, via standard weight-estimation formulas used for mounted gemstones, the seven Emerald Cuts had a total weight of approximately 24.50 carats. The six Old Mine Cut diamonds weighed approximately 16.56 carats. 41.06 carats total weight . . . Initially he had quickly eyeballed and guesstimated the total weight of the diamonds at 38 carats with his first look at the brooch. He had not fully considered the additional depth of the Old Miners.

Clearly custom-cut for this piece, the collection of diamonds was a *tour de force* of matching. Diamonds are graded for color on an alphabetical scale beginning with the letter "D" and descending, as yellow or brown saturation increases, to the letter "Z." A "good color" diamond, therefore, is actually the most colorless, rare, and valuable. All other characteristics being equal. All thirteen diamonds were in the colorless range, "D, E, or F," and Tom was ready to bet there was not an "F," and probably not an "E" in the lot. Magnificent. Stones like these were known as "Blue-White" before an empirical grading system and the associated nomenclature were developed. The average layperson started to see body color in unmounted diamonds around the Color "J." Nonprofessionals usually expressed seeing a relative dullness rather than more body-color saturation. Judging color in mounted diamonds is more challenging.

The other primary value-setting characteristic for gem diamonds is "Clarity." The relative freedom from various types of inclusions. These range from tiny minerals known as "pinpoints" to very small breaks in the surface of the material known as "feathers." The Clarity scale for diamond ranges from "Flawless," down through other grades, to three levels known as "Included." The lower levels of which, known as "I2" and "I3," are used in low-end commercial jewelry. On the border between industrial and gem, many of these could end up on an industrial diamond saw or drill bit. The ultimate Clarity grade assigned to a diamond is based on the size, nature (type), number, color, and position of the inclusions. Tom backed up the examination with the loupe in his dark-field binocular gemological microscope. Not only were there no readily visible inclusions, incredibly, there was absolutely no sign of wear on any of the diamonds. It was as if they had just come off the wheel and been mounted.

Unless Tom was horribly mistaken, these diamonds had to have been cut well before the standard grading language developed by the Gemological Institute of America was fully popularized and in use. These "non-quantitative" reports led to the modern notion of the "4 C's," Carat weight, Clarity, Color, and Cut, which, in turn, eventually led to a standardized pricing system. "Cut" does not mean "shape"; it refers to the exactness of a given diamond's proportioning, against established mathematical standards necessary for diamond to react properly with white light. Tom referred to diamonds as a "near-" or "pre-commodity" due to the now-accepted international language made possible by the grading system and price lists. The price lists, updated monthly, give a general baseline and starting point for pricing.

While certainly not fully fungible, the modern system allows for a general communication methodology, consistency, and understanding of diamond pricing and value.

No grading system for colored gemstones exists, due to the astounding number of slight color variations possible in these mineral compounds. All things being equal, a clean colored stone is more desirable and valuable than one with more obvious inclusions. And because of the varying characteristics due to the way colored gemstones form, there can be no standardized system for clarity grading or proportioning guidelines. The most important feature of a given colored stone is the purity of body color, known as hue. Value is determined predominantly from a given specimen's depth and purity of color.

Because diamond is the only gem mineral, or any mineral, for that matter, to be formed from one element, carbon, the range of possible optical, physical, and chemical variations is much more narrow than for colored stones. That results in a morphological consistency that led to and made the modern grading system possible. And, because diamonds are colorless, they must be cut to a specific mathematical formula. As a result, they react to white light, consistently yielding the optical properties of brilliance—internally or externally reflected white light, scintillation—sparkling as the diamond, light source, or observer moves, and dispersion—the breaking up of white light into its component colors . . . the rainbow effect.

Tom could not afford to start thinking about how to address the fact that the diamonds were not certified. On the one hand, any legitimate expert could see the quality but, on the other, the upside value would be lessened without gemological documentation. Diamonds need to be submitted "loose," meaning unmounted, to the better laboratories for grading. And touching the brooch mounting was unthinkable. When the time came, he would most likely assign values based on what he believed the lab grading would yield.

Due to their chemical composition and the way they are formed geologically, it is uncommon for gem emerald not to have noticeable or "eye visible" inclusions. And emerald is a gemstone that generally has more inclusions relative to other species. If one likes emerald, the presence of inclusions has to be accepted. Their included appearance is known as *jardin* in the trade.

Incredibly, there were no eye-visible inclusions in any of the emeralds making up the leaves of the brooch. The two leaves on the left side of the "stem" each contained five Pear Shaped and three Oval gem emeralds. The single leaf on the right side of the stem, providing perfect balance to the execution of the design, contained seven Pear Shaped and five Oval emeralds. The stems of the leaves were 18 karat yellow gold and seamlessly attached to the platinum spine of the main stem. All of the emeralds could have come from one incredibly gemmy crystal—the color uniformity, quality, and cleanliness were so magnificent. The mounting for each emerald was discreet. The tiny amount of yellow gold prong visible holding each emerald in its setting added a contrast and warmth to the cool green and to the platinum on the diamond stem.

Tom examined, measured, and estimated the weight of each emerald. The total weight of the 28 gems was approximately 48 carats. The individual weight ranged from approximately 1.30 carats. to 3.50 carats. Again, there were no visible signs of any wear. The polish was brilliant, and as new. Because emerald has less density than diamond, an emerald is larger than a diamond of the same weight. And ruby is denser than diamond.

It was just before 9:00 a.m. when Tom started to work on the rubies. He had to be at Christie's at 10:00 a.m. sharp. He started a new spreadsheet for his calculations and titled it "The Price of Wisdom Is Above Rubies" (Job 28:18). After putting his light on the "rose" blossom, he was not so sure.

Again, a collection completely homogenous in terms of morphology, quality, cleanliness, and, above all, color. The best he had ever seen, mounted or loose. Seven *cabochons* formed the center of the flower, and 16 faceted Cushion Cuts formed the petals. Also set in 18 karat yellow gold, a bit more prong was visible on the rubies' settings, which added contrast and depth.

After 40 minutes of measuring and calculating, Tom estimated the total weight of the 23 stones to be 71.30 carats, with individual weights ranging from just uder 3.00 carats to more than 5.00 carats. Any single ruby could anchor a world-class gem collection and would be the cover piece and anchor lot in a sale at the major auction houses.

This pure red, known in the trade as "Pigeon Blood," *ko-twe* in Sino-Tibetan, was largely the result of the lack of iron in the chemical composition of rubies from the Mogok Tract region in Myanmar. Formerly Burma. The absence of iron also means rubies from this region fluoresce a dramatic red when exposed to ultraviolet light. When Tom was finished with his calculations, he took the brooch to the windowless storage room and closed the door. He turned on the portable UV light, and the room exploded in a red glow. He could clearly see the details of his hands in the red fluorescent reaction. Fantastic energy.

Like diamonds, fine and important colored stones were subject to gemological documentation since the 1970s to be responsibly represented and sold. Colored-stone testing and examination is not for clarity, color, and cut. Country of origin and treatment are the important factors. A much more complicated situation compared to diamond, as each species has different treatments. Some treatments are considered acceptable, and some are considered heinous. And a definitive origin call can be subjective. The people treating gemstones have always been one step ahead of the laboratories.

Colored-stone treatments are used to stabilize gem material in some cases. In all cases, treatments are intended to improve the visual appearance of a gemstone. Enhancing gemstones is an ancient tradition, dating back more than 3,000 years. Treatments range from simple low-temperature heating to remove unpleasant secondary colors, to highly sophisticated treatments. One type, known as diffusion, actually coats a natural gem with synthetic material. The surface of a stone is exposed to certain chemicals combined with high heat in a furnace. Only the surface color changes. If a diffusion-treated colored stone were sliced in half, the inside would be a different, less-valuable color and likely more pale. These treatments are not detectable without sophisticated equipment.

Archeologists discovered heat-enhanced carnelian, a type of agate, dated to about 1,300 B.C.E. in Tutankhamun's tomb. Pliny the Elder, 1st century C.E., discusses in his writings many gemstone-enhancement techniques. These include foil backing, oiling, and dyeing. Techniques used on gemstones for more than 2,000 years that are still in use today.

Treatments vary from species to species, and, some, like the low-temperature heating of Aquamarine, are accepted in the trade as traditional. If a treatment is reversible, it is considered more positively than one that is permanent. Emeralds can be treated in many ways. Traditional oiling is meant to fill voids that reach the surface. This cuts down on light interference and iridescence. Cedarwood oil is most commonly used and is an accepted method. When a modern epoxy-like substance is used, known as Excel, the treatment is permanent and undesirable.

Of course, disclosure is at the root of ethical commerce. Hence, the critical role the laboratories play in the modern colored-stone business.

Back at his desk, Tom entered final notes into his computer, including the details of the pin and clutch system. Pictures of the front and back of the brooch, the tiny plaques with "VC&A France" and the purity marks, platinum and 18 karat yellow gold. Also, the Bigorne stamp. This is a two-horned, or beaked, anvil symbol with both a flat and a rounded striking area. These anvils were used when placing hallmarks and assay marks on metal. From 1818 to 1984, the French instituted a system whereby they engraved their anvils with insects. In the case of the small anvil used to mark jewelry, it was incised in a zigzag pattern depicting rows of insects.

Immersed in his analysis, Tom had not thought about how to manage Marla Wingate. What his plan would be for marketing and selling, or the fact that the brooch was not known.

Tom returned the brooch to the safe, closed the door, and spun the tumbler. If there ever was a case where the value of the whole was greater than the sum of the parts, this was it. He rubbed his eyes and noted he had 10 minutes to get to Christie's.

Because it was early, Tom did not bother going to the employee entrance. Gil, the Doorman at Christie's, saw Tom make the turn into the entrance plaza and waved him over past the small crowd waiting to get into a photography sale preview. He smiled, opened the door, and shook Tom's hand all in one motion.

Tom made his way to the main gallery, where the upcoming sale would be previewed for the public. He and Dawn Lawrence, the North American Jewelry Department Head, saw each other at the same time. Dawn pointed Tom toward the entrance to the back offices and waited for him there while he shook hands with two of the jewelry-department experts. They hugged as she gained entry with a key card. He was let into a small, empty office, where the lots he was interested in, including the blue diamond everyone was talking about, lay on a tray waiting for him. The gallery was already busy with employees setting up displays. One would not be able to move around easily soon enough. Especially after the lunch crowd finished their cocktails and showed up for some high-end tire kicking.

"Now, Dawn, that's what I call *service*. Thank you. And thank you for your kind email."

"You are welcome, and our pleasure. Heidi is incredible and always makes things easy. You did manage to shake everyone up."

"Did I, now?" Tom respected Dawn, but she spent most of her time posturing socially, and was becoming more and more arrogant as time went by.

"I'm sorry. I simply meant . . ."

Interrupting, "No, my apology. It has been a long day already. My reactions since Wednesday evening have varied, and we are doing our best to move forward. I have more meetings coming, but the police feel I am in no danger. I know you two talk, so I'll tell you: Heidi seems to be having a bit of a rough time, and I am concerned about her."

A young woman appeared in the door, and Dawn nodded to her. "May I take you to lunch the week after the sale? We are due for a catch-up."

"Of course."

"You should have everything you need, and, if not, John will be right outside. Coffee?"

"No, thank you, and I really appreciate your help today. Do you want me to tell John after I finish each piece so they can get back outside?"

"No, no. I know you'll be quick. Please say goodbye on your way out." They air-kissed, and she was gone.

Tom unpacked his catalogue, loupe, and penlights, and sat down. He was too tall for the desk, like every other desk at Christie's. But he was comfortable, and the office had good natural light. A microscope was on a small table in the corner, under a large photograph of Elizabeth Taylor wearing one of her necklaces from her estate's sale at Christie's in 2011.

Of the 16 lots he'd asked to see, only three of them warranted a full examination. And the Blue Diamond wasn't one of them. While not readily apparent in the face-up position, the stone was zoned, alternating bands of colorless and gray-blue material. Typical for Type IIb diamonds, which account for only 0.1% of all-natural diamonds. And it had quite a different body color, depending on the direction in which it was viewed, and the type, artificial or natural, of light used. Extremely rare does not equate to beauty.

Tom made his notes on the three interesting rings, all sapphires, and packed up. He opened the door and told the Admin he had finished; he was let back into the gallery.

CHAPTER 18

Saturday Midmorning

IT WAS 10:40 A.M., but there was already a good crowd viewing the jewelry for the upcoming sale. Tom could see across the gallery to the main entrance, where there was a regular stream of new arrivals. Saturday public viewing for the Winter Magnificent Jewelry Sales at Christie's and Sotheby's was extremely popular for New Yorkers, visiting out-of-town trade buyers, and local trade people who had nothing better to do or wanted to rub elbows and showboat. The champagne was flowing.

Tom decided to take a quick spin around the edge of the gallery on his way out. He wanted to get a look at the catalogue's cover piece. An Edwardian tiara made from large natural Persian Gulf pearls and Mughal emeralds. He spied it in a vitrine of its own in the center of the room, and, as he approached the case, someone put his hand on his arm. Tom turned. Yuri Propakov.

"Mr. Strawbridge, we were all so sorry to hear of your ordeal. You were not hurt at all?" Tom was not a Slavic-accent fan, and Propakov smelled like stale beets.

"Thankfully. If you will excuse me, I have an appointment."

"Of course, but tell me, is what they say in the paper correct? The police told me nothing."

"More or less. I am not able to discuss it."

"Of course. Tell me—may I see you at your office later? I think you would like to work with the Alexandrite, no?"

As Tom was trying to understand what he was hearing and gauge his anxiety about potentially being alone with Propakov, he felt a tap on his shoulder. Max and Sureka walked past, waving and smiling. He looked at Propakov, whose eyes had not moved from Tom's face. Max's perfume hit him.

"What are you talking about? That stone was yours?" knowing full well he was, at least, controlling it, if he was not the owner.

"Of course."

"We'll see." Tom might speak to Kessling again.

A very well-dressed, elegant older man with slicked-back silver hair approached and shook Propakov's hand.

Tom tried to move away, but Propakov said to Tom as the man extended his hand, "Mr. Matteo Keller, please meet Mr. Tom Strawbridge."

"Ah, the famous Mr. Strawbridge. Finally, I have the pleasure."

"Thank you," withdrawing his hand. "I'm sorry. I have an appointment and cannot be late."

"Mr. Strawbridge, I would like to speak to you soon. I want investments."

"Perhaps we can discuss that at some point. Goodbye, gentlemen." Tom walked through the crowd toward the door.

Tom blamed himself. He should have left immediately. What was the story with Propakov and his friend? The Alexandrite?

Before reaching the gallery door, he saw Marla Wingate with a friend, Kessling, and the Provsts. None of them saw him on his way to the street.

Waving back to Gil, Tom turned right on 49th Street and headed toward Fifth Avenue. His cell phone rang. It was Napoli.

"Detective."

"Hello, Mr. Strawbridge. I want to mention a few things. . . ."

"Detective, I'm on the street, heading back to my office. Can I call you in 15 or 20?"

"I'll call you. How is 11:15 a.m.?"

"Good."

The sidewalks were mobbed with tourists, as usual during the holiday season. Tom had to pick his way through the crowds with so many people gawking at the Rockefeller Center Christmas Tree. It would get worse after Thanksgiving.

Tom had temporarily forgotten about the robbery scene and his unease until Napoli called. He wondered if something about the meeting had changed, or if it had been canceled. Unlikely. He would find out what the purpose of the call was soon enough.

As he approached Fifth Avenue, he could hear the music blaring from the Sax's holiday displays. People were densely packed, many taking pictures. At the corner, he turned south down Fifth Avenue and was passing the entrance to 608 almost immediately. The scene of the crime. He made it a point to look into the reception area as he passed. It was empty, except for a maintenance man sitting behind the reception desk.

Approaching the corner of 48th Street, the river of people crossing the street was parting and re-forming. Closer, he saw a short, well-dressed woman waiting patiently. She had a purse in one hand and a long white cane in the corner of her elbow on the opposite arm. Blind. And not one person was even thinking about helping her. Just then, a man staring down at his phone bumped into her. She was jostled. Tom was enraged. He put his elbow into the man's side, who had turned to see what had run into him. That bounced the man into a couple who were moving fast. Insults.

Tom came to the woman's side and asked if she were all right and if he could shepherd her across the street.

"Thank you. I hate to come to midtown this time of year, but I work all week. Please put your arm out, and I will hold onto it."

The light had changed, and they waited.

"Always unpleasant after Labor Day. No let-up until Christmas."

As they walked along, Tom slightly in front of her, she said, "I'm going to my jeweler. She's on the corner of 47th Street."

"We are a little more than half a block away."

Up ahead, a bag person standing in the street just off the curb started angrily and loudly raving at the passing crowds. The blind woman's hand tensed around his forearm.

"What is that?"

"It's just a homeless man in need of medication." The man began flapping his arms wildly as they passed.

"That is so sad. You really have to feel sorry for some people."

"Where exactly is your jeweler?"

"In the exchange on the southwest corner. The door on Fifth Avenue, please."

As they made their way through the crowd and to the door, Tom noticed two Asian Saleswomen looking out the window of one of the small booths. They were looking at the blind lady with less-than-charitable expressions.

He held the door for her and put her hand on the handle.

"Thank you. You've been a gentleman."

"Goodbye, and the pleasure was mine."

She smiled.

Tom turned around and crossed Fifth Avenue diagonally and was soon in the lobby of his office building. He waved to the weekend security men as he got on the elevator.

David Mitchell texted him, saying it would not be necessary to meet ahead of the Monday meeting. Fine. There were no messages on the answering machine. He was in a chair in the showroom reading *The Wall Street Journal* when his landline rang. He walked back to his office and picked up the phone as he sat down.

"Good time, Mr. Strawbridge?"

"Yes, Detective. What's up?"

"We have some information put together for you on Igor Yatkin and one of his associates. And some press on the Pink Panther gang. Is there a chance you could come by the 17th Precinct House and pick it up today? We'd like you to have a look at it before Monday."

"Why would I need these things?"

"We'll discuss that on Monday. Can you make it—167 East 51st?"

Tom had a few calls to make and a few phone messages to leave; then he was heading to the Club for lunch and a steam.

"Detective, I'm sorry. I am loaded up here today, and I have no one to send. And tomorrow . . ."

"Never mind. I'll have an officer leave the material with your apartment Doorman."

"Why is this so important?"

"Monday. Were you able to find anything out on Propakov in the trade?"

"I'm waiting for a call or two more. Nothing significant."

Tom's phone rang again. "Detective, I have to run. Thank you."

"Hello?"

It was David Mitchell. "Hi, Tom, just checking in. You okay?"

"Thanks for the call. I was just on with Napoli. He wants me to read something on the Yatkin guy you mentioned. What do you think?"

"Is it just the background information I asked him to get you?"

"No idea. Sending whatever it is to the apartment."

"Well, when you have a look at it, give me a call, OK?"

"OK. If I have the time to look at it. Won't be before tomorrow."

"How are you feeling, anyway?"

"Basically okay. I ran into that Propakov at Christie's."

"And?"

"Nothing. I didn't hang around. He introduced me to another guy, Matteo Keller. Slick. I was about to google him."

"Here, I'll do it now. Hmmm. Former private-equity Portfolio Manager at APAX in London. . . . started his own group in 2002. Whoa, his list of deals is impressive. 70. I'll send the link."

"He told me he wanted investments."

"What kind?"

"Not sure what he meant."

"All right. I'm home tomorrow if anything comes up. Maybe the Giants can win."

"I'm about to head out. Thanks again for the call."

"Bye."

A quick look at the appointment calendar showed only four client appointments in the upcoming week. One Monday afternoon and three Friday. All of them were new, which was good. Light for the season. Part of the reason for the light schedule was the sales next week. He always blocked out both Tuesday and Wednesday during the "Magnificent" auction week because of all the international dealers who wanted to visit. He noted that the appointments the following week were comparatively heavy.

Tom reflected on how the buying patterns had changed for the public. There was no question that people were wearing less jewelry and that collecting, in its own right, had become more important. It would be interesting to see how the ladies at Marla Wingate's would be turned out.

He started to anticipate dealing with the holiday crowds for the 10-block walk to the NYAC. Then he thought of the blind woman he had met earlier. An amazing person and character model. Just navigating this city. And working. Blind but compassionate about the homeless man. And she was able to enjoy jewelry as well.

He switched off the computer and stood up. The building's intercom buzzed. Odd—his company was by-appointment-only on weekends, and only properly identified delivery men were allowed to make their rounds unannounced.

"Hello."

"It's Lenny. There's a man here who wants to see you. Shall I send him up?"

"What's his name?"

"What was the name again, Bud?"

Tom heard a second voice say, "Propakov."

CHAPTER 19

Saturday Midday

TOM WAS ANNOYED. And concerned. Even though there was no chance he would receive Propakov under the circumstances, he was tempted. He would love to see the Alexandrite in his own space and in his own light, and see if there was any way he could work it. Tom had a buyer—and probably more than one. If Propakov was telling the truth.

Tom told the Lobby Man to say he was in meetings for the rest of the afternoon.

He considered calling Mark Kessling but decided not to, in case he might have a shot at the stone. Tom would want complete discretion. Provenance and proof that the Alexandrite was not stolen was unlikely. This was a stone that would make people do things they normally would not, because of its quality, size, and undeniable energy.

Not willing to risk another encounter, Tom called the lobby desk. Propakov had left immediately. When Tom got to the lobby, he took the service exit just in case. It came out on 45th Street, and he headed toward Sixth Avenue. The crowds were heavy along Sixth Avenue, especially around Radio City Music Hall, as he made his way up to the New York Athletic Club.

Like everywhere in New York City during the holidays, the Club was packed. It was just after 1:00 p.m., and the Tap Room was a madhouse, with five college-football games on the televisions. Four and five deep at the bar, and an oppressive din. Tom went upstairs. The main dining room was also crowded, but the *maître d'* knew Tom and gave him a table in the far corner by a window. Central Park looked spectacular, even with most of the leaves down.

Mirko, the Head Bartender, came over and shook Tom's hand. He had previously worked at Elaine's, the infamous hangout popular with celebrities. Tom was a favorite of Elaine's until she died, and the place shut down. Tom and Mirko had known each other forever.

"Good Lord."

"Tell me about it. I'm incredibly lucky."

"How do you feel?"

"Coming along. Honestly, it'll take time."

"Well, let me know if I can do anything. What can I get you?"

"You know, given the week I've had, make it a Beefeater's and tonic, please."

"On its way."

A waiter came over with a menu, and Tom put up his hand. "Just a BLT, please."

Mirko brought his drink. Tom had a $20 bill ready. He took a sip and looked out at the Park.

Finishing lunch, Tom headed down to the locker floor. The lounge was packed—more football—but the locker area wasn't too bad. He went to the gym and immediately saw one of his few friends at the Club sitting on a bench against the wall with the gym manager, Hasan. Frank had introduced himself to Tom literally during his first visit after joining the Club by saying, "Francis Magowan Brunelli. Half-Irish and half-Italian. Perfect for the Club."

"Before you give me a hard time, Frank, I was going to call you later. Hi, Hasan."

"What kind of a-hole is involved in a shootout and doesn't return a friend's call?"

Tom sat down and filled them in on some of the details of Wednesday night's elevator experience. Hasan sat gape-mouthed while Frank speculated wildly about what the police might want. Tom quickly had enough and excused himself, heading to a rowing machine. While not too crowded, the steam room was annoying, as two members were talking loudly about politics. They hadn't listened to the news or read a paper in some time.

Tom left the Club at 2:45 p.m. and decided to walk home through the Park, preferring those crowds to the ones he would meet heading east. There was no chance of a cab. It was brisk, but there was no wind.

He turned his phone back on. Cell phones were not allowed in the Club, and it showed he had two voicemails. The first was from Max. He deleted without listening. The second was from Lily. He walked across Central Park South and turned into the Park at Sixth Avenue and headed north, toward the Carousel.

"Tom, it's Lily. If you get this in the next hour, give me a call back. If not, I will call you tomorrow if that's OK. We are setting up for the charity event I invited you to, and I won't be able to talk again today after then." Then, excitedly, "Tom. I found out about the brooch. I have said nothing to anyone. Bye, Tom."

She had called at 1:45 p.m., too late to call her back. But good news. While he would have liked to have been armed with whatever Lily had found out before he saw Marla Wingate, he would do as she asked and wait until tomorrow.

By the time Tom was passing behind the Metropolitan Museum of Art, he had more or less determined the two best approaches to the handling of the brooch. In either case, he would get the colored stones tested for treatment and origin. When the homogeneity of a collection of colored stones of a given species in a mounted piece is very similar or identical, it is unnecessary to do complete testing on every gemstone. The emeralds and rubies in the brooch were a slam dunk in terms of origin. Muzo Mine, Colombia, for the Emeralds, and Mogok Tract, Myanmar (always *Burma* in the trade) for the rubies. And even though the likelihood of treatment was low because of the apparent age of the brooch, the partial-sample testing needed to be done to remove any kind of speculation. Since the necessary testing work could be done without unmounting the colored stones, there was a low risk of damage.

While many of the better-known diamond-grading labs examine mounted diamonds and issue reports, the Gemological Institute of America grades only unmounted diamonds. Touching the brooch's mounting to temporarily remove the diamonds would be a travesty, and the current condition and perfection of the jewel would be fully compromised. Tom would do the formal diamond grading in the mounting himself and then get the opinion of George Saluto. George was working at the Gemological

Institute when Tom started and was now the gemologist for one of the most important international diamond dealers. George had no technical equal. Between the two of them, the diamond grading would be as accurate as any top *diamantaire*, or lab, could do with mounted diamonds. Tom would make it worth George's while. The lack of diamond-grading reports would be ameliorated by Tom's and George's grading, the condition of the piece, and the superlative and obvious quality of the diamonds.

Tom would then ask the Gemological Institute of America to produce one of their fancy Monographs on the piece. These can be created only for exceptional gemstones or extraordinary pieces, and any gemstone or piece must be "qualified" by the laboratory. They are beautifully hardbound books with an accompanying D.V.D., filled with professional art photographs, gemological information, histories of the mining locales, etc. He hoped things worked out so that Van Cleef & Arpels could write, if not the history, an analytical commentary. Images of the original design, if they existed, would be incredibly additive.

In all likelihood, Tom would set two selling prices. One for the trade and one for anybody else or any institution. A sale to the trade was unlikely, but the base value would be established by setting the lowest price he would accept for the brooch. This all assumed Tom would be able to successfully buy the brooch to begin with.

The more appealing of the two approaches involved offering the brooch for private sale to his existing customer base. He could think of only three, maybe four, clients who might have the interest and the resources to buy it. He would not ask any of his colleagues for introductions, but certain H.N.W. aficionados, the Sultan of Brunei, or the Queen of Saudi Arabia would likely have interest. Tom did not want to give anything up, as that would mean paying a heavy commission and, in effect, taking on a partner. Too risky, if he could not control the process completely, from start to finish. If one of his own privates was not interested, it would be approach number two.

The less-appealing approach was a sale at one of the major auction houses. Auction houses charge a commission, generally north of 20%, to both the seller and the buyer. And there are usually insurance and photography charges for the seller, on top of the commission. But, just like everywhere else, the competition for exceptional goods is stiff. As a result, for dealers like Tom, the seller's commission is often lowered or waived entirely, in return for placing fine and desirable pieces with a given house. Similarly, private art collectors can often negotiate sweetened seller's-commission deals. And frequently get advances on the projected sale proceeds as well. Both Sotheby's and Christie's would be bending over backwards to have the opportunity to offer the brooch for a major sale. They would be more than happy with taking a buyer's commission only.

While a public sale would most likely guarantee the highest selling price possible for an item like the brooch, there was a caveat. They were public. And that meant Marla Wingate would undoubtedly hear about the sale eventually. Any other dealer would, in this situation, tell his client that he sold the piece, and the new buyer must have put it at auction. Another common ploy by dealers in a situation where they have not treated a private seller ethically is to wait a period of time and then sell the item via auction in another country. There would be no hiding or forgetting this brooch once its existence was known. Tom would never do anything like that. Not because he was a choir boy, but because there was substantial risk. He intended to treat Marla Wingate well, but there was no way to predict the actual upside. Once he had the colored stones documented and established the values, he would start to consider his target profit margin.

Auctions also would expose the brooch to the widest institutional audience, including museums. In the span of Tom's career, the interest in jewelry acquisitions by museums had increased dramatically. Largely based on the ability to draw crowds.

Maybe his low value would be the auction reserve price. The hidden minimum price that the seller is willing to accept for an item. There was a chance he would offer it to Van Cleef at that amount, but a public auction was the best chance to achieve maximum value.

Auction catalogues show an anticipated range of prices. The reserve may be below the low end of the range, or it may be the stated low value. Buyers never know in advance. If the reserve price is not met, the item is "bought in," meaning it did not sell. Sometimes unsuccessful sellers are approached by the auction house post-sale with an offer that has been submitted after the sale has ended. They then have the opportunity to accept a lower price.

He needed to think some more, but he could always offer Marla Wingate a percentage of the profit on an auction sale over a certain guaranteed amount.

It was 3:20 p.m. when Tom entered the lobby of his building.

"Hello, Mr. Strawbridge. I have a package that was delivered . . . by the police." John, the Doorman, let it hang.

"Please send it up and have them leave it on the hall table. Thank you."

Tom sat down with the mail, and, before he looked at it, he texted Lily.

"Lily. Thank you for the call. Interesting news. I will be around most of tomorrow, but early afternoon is best. Looking forward."

CHAPTER 20

Saturday Afternoon

TOM FINISHED GOING THROUGH THE MAIL and was looking at an image of the brooch on his phone when the picture was displaced by a call.

"Hi, Tom." Max.

Trying to get ahead of it, Tom said, "Max, I am so happy for you and wish you all the best of luck. That is a lucky man. I am thinking about wearing your tie tonight. Thank you again."

"Thank you, and you are welcome. Heidi is at her parents' summer place in Sconset until tomorrow. I was hopeful you could stop by later with the other part of my gift. . . . You did enjoy yourself Thursday, didn't you?"

Tom was tempted, but he was glad he had plans. "Will your fiancée be there?"

"Funny. You don't seem like that type."

"You know what I meant."

"Tom, you're a man of the world and knows what's what. Marriage is one thing, and . . ."

"Look, Max, you are amazing in every way, and you know it. I have plans with clients tonight, but thank you for the call." Tom did not want to antagonize her. And he didn't want to indicate if he was closing the door or leaving it open.

"How about after? Tomorrow is Sunday, you know."

"Let's be in touch, OK?"

"I'm happy to come over if that's the problem."

Relentless. "Max, no. This is a rough weekend. Bye."

"Bye, Tom. Call me if you change your mind."

Based on her gift, he knew she wasn't going away, but he didn't see this coming so soon. He would have to be careful here and handle this one very skillfully. She had a lot at risk, so he hoped the odds of her becoming a "clinger" were low. But she was still used to getting her own way.

Tom had almost two hours before he needed to be at Marla Wingate's. He retrieved a thick Redwell from the hall the Porter had left and went to his office to put it on his desk. Maybe because of the text from Lily, Tom decided to start looking at the materials. Inside the Redwell were two Manila envelopes, one thin and one quite thick. There was an envelope stapled to the inside of the Redwell. A note from Napoli: "Mr. Strawbridge, please return these to me Monday, and do not discuss with anyone. Detective Napoli." He sat down at his desk and took out a pad and pencil.

He started with the thin one. The contents included information, much of it redacted from Interpol, the F.B.I., and the N.Y.P.D. There was a D.V.D. marked *Wafi Mall 2007.* This was the Pink Panther information. He dug in and was done with all the reading in 35 minutes.

Several major heists were described, from Japan to the Middle East to Northern Europe. Nothing in North America, and there was nothing about Wednesday night. In Tokyo, they got away with the Comtesse de Vendome necklace. The press called it "the greatest robbery in the history of Japan." Because of the number of redactions, Tom came away with a choppy and patchy sense of the gang.

The Pink Panthers, known as *Les Pinks* in Europe, were a shadowy syndicate of jewel thieves primarily from the Balkans. Over the past two decades, Interpol estimated that they had successfully pulled off more than 150 jobs worldwide, the loot worth hundreds of millions of dollars. In 2003, London police found a stolen blue diamond ring hidden inside a container of face cream, a move lifted from an Inspector Clouseau film. The *Pink Panther* moniker was born.

In summary, Interpol believed that the core group of the Panther operation consisted of 20 or 30 experienced thieves. Many dozens of other facilitators in various European cities, including Brussels, provided logistical assistance. Local associates of the Panthers obtain weapons and cars, rent hotel rooms, and make other arrangements.

Regardless of the complexity of the job, the criminals generally leave few, if any, clues. Or fingerprints or viable D.N.A. traces. After the second Harry Winston robbery in Paris, the police found the service stairway covered in green powder. It was an inside job, and the group had broken in the night before and spent the night in the stairwell. They emptied fire extinguishers all over the stairwell before they left to erase any traces of potential evidence.

Some of the Pink Panthers had fought in the Kosovo War, which explained their paramilitary aggressiveness. Retired, Pavle "Punch" Markovic was a founding member and talked openly about the Panthers' infrastructure. He was a self-declared "gem heist mastermind." He said, "There's no head, there's no tail, and there's no beginning. You're talking to the *it*—you're talking to the highest of the highest. It's me. What I did I was the best."

His skill base included shutting off alarms and security systems without detection, lock picking, and opening vaults. He claimed to be able to crack a safe in 16 seconds. "I am probably the fastest in the world," he said. "I could take the world apart and put it back together before the afternoon." Tom mused he would pay to see anyone crack a modern safe in 16 seconds.

Just as important as their robbery skills, the Panthers knew how to move hot property. Buyers were limited to an extremely wealthy and ethically challenged circle. High-profile jewels, like those sold by the world's elite luxury brands, are traceable in the open market.

Tom learned that the precise extent and membership of the Pink Panthers were unknown. Interpol described the mob as a transnational spider web: "You pull one thread, and you find a group of others." Some of the members were farmers, and others worked menial jobs. One of them, a Rajko Pavlović, credited himself for "forming a group of 'gentlemen thieves' with style. . . . Pink Panther is a system. We created a system. We were never violent." The French police call violent members "dirty boys."

Markovic's take: "I did hundreds of heists, smash-and-grabs, all different types of burglaries—anything that didn't hurt people." "Punch," his sobriquet, referred to his ability to rapidly crack vaults and safe-deposit boxes using borescopes, fiber optics, and a method he calls "the punch." "You know the thing that shoots cows in the head? I used to use that a lot, something like that, the hydraulic gun. You just punch locks right out, you know? I used to use a thermal lance: 8,000 degrees Fahrenheit, hot as the sun. It melts steel, concrete, vaults, safes, rooms, whatever you want. It'll melt a whole building in half."

Tom's 35 carat Ascher Cut masterpiece, *The Dude*, had been delivered to Paris the day before the first Harry Winston robbery. The Pink Panthers had inside intel and knew where the ring was in advance of the burglary. A hidden compartment at the bottom of the main safe. Tom was thrilled to learn they nicknamed it *La Grosse Pierre,* as the ring became known in the press. It was worth $8 million at the time.

Stolen diamonds end up in Antwerp or New York. Luxury watches can make their way east, to Serbia and Russia, hidden inside cars. Proceeds are generally laundered in Belgrade, where they are invested in cafés, restaurants, and real estate.

Since 2002, the Panthers had robbed close to 90 jewelry stores. Most of the heists followed the same *modus operandi*. A well-dressed man entered the store alone and put down a piece of wood to prop open the inside security door, allowing a few associates to enter. The first man through the door typically had a gun. The others carried hammers and pickaxes, for breaking display cases. The robbers hid the jewelry and watches in backpacks and left in a stolen car.

Occasionally the Panthers rely on a strategy called *vol au bélier*—meaning that they ram something heavy into a storefront window, such as a shopping cart filled with blocks of concrete.

The robbery in Dubai in April 2007 employed this technique. Two Audi sedans bashed through the gated entrance of the Wafi Mall. One Audi then smashed into the front of a jewelry store. The Audis are shown parked on the mall's polished tile floor. After a driver honked the horn twice, three masked men ran out of the store with the jewels. As shoppers stared from overhead balconies, the robbers jumped into the cars and sped out of the frame of the security camera. The store reported that the stolen items were worth $3.4 million. Tom was looking forward to the D.V.D., if it was more than he had found on YouTube.

Tom turned his attention to the other envelope. While about twice the size of the Pink Panther documents, it appeared to Tom that there were only about three pages of readable text after all the redactions.

Igor Yatkin was a Russian Arms dealer, entrepreneur, and former Soviet military translator. He reportedly used his air-transport companies to smuggle weapons from Eastern Europe to Africa and the Middle East. He had been doing this since the collapse of Communism. He had been nicknamed the *Merchant of Death* and *Sanctions Buster* for his reported wide-reaching operations, extensive clientele, and willingness to bypass embargoes. *Like a movie*, Tom thought.

Yatkin had been arrested in 2006 in Thailand on terrorism charges by the Royal Thai Police in cooperation with American authorities, specifically the F.B.I. The United States Ambassador requested deportation under the Extradition Act with Thailand, which was mandated by the Thai High Court in 2008. Yatkin was accused of intending to smuggle arms to the Revolutionary Armed Forces of Colombia (FARC) for use against U.S. forces.

He consistently denied his charges, but in 2009, Yatkin was convicted by a Grand Jury in a Manhattan federal court. The charges were conspiracy to kill U.S. citizens and officials, delivery of anti-aircraft missiles, and providing aid to a terrorist organization. He was sentenced to 25 years' imprisonment in 2009.

While being transported from Sing Sing Prison in New York State for an appeal hearing in Manhattan in 2010, he escaped. The prison van carrying Yatkin and three guards was forced off the road just after it turned onto Route 9 heading south, less than three miles from Sing Sing. According to the guards, at least five armed men surrounded the van and shot the driver in the shoulder. Yatkin was in the back with one guard, chained to the wall of the van.

The armed crew quickly broke open the back doors to find the lone guard in the back staring at the floor with his hands behind his head. They freed Yatkin with bolt cutters, which were left behind, and secured the hands of the two guards who were not wounded. They threw the guards' weapons into the woods and took their radios. Before leaving, they laid the wounded man on the grass and shot out the van's radio. Investigators determined the entire event took less than four minutes. It was after 3:00 a.m., and no one saw anything.

The men and Yatkin ran to a car across the road and headed north for two miles, where they turned left down a small road for a two-mile drive to the banks of the Hudson River. The car was left at the scene. There, they got onto a stolen float plane, later discovered off the New Jersey shore. There were reports of a low-flying float plane crossing Long Island sound around 3:30 a.m. Yatkin had not been seen since.

Better than a movie.

CHAPTER 21

Saturday Evening

THE D.V.D. HAD BEEN SWEETENED, so the sharpness was much improved compared to the YouTube clip. And there was additional security footage from outside the Wafi Mall showing the getaway cars exiting one of the entrances and speeding off in opposite directions.

It was 5:50 p.m., and Tom repacked all the materials and put the Redwell in his briefcase for Monday. He changed for cocktails and dinner. He did not select Max's gift tie. He wondered in what way he could have any involvement with whatever the Detective wanted and why he'd been asked to review the information.

At 6:15 p.m., Tom left his apartment with his hostess's gift for the ten-minute walk to Marla Wingate's building. Opposite the Central Park Zoo, 834 Fifth Avenue had been built in 1930 by Rosario Candela and is considered his masterwork. It is a special building in a city of special buildings, and Tom always liked going there for social events or sales calls. He had three good clients in 834.

He was passing under the canopy of the Carlyle Hotel as Ashley Prescott appeared from the revolving door. She was dressed casually, but spectacularly well. Tom was glad to see her. "Ashley, what a nice surprise. Bullshots at Bemelmans?"

Chuckling, Ashley said, "Nice to see you. No, I'm staying here. It bothers Dad, especially since Mother died, but even with his huge apartment, I need my own space. I'm meeting him and my Aunt for dinner at Cipriani. You have plans, of course?"

"I do, but I would really like to see your Father again at some point." 834 was only five blocks above Cipriani, but Tom did not want to offer walking together to his host's. "May I put you in a cab?"

"Thank you—this is Dad's driver," pointing to a big Bentley parked near the corner.

"Well, how's the husband-shopping going?" He gestured toward the car.

Smiling at the question, she replied, "Would you believe the jerk-quotient is leveling off at 98% for available men in this town?"

"You don't say?" arriving at the car.

The driver had arrived at the curbside back door and was holding it open. "How long are you in town again?"

"I leave Friday evening for Texas."

"Cocktails Thursday? I'll have to confirm, but I'm sure that will work."

"Good."

"Please text me a good number. Do you still have my card?"

"Yes, I will."

"Have a good time, and remember me to your Father."

Drinks would be easy, and she would be a good person for Tom to know. An unusual combination of looks, grace, and brains. Tom spent the rest of the walk thinking about any single men he should introduce to her but came up empty. She was going to have a tough go, if she was even serious.

He arrived to 834 at 6:29 p.m., and one of the Doormen stepped aside to let Tom pass. The Concierge said, "Yes, Sir," and quickly found Tom's name on the guest list. "16A, Sir. Rodney will show you up."

The top floor. Tom recalled someone, perhaps one of his clients in the building, saying there were only two apartments on the top floor. In any case, Marla Wingate was very wealthy.

Rodney, the Elevator Man, said, "Good evening, Sir. Good to see you again."

"Thank you."

The door to the apartment was across from the elevator, and it was open. Tom walked in, and a Maid appeared and asked for his scarf. As she moved away, another, in a slightly different uniform, asked for his drink order.

Looking across the room and out to the Zoo, Tom was struck by the enormous, outsized windows. He realized they had been scaled up to complement the ceiling height and room size. Looking to his left, he saw Marla Wingate approaching him, smiling. She was dressed very smartly, in understated Dior. He noticed at least five or seven people, and they were distanced throughout the enormous room. The bar was set at the north end of the room, in a double doorway leading to another huge room.

Tom extended his hand, and she, ignoring it, took his arms and kissed him on both cheeks. Her fragrance was incredible, and it was unfamiliar to Tom.

"So good of you to join us, and me, for dinner!"

"Wonderful, and thank you again for the invitation. Here is a little something. I hope you can use them."

Tom was surprised to see her remove the box from the Schweitzer linen bag and open it on the spot. Inside were eight magnificent Italian linen placemats with a discreet lavender brocade running around the edge. She seemed to be genuinely impressed as she thanked him. A servant appeared and quickly left with the gift. Apparently, this was not a first.

"Tom, please excuse me—we'll have plenty of time later. Everyone is looking forward to meeting you. Maybe you'll know some of the other guests? The list grew a bit."

His drink arrived. "Please see to your guests, and thank you again."

He started down the left wall and quickly saw that Wingate had a serious art collection. Eclectic. He first passed a Lichtenstein and then stopped at a Pollock. In the middle of the south wall, he joined three other guests looking up at a version of *The Three Musicians*. Not much of a Picasso fan, Tom understood the magic here. Spectacular, and the color palette, heavy on bright, cool greens, was incredible.

The others introduced themselves, and they all discussed the painting. They had all seen it before. One of the two ladies, who clearly had had plenty to drink, announced that the painting was one of the first acquisitions of Marla Wingate's ex-husband when he started to collect. "Very rich and handsome, but what a bore."

Tom continued around the perimeter of the room, and, arriving at the windows looking out at the Zoo and Central Park, he guessed the room to be about 45 feet wide and 100 feet long. He noticed a familiar man looking at him. When the man caught Tom's eye, he walked over. As Tom finished his drink, a Servant appeared and held a silver tray. "The same again, Sir?" An older English woman.

"Thank you, please."

"You're Tom Strawbridge."

Tom smiled.

"Roger Gillespe."

"I'm sorry—have we met?"

"Yes, at the Club, but I can't remember when. I'm in insurance, AON, and . . ."

"I remember now—you work with my good friend, Don Richter, don't you? You were having an event, and we all ran into each other in the lobby."

"That's it. Have you seen Don?"

"Almost never since they moved to Larchmont."

"Right. I only see him at the Annual Meeting myself. Good man."

"The best." This guy was nice enough.

"I've always been fascinated by your business. The gems end of it, anyway. My ex had a serious habit and was dedicated to Murray Ellenhorn. Did you know him?"

"Yes."

"Well, I'd ask what you thought of him, but I found out when we had her collection appraised during the divorce. Shyster."

"I'm afraid he doesn't enjoy the best reputation. He did make a fortune when he sold his business. He then just poked around the trade until he died."

"Sorry about that mess. Scary."

"Very. I am not at liberty to discuss it."

"Understood. May I have your card? It looks as though I'll be taking the plunge again, and I need a diamond."

"Of course. Why don't I take you to lunch so we can have a conversation before we look at anything? We can do that in my office as well."

"Great." Tom handed him a card, and they shook hands. "How do you know Marla, by the way?"

"Through one of my clients."

"Well, then you know her enough to know what kind of diamond she'd like." He waved and turned to go.

Interesting. Tom wondered if Gillespe would be at dinner.

Immediately, Ann and Mike Ross came over to Tom. Ann introduced her husband, who said to Tom, "Guess you feel lucky to be here?"

"Oh, it's a very nice party." Ross's flat face flattened further. "Ann. I am going to the bar. What would you like?"

"Vodka on the rocks."

He turned to Tom, who said, "I'm all set." Tom's new drink arrived at that moment.

Ross left, and his wife made an exaggerated eye roll. "Don't mind him. An acquired taste."

Tom smiled. "You look absolutely marvelous."

She was very pleased. Smiling, she said, "You're quite dangerous, aren't you?"

"Oh, I don't think so. Let me apologize for the other night. I . . ."

"Tom, how are you doing?" She had an easy, genuine manner that made Tom assume the "acquired taste" must have deep pockets. Just then he noticed her earrings, vintage Seaman Schepps.

"Those earrings are wonderful. One of my favorite makers." She blushed and held up her ring. At least a 10 carat Pear Shape very poorly made, and Tom estimated H-I Color. He took her hand, "Magnificent." It was hideous, and it was hard to tell what was worse—the diamond or the mounting.

"Oh, this was Mike's mother's." That explained that.

"I am doing well, thank you. The police are annoying but don't think I'm in any danger. It's become surreal at this point, but I am lucky."

"Well, everything has changed. And the quality of life here is well, spotty."

"It has affected my world. Years ago, every lady here would have been accessorized to the extreme with fine jewelry. But it's everything else as well. Look at that dress."

She turned to see a woman in a monstrosity that was too casual, without design, and embarrassing. She looked back to Tom quickly and looked like she was about to have a church laugh.

"Bad taste is worse than no taste, I always say."

"Tom, you are dangerous, and charming." Looking over her shoulder, they both saw Mike Ross returning and, leaning in, Ann said, "You know, Marla is very taken with you," winking.

CHAPTER 22

Saturday Night

CHOOSING NOT TO ASK ANN Ross about Gillespe, Tom now assumed it would just be he and Marla at dinner.

It was 7:45 p.m., and Tom had met almost everyone and secured two new client appointments and a dinner invitation. More questions than he would have liked on the robbery. Most of the guests had gone, and Tom was debating another drink when the English Maid came over to him, smiling, and said, "The lady asks that you follow me to the study."

He smiled back. "Of course. How long have you been with Mrs. Wingate?"

"Please. I started with the family when her mother was sixteen. I'm Alice."

They walked toward the double doors behind the bar. Tom glanced over his shoulder at the entrance to the room. Marla Wingate was looking directly at Tom and the maid. She was seeing several of the guests out.

Tom followed Alice through the room behind the bar. It seemed like a twin to the cocktail room. More impressive sculpture than impressive paintings. Then down a hall and into the study. This was a corner room and spectacular. Immense windows between bookshelves on the west and north walls. There were two massive desks at each end. Two doors led out on the wall opposite Fifth Avenue and the Central Park Zoo.

"What may I bring you?"

"Just a club soda, Alice. Thank you."

"Please make yourself comfortable. She shouldn't be too long."

It was just before 8:00 p.m. Tom walked to the window closest to the corner. It had a clear view of the sea-lion pool in the Zoo. He checked his phone. Nothing from Mitchell or Napoli, and his business emails were unrelated to the robbery. As he was looking at his screen, a text arrived from Ashley Prescott. It was her contact information.

Alice returned with the club soda. Tom sat on the edge of the windowsill, looking down on the traffic headed downtown. He had a flash of turning off Fifth, three blocks south on the night of the shooting, and heading to the Melrose. He remembered how rattled and anxious he was, and how he had perspired.

It was just after 8:05 p.m. when Marla Wingate came into the room. She smiled broadly. "Alone at last. Sorry for keeping you waiting."

Tom smiled slightly, not sure what to make of her comment. "I've been enjoying the view. And your apartment. Splendid."

"Thank you," as if only a fool wouldn't be impressed. There was something different with her from earlier and from when she was in his office. Tipsy?

"Maria needs a few more minutes. Would you mind if I have a quick change of clothes?"

"Not at all."

"I'll be quick. Drink okay?"

"All set."

Tom returned to the window and saw a man and a woman walk down the stairs to the Zoo and disappear into the bushes around the Administration building.

It was 8:20 p.m. when Marla Wingate returned wearing a surprising, and striking, lavender ensemble. The main article was a largely diaphanous, mid-thigh, dressing-gown/housecoat hybrid. The edges were trimmed in lavender fur. Under the sheer material, her top was covered. Her bottom was not. Impressive. An oversight? If not, she must have been planning on a directional change. On her feet were three-inch lavender stilettos. Tom purposely said nothing.

"I am much more comfortable. Thank you for waiting. Would you like to take off your tie?"

"I'm fine. I would like to wash my hands."

Pointing to the door, "Through there, third door on the left. I'll see you in the dining room. Alice will show you."

When Tom left the washroom, Alice was waiting at the opposite end of the hall from the study. They walked a short distance to the wood-paneled dining room. Marla Wingate sat smiling at the head of an exceptionally long table. Tom's place had been set to her right.

He sat down, and Alice poured Marla, and then Tom, a glass of white wine. An excellent, sharp Sancerre. Marla asked if Tom had enjoyed himself, and they chatted about some of the guests. She was an entertainer and hosted "something" almost every month.

Shrimp cocktail, first class. Tom switched to red, and a full Burgundy was poured. They were served an extraordinary pork roast with Brussel sprouts. Then strawberry shortcake with wonderful fresh strawberries.

"We'll have coffee in the study, Alice."

Tom pulled out her chair, and as they were leaving, Maria, the cook, came in the service door. Ignoring Tom, she said, "Was everything to your liking, Mrs. Wingate?"

"Absolutely perfect, as always, Maria. Thank you. I am having three for brunch tomorrow . . . I've told you, haven't I?"

"Yes. Thank you."

Tom followed Marla out of the dining room. The absence of any covering had not been adjusted. Intentional or not, she was a very sexy woman. By the time they got back to the study, Alice was preparing the coffee. Marla sat in the corner of a couch, and Tom took the chair opposite her on the other side of a low table.

Alice handed Marla her coffee and looked at Tom. "Black please, Alice."

Tom thanked Marla again for including him and as a set-up, said, "Ann is wonderful, isn't she?"

"We've been friends since school. Mike is her second husband, unfortunate and insufferable. But he does leave her alone." Her expression didn't change. She crossed her legs. "Did you mention our dinner to her?"

"I did not." He thought about Gillespe and let it go.

It was 9:25 p.m., and Tom wanted to move things along. He explained he had spent several hours examining the brooch and was happy to report that it was of excellent quality and in perfect condition. He would work on establishing a value, assuming she still wanted to sell, in the next few days. He was as vague as possible. She was focused on his face, and her expression was not readable. She told him to "sell it" when he was happy with the price and assured him she would be comfortable with whatever he decided.

"Well, I'm dying to hear what you have to tell me about the brooch."

"Of course. But first, may I ask you a question or two?" Despite her odd demeanor that evening, Tom assumed she was curious about the process or his strategy. Until she said, "I asked Judy about you, and she really didn't know anything beyond your work together."

"May I tell you about my professional background?"

"Everyone knows about that. Are you married?"

"No."

"Have you been married?"

"Yes. Once. No children."

He was going to say something but adopted an expression of mild annoyance and waited her out. She reached for her coffee and caught Tom looking at her as she sat back. She tilted her head and smiled at him.

"Everything I told you about the jewel," as she called it, "was accurate. My 'Aunt' was actually my Grandmother's first cousin. I always called her 'Aunt.' After Grandmother died, she continued to visit our family once a year, most often during the summer. She was very fond of my Mother and me, having never married and having no children. She was wonderful to me, and very sophisticated but accessible and kind."

She crossed her legs again, and Tom stared at her nose, thinking to himself, *What does this have to do with the price of eggs?*

"After her visit the year I turned fifteen, I asked Mother why Aunt Dagmar had never married. She was exceptionally beautiful and attractive. Mother became very tense and said she would explain, 'when I could understand.'"

Alice appeared and asked if Tom would like an after-dinner drink. He looked at Marla. "I'm having one. Brandy please, Alice. Tom?"

Tom had rationed to this point in the evening. "A vodka on the rocks please, a big one if you don't mind?" Alice smiled and left.

"Well, of course, you can imagine I hounded my Mother incessantly. A girl of fifteen, you know."

She went on to explain "Aunt Dagmar's" Mother was American. When studying in Paris, the Mother had fallen in love with an aristocratic and successful Swedish businessman, and they married. Dagmar was born in Stockholm but spent most of her life in Paris. "His name was Carl Borg. Have you heard of him?"

"Of course. He helped save Paris at the end of the war, working with Hitler's man, von Brecht."

"Impressive, Tom."

"Not really. I've read about him, and he's portrayed in *Is Paris Burning?*

"Well before the War, he was appointed Vice Counsel in Paris and became Counsel General eventually. He and his wife and daughter were treated very well by the Nazis and were more or less left alone. They were not affected by rationing, and Borg's business was not disturbed."

Alice arrived with the drinks. "How is the cleanup going, Alice?"

"Jane broke a glass and is upset."

"Please put her mind at ease."

Alice smiled and left. "Please excuse me. I won't be a minute."

Tom stood up with Marla, staring at her forehead. This was not only a good story but if the brooch had something to do with Borg, and if that could be exploited, it would add to the provenance and, therefore, the value of the brooch.

Marla returned, slipped off her heels, and folded her legs under herself as she sat down. Tom didn't notice that whatever had been covering her bust was now gone until she was saying, "Where were we?" Caught. She was smiling as they touched glasses.

"Tall and very beautiful, Dagmar was sixteen in 1941. At some point a Gestapo and SS official named Becker saw Dagmar. He sent someone to explain to her Father that if he wanted to continue to enjoy his family's privileges and safety, it would be smart to support Becker's interest in Dagmar. Of course, commonplace at the time. While her parents had no choice, they were devastated and shamed.

"The brooch had been commissioned for the Queen of Yugoslavia by her husband, Peter II. Understandably, when the War broke out, commissions of many kinds were put on hold or canceled altogether. At some point, the jewel was appropriated from Van Cleef & Arpels. All this was told to me by Aunt Dagmar. While there were rumors Goebbels himself got the jewel, it ended up with Becker."

Tom drained his drink. "That is all really quite something."

"Dagmar adapted to her role as paramour. Rationalizing that she was protecting her family, she never lived with Becker. At some point, she was presented with the brooch. Her father put it in his office safe, where it remained until the liberation."

"Did Becker ever . . ."

"He was flying—Dagmar thought to Berlin—when the plane was shot down soon after she received the jewel. The family never discussed the whole thing until my Aunt was in her 30s, and then sparingly. While Dagmar was philosophical about it, she never had much interest in men afterwards."

Marla seemed more lucid than she had been all night. Tom was anxious from not being able to look below her neck. He asked Marla if she minded if he took off his jacket. She smiled, and he got up and folded his jacket over the arm of a chair.

Alice walked in. "Yes, Mrs. Wingate?"

"Mr. Strawbridge would like another, and I would, too. Thank you." Alice collected the glasses and left.

"Thank you."

"Of course. Here is the best part. Carl Borg did not remember the jewel until the fall of 1945, almost six months after the surrender of the Axis Powers. He immediately took the jewel to Van Cleef. He was a client, and friendly with Jacques and Pierre Arpels. Borg met with Jacques and told him he was returning the jewel. The story goes that, without even looking at it, Arpels put up his hand and closed his eyes. He, under no circumstances, would take the jewel back. Borg's family, especially Dagmar, had suffered too much embarrassment and humiliation. He insisted the jewel stay with Borg's daughter. He also made Borg promise to never tell a soul, even Jacques' brother. No one had asked about the jewel since it was appropriated, and it clearly was not the only item taken by the Nazis."

"Good Lord. The fog of war?"

"Apparently. Arpels said he had taken the designs, working sketches, and jewelry-shop work order, and sealed them in a special envelope, and they were in his personal safe. Permanently. Borg discussed everything with his family, and they decided to approach Arpels again in the future."

"Did they?"

"No. Borg and his wife started splitting their time between Paris, Stockholm, and New York. During a New York stay, Dagmar thought in about 1947, Borg became ill. No one was ever sure exactly what was wrong, but he had awful fevers and spent two weeks in the hospital. The Borgs called for their daughter, now twenty-two, while he was convalescing on Long Island. She was working for her Father, and, when she was collecting papers he had asked for from his safe, she saw the jewel box and thought it best to take it with her to New York."

"I've heard a lot over the years, but this is incredible, on all fronts." Tom took a drink. "Is this where the story ends?"

"The Borgs ended up staying with my Grandmother's family for more than four months, which initiated the annual Dagmar visits. The jewel never left the country after that. Aunt Dagmar told me it was kept in a private safe-deposit box at U.S. Trust, Carl Borg's bank. It stayed there until I inherited it when Dagmar died in 2003, and it was moved it to my bank. And it stayed there until I collected it and brought it to Tom Strawbridge."

"No further attempts at a return?"

"Carl mentioned it to Jacques on many occasions, and he was always met with the same reaction. Arpels would put his finger to his lips and remind Carl the jewel was "lost," and the entire affair was their little secret. He would then ask about Dagmar."

"Unbelievable. Thank you. I need to think this through. There are two main things: Proof of ownership and the existence of any of the paperwork. Does anyone know about the brooch?"

"No one, including my Daughter."

"Okay. Let's keep this between us until I speak to my attorney. I'll be in touch next week."

Marla leaned over more than necessary to get her brandy. "I was very, very fond of her—so lovely for such a tragic figure. Another drink?"

"No, thank you. I have to be going. Big day tomorrow, preparing for the police Monday."

"So soon?" It was just before 11:00 p.m.

"Unfortunately." He smiled as he put on his jacket and looked down at his shoes as she stood up.

She led him out of the room barefoot, and they walked to the front door. His scarf was folded perfectly and on the hall table. The elevator button was on the inside front wall, near the front door, and she pushed it as he put his scarf on.

"Do you find me attractive?"

"What do you think?"

"I'd say 'Yes,' but you haven't reacted to much."

"That, my dear, is where you are wrong."

"Is there a policy at your firm regarding fraternizing with clients?"

"That is part of it, and we are extremely strict."

"Well, thank you for coming."

"Thank you."

The elevator doors opened, and Tom walked across the hall and got in.

Tom turned around in time to see the dressing gown fall to the floor as Marla Wingate walked back into the apartment. He almost got off but looked at the elevator operator, who had missed the action and was looking up at Tom. They smiled.

He looked at his phone while still in the lobby. He thanked the Doormen and headed out to the street.

Part Five

CHAPTER 23

Sunday Morning

TOM WAS AWAKE AND UP before 6:00 a.m., walking in Central Park.

There was a lot going on, and he wanted to put tomorrow behind him, but he thought the fresh air would do him good.

Back in his apartment after his walk, he had a long conversation with a cousin, his closest relative. Besides discussing the robbery, he told her he was working with one of the great jewels of his career with a story to match.

It was 9:00 a.m. when they hung up, and Tom texted Lily, asking when a good time would be to talk. He was waiting until 10:00 a.m. to call Marla Wingate to thank her. And to make sure everything was good between them. His phone rang. It was her.

"Good Morning, Marla. How are you?"

"Shall we say, a little slow. Thank you for coming, Tom. Everyone enjoyed speaking with you, and I see you did some business."

"Again, thank you for including me—a terrific time. And your story. Marla . . ." She cut him off.

"Did I offend you, Tom? I don't meet men like you, and I value our relationship." Relieved that the relationship, and, therefore, his control and responsibility for the brooch, were intact, he stalled to plan his next move.

"No, you did not. In fact, anything but. I was waiting to a bit later to call and make sure I hadn't offended you. I loved being with you, and, well. . . . you are incredible. Did I mention lavender is my favorite color?"

She laughed.

"But no comparison to no lavender at all . . ."

"Thank you, Tom. Does our budding friendship have to be platonic?"

"Can we resolve our business, or at least establish a clear path forward first?"

"If you say so. Could you come for brunch today?"

"I'd love to, but there is too much work. I would like to see you soon."

"Let's speak this evening and set something up, OK?"

"Perfect."

"Goodbye, Tom."

Air cleared, he thought more about Marla. She was stunning, refined, smart, and funny. He wasn't leading Marla on to secure the brooch, but he wasn't sure he wanted a regular relationship with anyone. He snapped out of it when he saw the bag with Max's gift on his desk.

Lily had texted back and suggested 1:00 p.m. for their call.

He reviewed his notes from Christie's and decided he was interested in only one sapphire ring in Tuesday's sale. It was an 11.61 carat Emerald Cut, Ceylon, no heat. It was zoned, but the color and evenness of color would be improved significantly with re-cutting. The challenge would be to hold 10 carats. He knew he was not the only one to figure that out. He made his projected calculation for a finished weight of 9 carats and established his maximum bid, without buyer's commission. $67,500, $7,500 per carat. He'd go to $70,000. He would see how Heidi was after the weekend and decide whether she would have her first bidding experience.

Tom then took a look at the link David Mitchell had emailed on Matteo Keller. Very impressive, as Mitchell had said, and very rich. Very strong international private-equity business and a lot of interests. Highly diversified, his primary residences were in Monaco and Palm Beach.

Lily called a little after 1:00 p.m. They exchanged pleasantries and discussed the upcoming sales. There was a one-owner consignment of more than 20 lots of fine, vintage Van Cleef & Arpels at Sotheby's Wednesday. She would go for most of them.

For all dealers and retailers trying to buy at auction, it was competition from private buyers that made things difficult. Privates always felt they had to be getting a better deal with open competition in the public domain, as opposed to a retail store, which was, in some cases, true. And signed pieces from major brands further emboldened private buyers, as they were automatically relieved of the responsibility of having to develop their own taste and style. As a result, all things being equal between a branded and a non-branded item, signed pieces traded at a premium. In addition, the sale-room atmosphere gives the amateur a sense of "winning," which fuels the bidding approach of privates. And they did not have to resell and make a profit.

They talked a bit about the growth and popularity of online auctions and agreed that the major sales would always be "live" in a sale room, with phone and virtual bidding as alternatives.

"So, Lily, tell me."

"Tom, I haven't been this excited and intrigued in a long time. It took a while, but it came to me in the middle of the night Friday. At the end of our annual Officers Meeting in Paris the year after Pierre Arpels died, 2003, everyone was asked to leave who was not part of the jewelry group. We took a break, and, when we returned—there were about ten of us—the CEO was at the head of the table."

"This goes without saying, but, this is all in the strictest confidence."

"Lily."

"Sorry, Tom. This is really something."

"Since you've raised the question, you haven't mentioned the pin to anyone?"

"Tom! *Touché*."

She went on to explain that a series of materials had been found in Jacques Arpel's personal safe. They included fourteen or fifteen envelopes containing the paperwork for pieces of jewelry that had gone missing or had definitely been stolen. And three of the pieces had been appropriated by the Nazis during the occupation.

"You're joking."

"No. I went back to my notes Saturday. Two of the pieces had no information, other than that they had been taken. One of those, a necklace, miraculously surfaced last year at Sotheby's spring sale in Geneva. The selling family says it has been in the family for as long as anyone knows, and they claim not to know where it came from. It was seized, and the case is in the courts. The third piece, can you guess?"

"Is it too great a stretch to suggest it was the brooch you saw?"

She laughed. "In the pin's envelope, there was a letter written by Jacques Arpels saying the clip was the property of someone named Borg. Apparently, a customer and close friend of Arpel's. The letter did not make clear what had happened to the brooch, only that it was taken by a Nazi officer at some point and that Borg was the rightful owner.

"Tom, the letter, dated September 1945, was witnessed by what would have been the equivalent of our COO today, and by Jacques Arpels' personal attorney."

Tom could not believe it. While not a guarantee, it appeared Marla Wingate had complete proof of ownership. From the acknowledged owner's Daughter to Wingate via last will and testament.

"This is something, Lily. Thank you. Is there anything else?"

"Yes. All the work orders from the shop, the stone counts and weights, and two original designs. One of the front and one of the back. They were extraordinary and actual size. Tom, I know you can't say how you came by the pin at this point, but we are going to have to determine how I move forward in the firm. I'm fine with this for a while, but at some point, I should at least let the CEO know."

"Thank you, Lily. I appreciate that, and I will work as fast as possible and get back to you. An amazing story for a fabulous piece."

"It may be the best piece I've ever seen. Definitely the best VC&A piece."

"I know. Lily, do you think there'd be any chance you could take someone in Paris into your confidence and ask them to scan everything and send it to you?"

"Tom, I could do it, but I won't."

"Forgive me for asking."

"No worries. And I don't have to tell you, we would be a most willing buyer and would even consider making you a partner at 50% on the profit."

"Very generous. Thank you. I can't thank you enough for all this, Lily. Are you going to Christie's Tuesday?"

"You are most welcome, and yes."

"I'll see you there."

They hung up, and Tom started making a list of questions that needed to be answered. He started to outline the details for his two primary selling strategies. A huge amount of information in less than twenty-four hours, and it was all favorable—and consistent. He spent some more time considering what could transpire that could interfere with or prevent him from concluding the deal.

It was 3:15 p.m. He walked around the block, ended up at the local market, and bought his dinner. He hadn't been able to decide if he wanted to eat out or cook. He now had options. He did know he wanted to be alone.

He decided to make dinner at home, and, after cleaning up, he picked out his clothes for the morning and called Marla Wingate. They made plans for dinner Thursday. After pushing hard for her place, they agreed on Sistina, one of the best Italian restaurants on the Upper East Side, at 7:30 p.m.

He was in his study reading out of the Meylan book on Van Cleef when the phone rang.

Propakov.

Part Six

CHAPTER 24

Monday

PROPAKOV'S VOICEMAIL WAS A PLEADING but polite request for a meeting to discuss "a number of things." Including the Alexandrite. Tom texted him and asked if Propakov could come by at 2:30 p.m. that day. It was clear he would have to see him sooner or later. Tom would confirm by 1:00 p.m., giving himself an out should the police run late.

Tom was in the office at 6:45 a.m.

He got the offices opened and, while making a coffee, looked to see what the new client for that afternoon was looking for. His notes said, "Not sure—something important. A ring or a bracelet? But must be well priced."

Classic. No idea and unrealistic expectations. This is when Tom wished Heidi were up to speed. Then she could do the heavy lifting and screening necessary for the early stages of most sales. When the client was not event-driven—anniversaries or engagements, etc.—or product driven ("I want a pink sapphire ring"), the narrowing-down and selection process was usually tedious. He could then come in and solidify a plan, finish, and close. The current situation had to change. He wondered what frame of mind Heidi would be in after the weekend. Nothing to prepare before the clients came.

He heard Heidi come in around 8:30 a.m. She came back to find Tom putting out jewelry in the display cases.

"You do this so much better than me."

"Morning. How was the weekend. OK?"

"I went to my parents' on Nantucket."

"Oh. Fun?"

"Yes and no. I don't know how Dad stands it. She's on point all the time. There were guests, though, so he and I got some relief."

"How about another coffee?"

"Sure. I'll get myself one, too, and then come back and fix the displays." She was smiling.

"Funny."

They sat in the showroom for a few minutes, and Tom told her what lot he was interested in at Tuesday's sale. He asked her how she was doing and was immediately sorry he did.

He quickly said, "Bad timing on my part. Sorry. I've got to check my briefcase for this meeting. I'll order an Uber for 9:10 a.m.—who knows what the traffic is like. The security screening there can take forever, too."

"I forgot about your meeting with the police."

He was surprised at this and said nothing.

"We'll talk about tomorrow's sale and everything else when I am back. Mr. and Mrs. Perez are new and at 3:00 p.m. Do you remember how they came to us?"

"Morgan Stanley referral."

"Right."

The Uber was waiting when Tom got downstairs just after 9:10 a.m.

Tom's phone rang as they merged onto the F.D.R. South. David Mitchell.

"David."

"Hi, Tom. Excited?"

"Knock it off. Pissed off."

"Geeesh. Try the decaf. Two things. I've got Jim Rossi, an Associate Partner, with me. He says he met you at the party when we opened the new space."

"No idea. Why?"

"Two sets of ears are better than one."

"What's the second thing?"

"Meet us behind City Hall at the beginning of that overpass to One Police Plaza so we can go in together. How far out are you?"

"In the 50s on the F.D.R.; traffic isn't bad."

"We'll probably beat you there."

"See you."

The Uber let Tom out on Broadway in front of City Hall, and he walked through the arcade and out the back. He saw Mitchell and his Associate standing off to the right, looking up at the Brooklyn Bridge. He walked to the other side of them and stopped and waited until they saw him.

"You guys took forever."

"Did you beat us?"

"No." They all shook hands.

The line for the X-ray machines was long but moving. Because of Detective Napoli's crack, Tom made sure he was carrying. When David Mitchell saw Tom take his holstered handgun out of his belt and put it in the X-ray tray, he shook his head. As they collected their belongings, an officer asked for Tom's carry license and immediately handed it back, waving him through.

"Did you have to?"

Tom shrugged.

The Officer at the main desk made a call and told the three of them someone would be down soon. It was 9:50 a.m. Rossi was chatty, and Mitchell asked him if he remembered his instructions. He said he did and repeated that he was to record, if permitted, everything, and, in any case, take complete notes. And if David gave him the "sign"—this turned out to be a raised eyebrow—he was to ask a question about the second-to-last name mentioned. Tom had no idea why and did not ask.

Just before 10:00 a.m, a very tall, fit, and attractive officer introduced herself as Captain Ramirez. Her uniform was perfect, and her captain's bars reflected light like mirrors. They followed her down the hall behind the main information desk, and she led them to a bank of elevators. When the next elevator emptied, she held everyone back and waved the three of them on. She got on and put two keys in the panel and turned them. As she hit 14, Tom said, "The top floor? I've only been to one and the basement before."

"I've only been up there a handful of times. And that's after twenty-one years."

Tom wondered if she had ever seen street duty.

She got off. "Follow me, Gentlemen."

They walked to the left, and she stopped in front of a wooden double door. There was an old style "C" painted on the door to the right, and on the left was painted in gold leaf "John F. Dickson Room." She knocked.

Almost immediately, Napoli opened the door. Waving them in, Captain Ramirez said, "I'll be right here, Sir," and stood aside.

Inside, Mitchell, Rossi, and Tom shook hands with Napoli. The three other people in the room were seated across the table—another detective, the Assistant to the Chief of Detectives and the Bureau Chief himself, Michael Wilson. Tom had seen his picture on the news and in the papers many times. He looked like a shark with a broken nose. Introductions, business cards, and handshakes.

Everyone sat down, and despite his prizefighter face, the Bureau Chief had a mild, slightly high-pitched voice. He began by thanking Tom very much for coming. Rossi produced his phone, and Napoli waved his hand, making the cutting motion in front of his throat.

"We are going to expand our group here after a few things are reviewed. We should be done in under two."

"Chief, Mr. Strawbridge is here voluntarily and runs a business."

The Chief of Detectives cut Mitchell off and said, "Well, let's get underway, then. Detective Napoli?"

"One." To Tom. "Did you review the materials I sent over?"

"I did. There wasn't too much to actually read there, so I poked around the internet as well." Tom slid the Redwell across the desk.

"Good. Everything is in there?" Tom nodded. "Two. Did you find out anything on Yuri Propakov from your associates?"

Tom opened a folder and read the high points from the summary he'd prepared from his phone conversations with Benny Kosuk, Dennis Mangini, Serge Wienkof, and also Mark Kessling.

When Tom finished, he counted out four copies and handed a total of six to David Mitchell. "Those copies are for you if Mr. Mitchell approves. Even though you have them, I included contact details for all of them." Tom handed them over as he said, "Not a lot there." Mitchell smiled and put the copies aside.

"Anything more?"

"No."

"Two, as it turns out, we knew a little bit more about this case than we've let on." Napoli went on to explain that Interpol had turned the woman-half of the couple, a Croatian, who set up Robbie Tabah. Pictures of some agents visiting the girl's Mother at her home outside Zagreb did it. And they knew the identities of the three Pink Panthers and had confirmed their involvement in several burglaries.

Tom started to get hot, shifted in his seat, and shot a look at David Mitchell.

"The reality is we knew about the Tabah job in advance and had both entrances to the building covered, ready to pick them up when they exited. The woman is heading to Witness Protection. We had the driver as soon as Milankovic and the other one went inside."

The Bureau Chief took over, saying, "We didn't expect Tabah's employee to take a shot at these guys and, well, you know the rest."

Tom was about to blow, and Mitchell put his hand on Tom's arm. Directing his question to Napoli, "Why, Detective, would you, and the Department, knowingly mislead my client? He has been cooperative from the start and has done what you'd asked." Rossi was scribbling furiously.

Standing and taking off his jacket, Tom asked, "So nothing you told me was true?"

The three cops' eyes were glued to Tom's holstered firearm. He walked to the end of the table and back.

"Have a seat, Mr. Strawbridge, and calm down. And," Napoli said, "the rental car part was true."

Tom may have detected a slight smile. "Well, David, is there any reason we can't leave? This is bullshit."

"Are we done here?" Mitchell asked.

Napoli said they were not done. He explained that it was common practice to hold back the full details from witnesses in certain crimes, especially violent ones, for a week or two. He said many, if not all eyewitnesses, remembered something more about a crime after a brief passage of time. It was believed that leaving out details in a crime caused the witness to fill in blanks, which could lead to memories forgotten or overlooked initially. Some people remember important details weeks or months later. He did not apologize.

Mitchell said, "Look gentlemen, that's all well and good, but you already knew everything before you misled my client. Why?"

"It was, up to now, an open case, with two serious assaults and one death. The two gang members are in Belgium and will be put away." Napoli looked at the Bureau Chief.

The Bureau Chief said the case was just about to wrap up and close. They had asked Tom to read the background information because he may have thought of or remembered something new.

"But that's not why we asked you here today, Mr. Strawbridge. We want your help with Igor Yatkin."

CHAPTER 25

Monday Morning

The Bureau Chief said, "Look. Just hear us out. Join us in the next room, please. And you are free to decide after that. You can also leave. But we have asked some friends from the F.B.I. and Interpol to join us and, if nothing else, I think you'll find them interesting. Also, you potentially stand to make a great deal of money."

Tom obviously had no idea what the Chief was talking about, and he looked at David Mitchell.

Mitchell shrugged and said, "Up to you."

Tom said, "Okay. Let's hear it."

"Good. Thank you," said the Bureau Chief. "Follow me." It was 10:50 a.m.

Rossi, Mitchell, and Tom collected their things while the four cops waited for them by a door at the south end of the room. The Bureau Chief led them into the next room, which was large. Around a huge table sat another nine people. The Chief pointed to empty chairs on the side of the table facing the window.

Tom and the lawyers sat down in the middle chairs. Out the large window, the Manhattan side of the Brooklyn Bridge was almost at eye level and looked to be just feet away.

"Help yourself to something, gentlemen," the Chief said, gesturing to a credenza covered in drinks and food.

David Mitchell and Rossi got coffee, and Tom took a water. When they returned to their seats, the Bureau Chief introduced the nine people, eight men and one woman, from left to right.

Each one was *Agent*, *Director*, or *Chief*, along with their surnames. Chief Inspector of Internal Affairs, his Deputy, Chief of Special Operations Bureau, his Deputy (the woman), the F.B.I.'s Executive Assistant Director Criminal Branch, an Assistant Director, and two Interpol Executive Committee Members. One from France, and the other from the United Arab Emirates and France's Chargé d'Affaires.

"Well, Mr. Strawbridge, what do you think so far?" Clearly expecting to assuage any anger or frustration by having assembled this apparently significant and impressive group.

"Honestly, Bureau Chief Wilson, that is an extraordinary look at the Brooklyn Bridge, don't you think so, David? Spectacular." Mitchell stared at the top of the conference table. "With all due respect, what exactly am I doing here?" Looking into each face around the room, he caught a glimpse of Rossi, who was grinning like a groupie for the Rolling Stones. Having worked with important political figures and major celebrities since early in his career, Tom was accustomed to power, prestige, and entitlement. "This was fun for a while, but what gives?" No one's expression changed.

Wilson explained that the Chief of the Special Operations Bureau (C.S.O.B.), Dermot Monahan, would begin by making a presentation. Monahan's eyes looked black, the eyes of a killer. He motioned to Napoli, who handed some papers to David Mitchell.

The C.S.O.B. got up, walked to the head of the table, and lifted the top of a notebook computer. Napoli and the other N.Y.P.D. detective started at opposite ends of the room and began drawing the shades over the windows.

Monahan thanked Tom and his associates for coming and explained that all the agencies represented today and several other governments and law-enforcement agencies were collaborating on the apprehension of several international criminals. The man was lucid, almost detached, and clear.

He waited while Mitchell read the Confidentiality Agreement and nodded and motioned at Rossi and Tom. While the three of them were signing the C.A.s, Monahan implored them not to discuss anything they were about to learn. There was to be no mention of any of the names they would hear. It was a capital felony to do so and would not only jeopardize years of work—it would potentially put people's lives at risk. Napoli collected the signed Confidential Disclosure Agreements.

The first slide of the PowerPoint said, "Operation Rapids" and showed the location of the meeting and date. The seal of each agency present was pictured in the header. The N.Y.P.D.'s was first. The next four slides showed a picture of everyone in the room and their title, and listed them by rank.

The next slide showed six images of a man in various settings, all but one clandestine. "This man is Igor Yatkin. The worst. You've read some about him, Mr. Strawbridge, but there is a lot more that is not common knowledge. You know the *Merchant of Death* became very wealthy with his air-transport companies, smuggling weapons after the Cold War and the collapse of Communism. Primarily from Eastern Europe to Africa and the Middle East. There is no definite information on his military career except that he graduated from the Military Institute of Foreign Languages. A polyglot, he was either a translator in the Russian Army or a Major in the Soviet Air Force, the G.R.U. As a businessman, he proved to be ruthless, a creative briber with no concern for international shipping laws regarding cargo or embargoes."

The next slide was an organizational chart showing Yatkin's other primary business interests. Sex and human trafficking and drugs. "It's the sex trafficking that gets everybody's attention. Several of our partner governments have received constant and enormous pressure from their citizenry," nodding to the Interpol Executive Committee Member from France. "He employs the Lebanese Mafia operating out of Sierra Leone to source most of the girls."

Monahan concluded on Yatkin by saying, "He'll never see the light of day again once he is recaptured. And if our Arab friends find him first, it will be a lot worse than that."

Next up was Matteo Keller. Monahan explained that Keller was self-made and seemed to have the golden touch. Very well connected, both privately and politically, he was never short of capital. "We don't have much on him, except we can prove his money has been used to back individuals buying antiquities, stolen art, and jewels. Ironically, he is on the Board of the Art Loss Register, artloss.com. Check it out if you get a chance."

David Mitchell, clearly intrigued, said, "He isn't too hard to find. Our associates in Geneva found out through Barclays about a recent meeting in Monte Carlo. It seems Benjamin Friman was the organizer. And Yatkin, Keller, and Propakov were all in attendance."

"Friman is another story and not of interest in this operation. We know all about the meeting and have a lot of support in Monte Carlo. We'll come back to Yatkin and Keller later. On to our friend, Yuri Propakov."

Monahan explained Propakov had been a mid-level government official in the Russian Natural Gas monopoly, Gazprom, which produced more than 90% of Russia's natural gas. The main importers are Germany, Ukraine, Belarus, Italy, Turkey, France, and Hungary. Propakov had traveled extensively to those countries and to Northern Europe. After the end of the Cold War, he worked for one of the original oligarchs, Vladimir Trepov, who continued to wield power and remained one of the country's richest men. He was already powerful enough during Yeltsin's presidency to shape economic policy.

"Propakov made a fortune on one of Trepov's nickel deals and struck out on his own. He is well connected and has an eye, especially for jewels, and a strong clientele." Monahan cycled through three or four slides showing Propakov at various art fairs, showrooms, salons, and auction houses around the world. The last slide was Tom with Keller and Propakov in the preview room at Christie's from Saturday.

Tom's expression was flat.

Monahan, scanning the room, said, "Any questions?

"Here's the bottom line. The Pink Panthers steal, and Propakov fences for them and others, either buying outright or returning a cash profit later. Sometimes Keller finances the purchases. Propakov never seems to use his own money. And Yatkin buys. He always has cash to clean. If he buys, from anyone, Keller is involved. Everyone loves cash, so nothing, especially tracking, is ever easy."

"We don't believe Propakov is dangerous, but he needs to go down. Keller is not dangerous. But to make anything stick, we'd need to catch him buying stolen merchandise and prove he had prior knowledge. Not easy. The primary mission here is to find Yatkin, recapture him, and put him away.

"Yatkin's organization is formidable, and he has a lot of people on his payroll who don't work for him directly. Ready to provide a service or information, these people are otherwise perfectly legitimate. His paid regular staff seems to be of two types—those who know and those who don't. Keller is independent.

"New slide. Boris Resnikov is Yatkin's right hand, and while a brutal anti-Semite known for some rough stuff, he has no record. One of his main responsibilities is to keep Yatkin's daughter, Marina, safe. She's twenty-six and lives alone in Palm Beach. We've spent a fortune surveilling the compound, and it is tight. I'm convinced Yatkin visits. The whole crew is slick, and we have people working inside four of the surrounding estates. When Marina travels, it's in plain sight with Resnikov. Sometimes one or two others."

"Excuse me, Chief. Where do I fit in here?"

"In a minute, Mr. Strawbridge. We have looked at detaining the daughter to pull Yatkin out. We don't think it would work, and we'd be killed in the press. Our best plan is to draw him out, via Propakov and/or Keller, with some one-of-a-kind buy or extremely important item."

Mitchell, "Are you suggesting my client involves himself with these criminals?"

"I'm suggesting Mr. Strawbridge consider helping us, directly or indirectly. If an item of jewelry or art were compelling enough for Yatkin, a meeting might be arranged, leading to his recapture. It would have to go up the line from either Propakov or Keller."

Tom, "With all due respect, Chief Monahan, would the Hope Diamond or the Mona Lisa even pull this guy out? And how would any item be protected, even if something that compelling was available?"

"We have some ideas. If you'd be willing to help, there is more we can share. Including some of what we know of Yatkin's movements.

"So, you're asking my client to get involved at some level?"

"We are. There is a substantial reward, and, depending on your level of involvement and the success of the operation, you could make a great deal of money, Mr. Strawbridge. The reward cache is funded by more than a few governments and several international agencies, including the Renew Foundation. The reward fund stands at about $35,000,000."

"I'm assuming you want me to be the consultant and expert on anything gemstone or jewelry related?"

"That and maybe more. I'll be blunt. You handle yourself well; everybody knows you and comes to you for important things. We are asking you to engage Propakov, whom you have met, and see if he wants to do business. By the way, we know he went to Kessling to get to you. We got that from a phone conversation."

David Mitchell and Tom looked at each other, and Mitchell raised his eyebrows.

"Do you think you could organize a meeting with Propakov?"

"He's coming to my office this afternoon."

CHAPTER 26

Monday Morning

Tom told them about Propakov's voicemail leading to the meeting planned for later that day. He also explained Matteo Keller mentioned investments when they met at Christie's.

"Mr. Strawbridge, please go ahead with Propakov, and get back to us."

"With all due respect, Chief Monahan, I don't want to become a Junior Detective here. I have a small business to run. Our trade is difficult and dangerous enough without exposing myself to these criminals."

"We understand your concerns, but we have a very narrow window here, and . . ."

"Meaning what?" Tom interrupted.

"Meaning we have solid intelligence that Yatkin is currently in the States, and we want to get him back. Now. And remember the reward."

Mitchell asked the C.S.O.B. if he could have a private word with his client.

Monahan pointed at Napoli and waved his hand toward the door to the first conference room. Tom and David Mitchell walked into the room and, leaving the door open, walked to the far end.

"Tom, let me take it from here. When we go back, ask about the reward, and then say nothing else until I prompt you or ask you a question." Mitchell looked over his shoulder to see Rossi waving his hands and talking nonstop. "I'd say they have an idea, but until we know what they are thinking, I don't want you committed. Got it?"

"Yes, got it."

Once seated, Tom asked, "If I continue to assist you, how much of the reward can I expect?"

The instant he stopped talking, David Mitchell said, "Chief Monahan, Mr. Strawbridge will be happy to tell you about his conversation later today. However, your request for Tom's continued help has no details or specifics. Whatsoever. If you have a specific plan at this time, please fill us in. Otherwise, please understand, my client does not care to participate further."

Monahan looked at Bureau Chief Wilson and nodded.

Wilson explained that their multi-agency task force did have a series of ideas and further explained they had resolved initial concerns and complications regarding jurisdictions and responsibilities.

"Normally, in a case like this, we keep what is known as a 'sterile corridor.' Basically, the intelligence work and the operations sides operate independently, with no knowledge of the other team's work. The goal being an investigation free from infection by corruption, where informants are kept quarantined from police officers. And, before you say it, Mr. Strawbridge, it does sound like big government."

"So, Tom would be considered an informant?"

"Not in the strictest sense of the definition. Given the enforcement agencies involved, the international aspect to this case, and that Yatkin has already been convicted, our path ahead is straightforward. We would like Mr. Strawbridge to present something to Propakov of sufficient value and interest so that Yatkin hears about it. Either directly or through Keller. Our hope is, via surveillance of various types, to find Yatkin's whereabouts and bust him. We have enough to pick up and hold Propakov right now. If this moves forward, the item or items should be discreetly presented as stolen, so if Keller is involved, we'll have him, too."

"And where is Tom to get the bait, if you will? And what about his insurance?"

Monahan put up his hand, taking over for Wilson. "We could help with art, but not with jewelry. That would be up to Mr. Strawbridge. The taxpayers will cover the insurance."

Mitchell, "Let us consider what you've suggested, and we'll get back to you."

"Please also think about letting us put some devices in your office or, at the least, giving us access to your security system. Please get back to us by 10:00 a.m. tomorrow." Monahan leaned in, looking ominous, as he said, "And remember. We don't have to ask you for permission for surveillance, Mr. Strawbridge."

Everyone stood up. The Interpol and F.B.I. people made attempts at smiles as they shook hands. Captain Ramirez was outside the door and led them back to the elevators and down to the main floor of One Police Plaza.

Outside, David Mitchell said, "You get everything, Jim?"

"I did. By the way, did you notice Wilson's body language? Nervous as a cat."

"He's probably on the hook for Yatkin's escape and needs to make this happen. What do you think, Tom?"

"If all I need to do is interest Propakov in something, God knows what, so they can track and surveil him, and the reward is substantial, I don't know. What do you think?"

"I think you have to consider doing what they ask. It's a big case and really important; you'd gain a lot of political capital. And maybe a payday. Jim, please wait by the garage. I'll be right along."

"Tom, how do you want to handle this?"

"Do I have to decide now?"

"No. But I've already got four hours in."

"Oh. Of course—your fee. Silly me. Okay, I'll think about it."

"Call me immediately after your meeting with Yuri Propakov, OK?"

Mitchell walked to the right, around the back of City Hall, toward Chinatown, and Tom walked back through the arcade and arranged an Uber. Six minutes. He called Heidi—all quiet, and the Pérezes had confirmed. Max had called his cell. No message.

Heading north on the F.D.R., Tom thought about the proposal and quickly decided he'd go forward if there was a guarantee of a significant reward. If not, he would try to get Propakov back to his office one more time, and that would be it. He assumed the police would be watching his building later today, anyway. In fact, based on what he'd seen earlier, they were probably watching his building and him constantly. How he'd pay Mitchell, straight hourly or contingency, depended on what arrangements could be made and guaranteed regarding any reward. Tom was leaning toward hourly unless something changed dramatically.

Heidi was chatting with the FedEx lady when Tom got back to the office. It was 12:25 p.m. He put in a call to George Saluto and left a voicemail. His cell phone rang. Max.

"Max. All good?"

"Very good. My fiancé and I are having a small—let's call it an *announcement party*—this Thursday at Bar Wayo. Can you join us?"

"I'm not even going to get into what you are doing, but, honestly, no. I have drinks and dinner Thursday."

"Too bad. I'm sure we'll still be going after your dinner, so feel free to stop by later. You could see Heidi and me home?"

"Not this week, Max. It's a sale week."

"I'm going to text you some dates and times for us to meet. We need to have a talk."

"Okay. By the way, how is Heidi doing?"

"I think fine. She's still terribly upset, mostly about you, but she'll be OK."

"Thanks. Give me a heads-up if there is anything I need to know."

"We can talk about it at our meeting!"

"Fine, Max. Goodbye."

Tom ate a sandwich at his desk and read the notes from the meeting Rossi had put together and just emailed. No surprises.

At 2:25 p.m., Tom saw Propakov in the hallway. As he rang the bell, Heidi buzzed Propakov through the mantrap. She took his coat and showed him to the showroom. Tom let him wait a minute. He picked up a pad on his way to the showroom. He was met with the stale-beet smell at the door. They shook hands, and Tom, putting down the pad, excused himself and walked to Heidi's desk.

"Can you break out the Febreze? This guy reeks."

"No kidding."

"And please hit the showroom after he leaves, before the clients arrive."

"Will do."

When Tom returned, Propakov was leaning over the main showcase, looking at a pair of vintage earrings by Suzanne Belperron. They were cream-colored chalcedony, dotted with round sapphires and diamonds.

"Would you like something to drink, Mr. Propakov?"

"No, thank you, and 'Yuri,' please. How much are these, Mr. Strawbridge?" he asked, pointing at the earrings.

"The trade price is $32,600."

"Strong, no?"

"No. 1937, one of a kind. I want you to know I have an appointment in a half hour." Tom sat down at one of the desks, gesturing toward the other side to Propakov.

"Is there any room there?"

"Maybe a little. For cash."

"Aaaah. Cash has become so difficult. I will ask a buyer of mine. Could I take them on memo?"

"Why not? What can I do for you today?"

Propakov sat down and took a parcel paper out of his jacket's inside breast pocket and handed it to Tom. The Alexandrite.

"I will be leaving New York after the Sales and would like you to hold the stone and work with it."

"What's the price?" Tom took out the stone and louped it for condition. Still perfect, bright polish. It had an incredible energy of its own and looked like a top gem emerald in the showroom's ambient light.

"$30,000. per carat. Cheap, no?"

"Fair. Do you have a memo?" It was cheap.

"No."

Tom rang for Heidi. "I'll call you with any offers and for sale approval, of course."

"Thank you."

Heidi came in, and Tom put the parcel paper on a black-velvet tray and handed the tray to her.

"Do you have a card?"

"No, I do not."

"How do we make out the memorandum?"

"My name and number will be good enough."

"Heidi, please make out a reverse memo to us from Mr. Propakov," writing his name and copying his number from his phone on to the pad. "$30,000 per carat. Thank you." A reverse memo is one made out from the party taking goods, but on their own memorandum form. They are used when the lending party does not have their own memo forms. It's a simple matter of writing in the word "To:" in front of the business name and "From:" in front of the blank spaces where the recipient's information would normally go.

"The man you met Saturday. I've taken the liberty of asking him to join us." Tom was mildly annoyed but not surprised.

"Keller. Is that it?"

"Yes. We have worked very closely together for some time, and he is a very good man to know."

They discussed the upcoming Sales for a few minutes when Heidi showed Matteo Keller into the showroom.

"Gentlemen!"

Tom, shaking hands, "May we take your coat, Mr. Keller?"

"No, no. May I put it here?" pointing to a chair in the corner.

Keller was very smooth and supremely confident.

Keller handed Tom his card. "I like to keep a certain portion of my money in hard assets. I have all the gold, platinum, palladium, and white diamonds I need. I am, therefore, always on the lookout for important fancy-color diamonds, important colored stones, and the best vintage pieces. After the Edwardian Period, please, unless it's exceptional and unusual. I am happy if I can liquidate at 90% immediately after purchase. Not always possible, but this is my goal."

"And, what kind of money are you looking to invest?"

"That, Mr. Strawbridge, is up to you. We are well capitalized and pay quickly."

"Can you ever pay in cash?"

Propakov looked at Keller, but he did not react. "On occasion. You know how difficult cash has become."

"Yes. And tell me how you came to me?" To neither one specifically.

Propakov said, "Everyone knows you, and I asked Mr. Kessling to introduce us."

"All right, gentlemen. I don't have anything in the office that you would find interesting at the moment, but let me think, and I'll get back to you." Tom stood up.

"Might you have something before the weekend?"

"That depends, Mr. Keller. I know you are serious, and I will be in touch either way. I'm sure we'll see each other at the Sales this week."

Tom walked them to the door, and Heidi handed a sealed envelope to Propakov containing the memo she had executed and signed. That got Tom thinking. They shook hands, and the two men left.

Before they had reached the lobby, Tom had texted Propakov asking how many people knew about and had seen the Alexandrite. Did Matteo Keller know the stone?

Tom jumped on the phone to David Mitchell and relayed the details of the meeting with Keller and Propakov.

"Interesting. So, no surprises?"

"No surprises."

"OK. I'll put that in writing for you and email it over so you can have a look before I send it to Wilson and Monahan."

"Thanks, David."

"And don't speak to them—Napoli, either—without me, OK?"

"Good."

Heidi was at the door. "Mr. & Mrs. Perez are in the showroom. She is having a champagne, and he has coffee."

"Well?"

"She's a big girl."

"How's the air?"

"All clear."

Tom got up to go to his clients as a text from Yuri Propakov came in. "You, Kessling, and the couple. That's it. Old stone, unseen since the 1930s."

CHAPTER 27

Monday Afternoon

TOM WALKED INTO THE SHOWROOM and introduced himself to Mr. and Mrs. Perez. They were upper-middle aged and extremely well-tailored. Her taste was another matter, and she had too much perfume on.

Tom sat down, smiling. "How are your beverages?"

"I'd love another champagne." Tom hit a button next to the desk phone that started a light blinking on the wall opposite Heidi's chair.

"It's a pleasure to meet you, Mr. Strawbridge. Our people at Morgan Stanley can't say enough about you. You can imagine that when we asked them, more personally than professionally, if they knew any fine jewelers, we discovered they have preferred vendors for almost any service."

"'Tom,' please. And the pleasure is mine. Morgan Stanley has been very helpful to us. I won't deny it. We do a lot of entertainment and educational events for them, and their clients always enjoy themselves." Heidi walked in, excused herself, and deftly refilled Mrs. Perez's champagne flute.

She turned to Mr. Perez, who put up his hand and handed his coffee cup back to her.

Tom had been trying to determine what it was about Mrs. Perez that was distinctive. It hit him. No neck. At all. A necklace would not be an option. She had on earrings and two bracelets, all David Webb enamel. And all variants on the frog theme. Plus, two immense rings, one on either hand. A large round diamond on her left hand, and a *cabochon* emerald ring on her right.

"You have wonderful jewelry, Mrs. Perez. Is there something special you are trying to find?"

"Thank you, Tom. I love jewelry." One of the many client statements Tom could go without hearing ever again. "I was thinking . . ."

Tom interrupted, "Forgive me. But we recently purchased something that you must see. It may not be for you, but I know you will enjoy seeing it, given your excellent taste. Let me see if it is still in the vault. Will you please excuse me?" Mrs. Perez was visibly excited.

Heidi joined Tom in the vault room. "What are you thinking?"

"I am thinking that I'd love to truncate this sale. Where is that Chanel Maltese Cross brooch I had to buy in that lot from Empire Diamond? Here we go." Tom took a black leather box from one of the shelves and stood up. "I am going to check this. Go in and chat them up, okay?"

Tom took the piece to his office window and louped it. Minor and normal wear for a piece from the late 1930s. Everyone is familiar with the countless costume Maltese Crosses produced by Chanel until they stopped producing costume and changed to fine jewelry in the 1980s. But vintage examples made from precious metals and gemstones are impossibly rare. This particular Cross had four long Emerald Cut emerald arms, above commercial quality but just barely, and four large Drop Shaped natural pearls between them. The gold work was heavy. The center was a Square Sugarloaf *Cabochon* amethyst. Not the most attractive, but wildly desirable and collectible. He looked up his cost. He had averaged it over the price of the entire 16-piece lot. $19,000.

Heidi stood up from behind the desk as Tom came into the showroom. They let Mr. Perez, who was gushing at Heidi, finish a story about how rich he was.

"Something more, Mrs. Perez?"

"Maybe one more." Heidi left for the champagne.

"Now, you were saying, Mrs. Perez?" Tom put the tray with the brooch's box on the corner of his side of the desk. Both Mr. and Mrs. Perez moved their eyes and stared, riveted on the box.

"Oh. I was just thinking about something unusual. I wear a lot of earrings." Mr. Perez seemed genuinely interested in his wife's jewelry habit. "What is in that box?"

Perfect. "Oh, just something I thought you might enjoy seeing, but let me go to the vault for some earrings." He started to stand.

"Could we see what's in the box first?"

Tom sat down and started by asking them if they knew anything about Coco Chanel. They did not know much, but Tom made them think they did. He patiently explained that the few, and very rare, examples of genuine jewelry from between the Wars were believed to be the result of competition between Chanel and designer Elsa Schiaparelli. The Perezes were mesmerized. World-class illusion.

Tom ended with, "She accomplished a lot in her life, including spying for the Nazis." He opened the box and placed it between them on the desk. He knew he had them before anything was said.

"Please, have a close look," as he handed the pin to Mrs. Perez. "Excuse me, I'll be back in a moment." She was turning it over in her hands, and he was leaning over and looking on.

Tom walked down to Heidi. "How's it going?"

"Well, you never know, but I think this is over."

"David Mitchell wants you to call him."

"OK." He headed back to the showroom. "Where is the champagne?"

"Coming."

"Apologies. Now, what kind of earrings are you thinking about?"

Mr. Perez, "Tom, how much is this piece? Mrs. Perez likes it very much."

"Have you tried it on?" Heidi arrived.

"Please help Mrs. Perez with the brooch."

Heidi filled Mrs. Perez's glass. Once the brooch was on, Heidi placed a tabletop mirror in front of Mrs. Perez and adjusted it so she could see herself and the brooch.

"A second opinion," Tom said, smiling. Thankfully, Heidi had placed the brooch well away from the area where Mrs. Perez's head emerged from her torso.

"Charming, don't you think so?" She was smiling broadly. "We have to get $135,000."

No reaction. Mr. Perez, "Some discount is customary, isn't it?"

"Sometimes, yes. Unfortunately, not in this case. We have just acquired it, and that is what I would ask from the trade. I'm quite sure Chanel themselves will be the buyer—I just haven't gotten around to contacting them. You have a home in Connecticut? Delivering the brooch would save the sales tax."

"May we have a minute?"

Tom and Heidi stepped into the hall. "What do you think?"

"Not sure now. If she likes it, we're closed." Tom went back into the showroom a few minutes later.

"Any thoughts?"

"We'd like to buy it."

"Wonderful."

"Would you say this is a good investment?"

"Mr. Perez, we don't sell investments. I can tell you, though, that this is a rare opportunity, and it is very possible you could make a profit tomorrow. If you are undecided . . ."

"No, we'll take it. Payment? And you'll have it sent?"

"Whatever you prefer; we generally prefer wire transfers. You let me know when you would like the pin sent, and you will have it. We will cover the insurance, $250,000. And live with it for a week or so before we discuss payment."

Tom showed the Pérezes to the door. They shook hands with Heidi and left. It was close to 4:30 p.m.

"Well done, Boss."

"You know what they say, 'It's not easy.'" Heidi smiled.

A good sale and remarkably easy. The perfect clients for that piece.

Tom called David Mitchell.

"Did you look at my email?"

"Yes."

"Good?"

"I would just emphasize, in the summary, that they both project an air of extreme confidence, and that Keller is unusually charismatic and smooth."

"OK. Got it. I got an email from Chief Wilson, cc'ing Monahan, and he wants to know what we are thinking by noon tomorrow. They are going to smell blood in the water when they hear Keller showed up."

"Oh, Napoli called."

"And?"

"Heidi got it. Wants me to call him."

"Don't. I'll email him and bcc you."

"What else?"

"Have you had any time to think about . . . ?"

"Your bill? No."

"Wise ass. What are you thinking?"

"At this point, I'm still not sure exactly what they're expecting."

"They want you to set Yatkin up, Tom. Get something, something 'stolen,' something interesting to him, via Propakov and/or Keller. The police track and get him back in custody. You know."

"Do they really think Yatkin will expose himself? Even if we found something super grand, rare, and expensive, wouldn't he just rely on Propakov?"

"Who knows? They are convinced Yatkin is in the U.S. right now."

"I do have something. I don't own it, but it would get everybody's attention."

"Well, think about it." Tom probably should not have mentioned anything, but no harm, as Mitchell was not curious and asked no questions.

"What about the reward, David? That is interesting."

"I'll ask in my cover email."

"Can you tell them we need specifics on any reward before I make a decision?"

"Is that what you want to do?"

"Why not? I don't want to be involved unless there is some upside. No goodwill or noble act on my part, David. When did you become the Saint of Altruism?"

"Not that. It's a very big case and an important chance to help collect a serious bad guy."

"Sorry, David. Not moved. I have the auction tomorrow, and—hold on, David."

Heidi was at the door. "There's a Roger Gillespe on the line."

"I'm just hanging up. Please see if he can hold." She nodded. "The sale starts at 10:00 a.m., so see if they get you an answer before then. If not, they'll have their answer."

"Goodnight, Tom."

Tom was frustrated by Mitchell's apparent interest in helping without some kind of definitive reason or purpose. Too bad.

"Roger. Sorry for the delay."

Tom listened while Gillespe explained how he was mad for Marla Wingate and was going to propose. What would Tom recommend? And, how much would he have to spend? A nice guy, but Tom could not see the two of them together.

A cushion cut, 5.00 to 7.00 carats was Tom's recommendation. Plain platinum mounting, about $180,000–$190,000.

"Great. How long will it take to make?"

"Once I find the right diamond, about a week."

"Thank you, and please go as fast as you can. Do I need to pay anything now?"

"No. Not until she is happy."

They hung up, and Tom texted Marla Wingate. "Just hung up with Roger . . ." as Heidi came in and sat down.

"Thanks for the excellent help today. Good sale." She beamed. "What are you feeling?"

"I'm good. My therapist says I need to confront my feelings when I get anxious about what happened. He doesn't think it would be a good idea for me to take any time off."

"All right. But keep me posted, OK? What about tomorrow?" Tom handed her a card detailing how he had arrived at the bidding price for the sapphire ring lot. $70,000 was underlined and circled. "Pretty straightforward. If you want to bid, you stop at 70."

"Would you go any higher?"

"Good question. In this case, no. I think it will be a great stone, but with the market the way it is, no need to stretch."

"I'd like to do it."

"Good. You go for the start of the Sale, mark it until I come, and save me a seat." Marking a sale is not bidding but following each lot and recording the hammer price in the catalog as they are sold. "It's Lot #43, so I'll get there well before 11:00 a.m., OK?" The major auction houses average about 40 jewelry lots per hour.

"Yes."

"This will be good. Anything else?"

"Yes. George Saluto called, said he was sorry to hear what happened, and will be back in town Friday." Tom put a reminder in his computer to call him then. Of course, if Tom eventually got the details on the diamonds and colored stones from the Van Cleef worksheets, everything would be a lot easier. He and George Saluto would only have to grade the diamonds, not re-estimate their weights.

"And then there is this." Heidi reached down to the pad on her lap, picked up an envelope, and put it on the desk in front of Tom.

It was the envelope containing the reverse memorandum she had created for Yuri Propakov.

Part Seven

CHAPTER 28

Tuesday Morning

IT WAS 7:00 A.M. Tuesday. Tom was at his desk, looking at the envelope containing the Alexandrite memorandum and thinking over the conversation with Heidi from Monday afternoon.

She had explained, "I went down to the service hall with the trash, and it was lying on top of the bin at the end of the public hallway. Open it."

Tom opened the envelope. The memo was intact and untouched.

"What the hell? Do you think he dropped it, and someone else threw it away?"

"Doubt it. Has our address."

If true, that meant Propakov had, for some reason, thrown out the only record of a valuable gemstone's whereabouts. Before electronic record keeping, the paper copies of a dealer's "open" memos were just as valuable as the gemstones or jewelry they described. The recipient's signature proving something had been "memoed out." Even with computer-generated memoranda, dealers had to physically sign a memo when goods were returned. In effect "closing" what had been a potential transaction. Without this record, Propakov had no record he had memoed the Alexandrite to Tom. But why throw it out?

Maybe he knew Tom was no risk, an honorable man of his word. Or maybe he didn't want a physical record of the stone. Either way, the odds were good that the Alexandrite had come to Propakov via less-than-legitimate channels. Out of curiosity, and expecting nothing, Tom googled "plus 20 carat gem Emerald Cut Alexandrite." Nothing. Then "missing plus 20 carat gem Emerald Cut Alexandrite." Nothing again. Propakov said it was from the '30s. Did he come across it somehow and buy it directly from the owner?

Maybe he discovered it in a museum and paid off a curator? One mineral dealer whom Tom knew in California cherry-picked historically significant specimens from The Chicago Field Museum and The American Museum of Natural History by trading in things absent from the Museums' collections. He made a fortune, as the curators were not business minded and had no idea of value or historical significance. This was before the days when museums considered gemstones and jewelry as "legitimate" objects for their collections. Eventually, though, museums started competing for donations and acquisitions with trade dealers and the public alike. Museums became interested once they realized the draw for the public of gems and jewelry. The lack of scientific worthiness quickly became unimportant. The only museum installation, of any kind, that receives more visits than the Hope Diamond in the Smithsonian is the Mona Lisa in the Louvre.

Tom checked his emails. He reread the one from Mitchell to Wilson and Monahan, detailing the meeting with Propakov and Keller. A separate one from David Mitchell to the N.Y.P.D. Chiefs, cc'ing Napoli, asked them to communicate directly with Mitchell for the time being. This was followed by an email from Napoli to Tom, asking for a call. Tom forwarded it to Mitchell.

Tom got a coffee and started to read *The Journal*. There was an article on the auction market, highlighting this week's Magnificent Jewel Sales and next week's Fine Art Sales. Auction houses use several metrics to measure their success, both internally and relatively. A given sale's success was dependent on many things, including the content of the sale and the current economic and market conditions. It is always important for the auction houses to hit their pre-sale estimates. It does not look good if they misjudge, and a lot doesn't meet the reserve. While better, it is also not good if they missed the high estimate by too much and the piece hammers well above the estimate. One of the most important metrics used to gauge a given sale's success is the percent of lots sold. A good showing with that statistic indicates to Management that the Experts know what they are doing. More importantly, the higher the percent of lots sold, the better it looks to potential private sellers comparing auction houses.

Tom's phone buzzed. It was a text from David Mitchell asking for a 9:15 a.m. phone call.

It was just after 8:00 a.m. when Heidi knocked on Tom's door. She was smiling, looked more relaxed, and was wearing her birthday scarf. She was incredibly well turned out.

"Morning. You have great taste," gesturing toward the scarf.

"Good morning. Another coffee?"

"If you don't mind, great."

"Can we review today again?"

"As soon as you're back."

She left, and Tom put the paper in the showroom on the way to wash his hands. Heidi was sitting in Tom's office, sipping her coffee, when he returned.

"Thanks for the coffee." She picked up her pad and started to look at her notes.

"Let's try this. Put the pad down, and just tell me what you are going to do at the Sale."

She recounted each step, from registering for the paddle, down to saving him a seat. Every registered bidder receives a plastic ping-pong racquet-shaped paddle with his or her assigned number for that sale. Many bidders do not use the paddle, preferring another signal to the auctioneer. In either case, if a bidder is successful on a given lot, the paddle is held up so their number can be recorded.

Heidi then reviewed the bidding prices. "We've talked about it, but when do you think it would be best for me to start? And, if it is close, but more than our stopping number, will you step in or signal me to go on?"

"Why not try what I do? Wait and see if the action settles down before our stopping point. If you have room, start then. I've always felt there is no point jumping in from the start, like most people. You don't have anything to prove, and it's possible more bidders might drive up the price, especially if there are privates involved. And eventually as you become known, your very involvement will get other dealers to jump in. I once went to a sale with serious interest on thirteen lots and never bid on a thing. And that speaks to your second question. No. We have to own a sapphire like that at the right price. If we get it, we get it, and if we don't, we won't look back."

"OK. I want to go a little ahead of time."

"Good. I emailed Dawn, and there will be no issue for you at registration. It's Lot #43, yes? I'll be there before 11:00 a.m., like I said, given they run about 40 lots per hour, just in case."

"Good. I'm excited, Tom."

"You should be. Don't show it, especially if you are successful. And if there is anything else before you go, just ask."

Heidi left the office, and Tom started to think about the requests from the various law-enforcement agencies. It seemed probable that the police felt Tom's reputation and station would be an asset in trying to expose Igor Yatkin. But they clearly had no sense of what it would take to interest Yatkin enough to risk exposure. Especially since Yatkin had at least two people aggressively bird-dogging and buying for him. Propakov and Keller would have access to anybody and anything Tom did, from major signed jewelry pieces to important fancy-colored diamonds. Would the brooch even be enough? It was the only thing available that Tom knew of that had sufficient value and provenance, outside of pieces already in private collections or museums.

His cell phone. A text from Marla Wingate. "Good morning. I just saw your text from last night. Can you call me?"

"Morning. Give me five."

Tom roughed out a value he would ask for the brooch and then added 30%. If he was going to work with the police, this was the bait. And if the brooch didn't interest Propakov and Keller, he was out.

He called Wingate. They exchanged pleasantries. He did not ask if she would attend the Sale. She asked what Roger Gillespe had said, and Tom told her all the details and, jokingly, asked her ring size.

"Tom, I'm not one to waste my time or anybody else's. I have been on one date, literally, since my divorce. Roger is a lovely guy, but we have never even had dinner alone. I am honestly not sure where this is coming from."

"Well, I think you'll make a lovely couple."

"Stop it. I'll have to talk to him, sooner rather than later."

Facetiously, "Does this mean you don't want the ring?"

"Not unless you're giving it to me."

"Okay, then. Is there anything else I should be doing with him?"

"No. I'm really looking forward to Thursday. Are you sure I can't convince you to come here?"

"Remember our deal. And I may have something serious to discuss."

"Fine, Tom. Goodbye."

Heidi called. "David Mitchell on the phone, on three."

"Good morning, David. You're early." It was just before 9:00 a.m.

"Tom, I had a talk with Dermot Monahan earlier, and I need to talk to you A.S.A.P."

"Shoot."

"Look, I'm five blocks away. Can I stop up? I only have ten, fifteen minutes tops. We have an interview nearby you at 9:30 a.m."

"I guess. Is everything all right?"

"I'll tell you when I get there. See you in five." He hung up.

Tom told Heidi that Mitchell was coming and to go ahead and head to Christie's whenever she wanted. She asked if he would attend the Sotheby's Sale tomorrow and if she should go. He didn't know if he was going yet. Since work was light, he suggested she could attend either the afternoon or the morning session.

Tom saw David Mitchell at the door and went down the hall to meet him. They went to the showroom and sat down at one of the desks.

"Monahan was more user friendly over the phone. We talked about everything, and there are three main points to tell you now. One, they are now certain Yatkin is in the Tri-State area. He wouldn't tell me much, but if I had to guess, they have I.D.'d the aircraft he is using. You can imagine how badly they want him back in custody. Two, they want you involved and are watching you and anyone else who is in contact with Propakov and Keller, around the clock. Nothing new and no surprise, but he wanted you to know. Three, they'll commit to a specific reward that would be guaranteed if any part of your involvement leads to Yatkin's capture."

"How much?"

"I'll come back to that. They confirmed they want you to tell Propakov, Keller, or both about something spectacular, real or imagined. They surveil and see what happens. See if Propakov and Keller contact Yatkin."

"Like I said yesterday, do they really think Yatkin would expose himself in any way that was traceable? But, how much?"

"$32,000,000."

"Guaranteed?"

"If your involvement leads to them learning Yatkin's whereabouts and to his successful capture. They gave me permission to draft a brief agreement outlining the terms. I can craft it so that it would be hard for them to get off the hook. And the potential embarrassment would be devastating for their public image."

Heidi came to the door in her coat and carrying a briefcase. "Excuse me, Mr. Mitchell." Looking at Tom, "I'm off."

"Good luck. I'll see you there soon."

"Goodbye, Mr. Mitchell."

"Tom, I think you have to try. They claim there is little to no risk and will stop if anything unpredicted or dangerous happens."

"Like me showing up in the Reservoir with no head?"

Mitchell grunted. "Look, I told you I have something major."

"And?"

"And I have to think about everything."

"Well, I got them to give you until 5 p.m.—OK?"

"I'll let you know right after the Christie's Sale. I'll be back early."

David Mitchell stood up. "I'll get the agreement done by then; Jim is working on it already. Oh, Napoli was calling to see if you are working on any other business with Keller or Propakov."

"No." Not wanting to mention the Alexandrite.

Tom walked David Mitchell to the door. He sat down at his desk and dialed Marla Wingate.

"Hi, Tom."

"Marla, are you free for an early cocktail tonight?"
"I can be. Shall I get my hopes up?"
"Funny. I want to discuss something. 6:00 p.m.?"
"Okay. Please come here, all right?"
"See you then."

CHAPTER 29

Tuesday Midmorning

TOM LOCKED AND ALARMED THE OFFICE and headed to Christie's. He wondered whether taking a gemstone on memorandum from Propakov constituted "doing business." He would mention it to David Mitchell.

Tom started thinking about how he would present the brooch if he decided to move forward. Introducing the idea that something incredible might be available, while describing it in general and then naming a price would reveal a great deal. The compelling thing about the brooch was that it more than stood alone as a world-class jewel, but its provenance put it in another category. If there were a meeting, what would prevent them from threatening Tom and stealing the brooch? Private security. All risk had to be removed from any potential showing. Matteo Keller indicated that he was leaving New York by the weekend, and Propakov had said "after the Sales." If anything were going to happen, it would have to happen fast.

Tom shook hands with Gil, the Doorman at Christie's, and walked down the main hall. Tom knew the Sale would be a scene by the time he got to the stairs leading to the main gallery, where the auction was being held. Reaching the top of the stairs, he could hear the auctioneer over the crowd milling in the hallway around the registration desk where paddles were distributed. The people around the double doors into the sale room spilled out into the hallway, and Tom made his way through until he was inside, at the back of the gallery.

The room was packed. Francois Puriel, the Worldwide Jewelry Department Head for Christie's, was over from Geneva and conducting the auction. Besides the 400 people in the room, there were monitors for real-time Internet bidding at various places along the side walls. And ten Assistants manning the bank of telephones for remote bidding to the right of the auction podium. The ceilings were very high in the sales gallery, and behind Puriel to the left was a large digital screen that projected an image of each lot as it came up for sale. Along the right margin of the screen, the current bid price of the lot was displayed in U.S. dollars, and below that, simultaneously, in seven international currencies. Directly behind Puriel and high on the wall was a large image of the cover of the catalog, featuring the money lot in the sale. The Edwardian pearl-and-emerald tiara.

Bidders and gawkers lined the walls and were two and three deep along the back wall. Tom was standing behind a small group, thinking he couldn't see an empty chair, when Heidi, on the opposite aisle, second-to-last row, stood halfway up and waved at Tom.

"Who's that? Wow."

"Works for Strawbridge. That guy gets more box than UPS."

Tom excused himself and walked between the two men and along the back row to the chair Heidi had saved. He'd seen the dealer who made the comment but didn't know him.

It was 10:55 a.m.

"Hi. How'd you do?"

"Fine, I guess, but I took a lot of heat."

"Well, thanks. Too bad. I think they were probably more interested in you than the seat."

She smiled.

Puriel, in his vacillating auctioneer cadence, "We have 265 thousand, 265 thousand to the lady in front. 265 thousand, all done? 265 thousand on lot number 36, 265 thousand." Crack! The sound of the hammer, which, in this case, was a wooden cylinder held in the palm of the hand, hitting the podium, signaling the successful sale of that lot. The final few moments of the sale of any particular lot can be tedious. The auctioneer makes sure all the remote bidders are up to speed, while he or she milks the crowd, hoping for someone to up the current bid or for a new bidder to jump in. "Paddle number 368. Thank you."

"Talk to anybody?"

"A lot of waving. I was focused on the catalog and defending your seat."

"All right, all right."

"That creep from Ben Nur Diamonds tried to chat me up."

"Lot number 39—a beautiful pair of South Sea pearl-and-diamond earrings. Signed Chaumet. I have a bid for 65 thousand on the phone, 70 thousand in the back of the room."

Bidding generally starts below the low estimate, and the increments of the next bid are increased by specific amounts. For example,

$5,000 to $10,000 by $500s, $50,000 to $100,000 by $5,000s, and $100,000 to $200,000 by $10,000s. Auctioneers frequently take less than the standard increment just to raise the selling price, especially if the bidding was well above the high estimate.

Tom was watching the action when he noticed Propakov, Keller, and a third man standing against the wall near the phone dais.

"Do you see your friends from yesterday?"

"I do. Look at that third guy. Central-casting hitman, right?" Heidi giggled. This guy looked really rough but was very well dressed. He was big.

They watched the sale progress, and Tom noticed all the lots he'd seen had hammered above the high estimate. One lot to go: "Lot number 42, a fine rubellite ring, with diamonds, platinum mounting . . ."

"Good luck."

"Thank you. I'm ready, Tom."

Just as Lot 42 was closing, Propakov caught Tom looking at his friend. Propakov smiled and made a small bow. Tom nodded back.

"Lot number 43. A fine Sri Lankan sapphire, with round diamonds and platinum mounting."

The estimate for the sapphire was $40,000–$50,000. And the bidding quickly reached $65,000.

"We have 65 thousand online, 65 thousand online. 67 five on the phone. Do I see 70 thousand, 70 thousand. 67 five on the phone, all in, 67 five, 67 five on the phone." As he raised his hand to hammer the lot, Heidi shot up her arm. "70 thousand in the back of the room, 70 thousand. All against the lady in the back at 70 thousand." Crack! "Sold to paddle number?" Heidi held up the paddle. "One, one, three."

"Well done. Are you going to stay? I want to get back."

"No. I want to go to one of the sessions tomorrow, so I'll leave with you."

"Okay—after this next lot."

They walked out of the sale room, and while Tom waited for Heidi to return the paddle, a colored-stone dealer, Jack Rubin, who had followed Tom out, came up to him. "Hi, Tom. Will you take 10% over hammer and the vigorish right now?"

"Hi, Jack. No, thank you. We are making a line, and we need that stone."

Rubin smiled in a disgusted way and turned away.

Tom waited for Heidi as she went to the merchandise-pickup office on the main floor to get their sapphire. Once outside, "How did I do?"

"Very well, poker face and calm. Did you cut it a little close?"

"I wouldn't have waited that long, but I knew he'd see me."

Heidi stopped to get sandwiches, and when Tom opened and disarmed the office, it was just before noon.

They would have lunch in Tom's office. Before he sat down, he got a bottle of Sauvignon Blanc from the refrigerator, opened it, and brought it and two glasses back to his desk.

"Congratulations are in order. Purely ceremonial."

Heidi looked surprised but flattered. He poured their wine and held up his glass. "Today was a big step forward. Well done, and congratulations." They clinked glasses.

"Thank you, Tom. I know I have a long way to go, but thank you for the confidence."

"You'll see there are very few times when something we're bidding on is critical for the business. It's always good to go in with a plan. On occasion, you will have to overpay. For the next sale, we'll go to the dealer sessions together and review the goods."

She beamed. "How are you doing, by the way? The shooting was a week ago tomorrow already. Unbelievable."

"Much better, thanks." She had a tiny bit of lettuce on her nose. "Dad has been really good about everything. I also added an extra session with my therapist. My Mother keeps asking how you are doing. What do I tell her?"

"OK. The police wanting my help and concentrating on that has moved things along faster. I don't think about it much, especially since the guy who saw me is locked up. Remember me to your Mother, by the way."

They finished lunch and the wine, and Heidi started to clear.

"When you have time, bring in the Alexandrite. I want you to spend some time studying that stone."

Tom was going through his emails, and the most recent was from Jim Rossi, cc'ing David Mitchell. It was the agreement for the N.Y.P.D. Tom read it. There were two questions for Tom at the end. What was a description of the item(s), and the requested insurance coverage?

He debated the level of detail and settled with, "A signed pin from the late 1930s, made for European royalty, never delivered or worn. Mint condition." He didn't need to try to interest the law-enforcement people after all. "Insured value: $93,000,000." He added, "Thank you, Jim. It looks like you got it all," to the email.

Heidi buzzed at 1:25 p.m. and said that Mitchell was on the phone. Tom asked her to have him call his cell.

"93,000,000?"

"Yes. I don't have too much air in there, and the piece and the story are second to none."

"I just spoke to Monahan and Wilson earlier. They had men at the auction you went to, watching Propakov. Did you see another man with them?"

"Yes. A well-tailored ape."

"That was Yatkin's, let's say, *Chief of Staff*, Boris Reznikov. Like they told us, he runs everything, apparently, and is responsible for Yatkin's daughter's security. He lives in the Palm Beach house and held everything together when Yatkin was in the clink. He has a record but has kept clean for years."

"Besides the fact he works for one of the world's worst dirtbags."

"They are sending both of us some of his details. They suspect Reznikov screens any requests to speak or meet with Yatkin. Including Keller's. They have had eyes on Reznikov for quite a while—even had a tracking bug on his car in Florida for more than a month. Not hard to find. Here's the good part. They picked up an unencrypted text from his hotel room—he's at The Sherry Netherland—to another room. And they think it was Yatkin. So, he is most likely here in town. And they got a positive I.D. on the daughter at Kennedy yesterday."

"What's the plan?"

"Once we get a sign-off on the agreement, they want you to get Propakov and Keller over and show them the item. Whatever they say, you are not to let the piece out of your sight. If they bite, you ask to meet the buyer."

"Ridiculous."

"That's what they want you to do, and you're to make it clear up front that you need 50% of whatever price you settle on in cash."

"Or no deal?"

"Right. Well, that's what they think, but Monahan said you would know best how to manage things. So do what you think best."

"I'm talking to the owner tonight, so, depending on where that goes, I should be able to offer it to Propakov and Keller."

"Oh, and they want to come over and put in some wireless cameras and voice monitors of their own. They say it will take 15 minutes. I'll tell you as soon as we have the agreement. They want to come tonight."

"Seriously?"

"I'll be in touch, Tom. Bye."

"One more thing, David: Propakov left a stone with me the other night."

"So?"

"So, Napoli asked if we'd done any business."

"Did you?"

"No. Just took the stone on memorandum."

"OK. Bye, Tom."

He buzzed for Heidi.

"Uli Bank called, and I set him up for 8:00 a.m. Thursday. He has a 1:00 p.m. flight. A 'Steven Hopper' called and wants to come in to look at diamonds. He thinks a round brilliant cut, for an engagement ring. He's Mr. Perez's in-house counsel. I told him Monday morning. "OK?"

"Fine—nice of them. They haven't even received their Chanel piece yet. Please send them a magnum of Veuve. I'll craft a note." Tom took a moment to reflect again on how his business, for the most part, grew by itself. Whether it was the trade part or the private luxury-retail component, his work continued to expand organically.

Tom asked Heidi to get the sapphire they'd purchased earlier. He unmounted the sapphire with a prong lifter and asked Heidi to put the mounting and the sapphire in the ultrasonic cleaner for five minutes. A prong lifter is a hardened steel bar with various gaps cut into it to pry up most mounting prongs, regardless of the angle or style of jewelry. When the sapphire and mounting were clean and dry, he put the sapphire in a stone holder that attaches to the stage of the dark-field microscope and positioned the stone for her. He explained the different inclusions, including the source-specific ones for Sri Lanka, and pointed out the color zoning. Working around the zoning was critical for a successful re-cutting job to maximize the most-desirable type and even saturation of body color.

As they were finishing up, Tom's cell phone rang. "Hi, David."

"OK—they signed. They balked at the amount but signed. I want to give them the go-ahead to come over." It was 3:15 p.m.

"When can they get here? I have to leave by 5:15, 5:30 the latest."

"He said 30 minutes, three people."

Hold on." "Heidi, the police need to come here. Can you stay if I have to leave before they are done?"

"Sure."

"OK."

"Let me know how it goes, Tom. Let's talk first thing in the morning."

"Bye, David."

Tom and Heidi finished talking about the sapphire, and Tom said they could go to the cutter together and discuss the stone with Marco, one of their lapidaries. He explained that one of Marco's strengths was to keep the outline of the "face" of the stone as symmetrical as possible. Tom told Heidi they would study the Alexandrite tomorrow or later in the week.

Tom was writing a thank-you note to the Perezes when his cell phone rang. Propakov.

CHAPTER 30

Tuesday Evening

TOM DIDN'T TAKE PROPAKOV'S CALL but immediately listened to the message. Propakov was checking in to see if Tom had found anything for them and asked if "we" could stop by before the end of the day today. He did not mention the Alexandrite. Tom would call or text him after leaving the office. He needed to prepare his story.

Tom decided to write up the provenance for the brooch accurately and present that, along with his description and weight estimations. If Marla Wingate approved of his plan, he would show Propakov and Keller as soon as possible. But there was nothing to say to them today.

Once finished with the provenance on the brooch and having typed up the description, Tom opened the email from Monahan that had the information on Boris Reznikov. In 2008, Russian Mafia members and affiliates were arrested and charged by the F.B.I., U.S. Customs and Border Protection, and the N.Y.P.D. The charges included extortion, racketeering, illegal gambling, firearm offenses, narcotics trafficking, wire fraud, credit-card fraud, identity theft, and fraud on casino slot machines using electronic hacking devices. Most of the men were based in Atlantic City and Philadelphia. They were also accused of operating underground gambling operations based in Brighton Beach, Brooklyn.

Specifically, Reznikov was involved with a crew charged with murder-for-hire conspiracies, cigarette trafficking, and using violence to collect gambling debts. It was believed that all those arrested were members of the Russian Mafia clan, *Shulaya*. Reznikov made bail immediately—$2,500,000—and had not seen the inside of a jail cell since. His case was defended by Ron Mooby, the famous criminal-defense attorney. He managed to get the case thrown out on day one of the trial for a Miranda Rights violation.

The rest of the information on him came from extensive surveillance and intel gleaned from vendors and service providers whom the F.B.I. in Florida had leaned on. After six years and seven months, they had only one possible picture of Yatkin, and the other man in the shot was Reznikov. He was really the Operations Manager, taking care of everything for Yatkin's property and his daughter. The F.B.I. believed Yatkin lived at the house in Palm Beach, but, like Bin Laden, they never found any D.N.A. evidence in the trash. And never heard or got a recording of his voice.

The last part of the document was heavily redacted but indicated that Interpol and the F.B.I. had planned a raid but could never get approval, based on the lack of solid or confirmed evidence of Yatkin's whereabouts.

Heidi came to the door and said that the police were in the reception area.

"How many? Are the safes locked?"

"Three, including Napoli, and yes."

"I'll be right there."

Tom put on his jacket and went to meet them. As soon as he got into the hall, he recognized Napoli's voice. The other two were plainclothesmen, and big.

"Detective, I didn't think we were not allowed to speak." They shook hands.

Napoli explained they had let Mitchell know he was coming, and he introduced the other two officers. Tom led them into the showroom and explained the office layout. The bugs and cameras they showed him were incredibly small and discreet. Tom led the two techs to the areas where any guest or client would be permitted and let them get to work. He went back to his office and found he did have a text from Mitchell about Napoli.

The four of them were standing in Tom's office when the younger of the techs explained that they'd set up six cameras. All on the ceiling or just next to light fixtures. All of the five bugs were attached to the bottom of desks or tables, except for the one in the long hall that was behind a framed picture. He explained they would leave one camera at the end of the public hall covering the elevators, on both sides of the hall, and Tom's front door. He said Tom didn't have to do anything, and because he'd agreed to let the N.Y.P.D. have access to Tom's security company's video, they were more than covered.

Tom had heard the front doorbell, but because he was not behind his desk, he couldn't see the monitors. Heidi tapped on the doorframe, looked at Tom, and widened her eyes. He waved her into the office.

"You won't believe this. The three men from the auction are at the door and want to see you."

All three policemen's heads turned to Tom. "Gentlemen, that would be Propakov, Keller, and Reznikov."

Napoli, "Dammit. Did you know about this—that they were coming?"

Tom shot him a disgusted look.

"Sorry. You've got to get rid of them."

"I know that, Detective. Heidi, tell them I'll be right out. Please leave them in the hall."

"Make yourselves at home. They can't see, so, if you want to go across to the utility room, you can watch on the monitors." He didn't want them in his office or behind his desk.

Heidi buzzed Tom into the hall. "Mr. Propakov, Mr. Keller—how are you?"

"This is Mr. Reznikov." They shook hands. "He is an associate of Mr. Keller's. Can we come in and have a word?"

Tom took control of the situation. "Impossible, gentlemen. I have an office full of guests. I saw you called," nodding at Propakov, "but I haven't had the time to get back to you. I do have good news. I'll have something quite exceptional for you to look at, probably by Thursday."

Propakov and Keller leaned in. "What is it?"

"Not yet, Mr. Keller, but you will be impressed. I assure you. Now, gentlemen, I have to get back." Reznikov had said nothing and looked uneasy and suspicious. He was sweating. Heidi, listening on the security speaker, released the outside door, and Tom stepped into the mantrap.

Back in his office, Tom sat at his desk and watched as the three men talked at the elevator bank.

The three policemen came in, and Napoli said, "Well?"

"Not much. Didn't say what they wanted, but they are teed up for Thursday. Pending me securing permission to work the item."

"The $93,000,000 item?"

"That's right." Tom was basically sure Marla Wingate would have no issue with his plan, but he wanted the optionality of an out.

The older tech held up his cell phone and told Tom they'd heard all but about six words from the conversation via the bug under Heidi's desk. He said they were going to their van around the corner to test all eleven devices. If they didn't call him within fifteen minutes, everything was set and working properly.

Tom asked Heidi to show them the service elevator, so that they could go out the back of the building. Napoli told the two techs to go ahead and that he'd be right after them. Once the men left, he sat down and explained that everyone appreciated Tom's willingness to be involved.

"Could be a good payday, Detective."

"Is that the reason?"

"You see, I don't have the selfless commitment and humility that allows one to serve others. I am very shallow."

"Mr. Strawbridge, we now know for certain Yatkin is in town. We just have to find him. We think he's here to meet with another Russian, regarding a stolen shipping container of sarin nerve agent. It has ended up in Newark, and we think there was a mistake on someone's part. After being produced in Poland and shipped out of Bremerhaven, it should have ended up in Oren before being forwarded to Iran. One conversation we got indicated Propakov himself failed to forward a code regarding last-minute shipping instructions."

"And?"

"When and if you meet with them, please keep your ears open for anything they might say. As we don't have a mechanism, we have to try to draw Yatkin out—or somehow get lucky and get a tip."

"I will try to get in front of him, no?"

"Probably won't happen, but between the item and the cash requirement, hopefully, we'll get a break."

Napoli asked how Tom was doing and stood to leave. "You do lead an interesting life, Mr. Strawbridge."

"I can't say I love knowing that I am being surveilled constantly."

Napoli shook hands and left. It was 5:05 p.m.

Heidi told Tom she would go to the morning session, 10:00 a.m. to 12:00 noon at Sotheby's the next day, and be back for the afternoon. He congratulated her again on their purchase and left.

Tom got a cab quickly, and traffic was on the light side. It was 5:45 p.m. when he got out at Marla Wingate's building. He called David Mitchell from the street and got right through. Tom updated him on everything, including the surprise visit. Mitchell listened carefully as Tom relayed the information about the sarin gas and Yatkin definitely being in town. They agreed to talk first thing Wednesday.

Tom knocked on Marla Wingate's door at 5:58 p.m. Alice opened the door.

"Alice—so nice to see you. Thank you."

"Very nice to see you again, Mr. Strawbridge. Follow me, please." Tom walked over the spot where Marla Wingate had bared all and reminded himself to stay focused.

"She'll be right along. Her daughter is here for the night. The usual?"

"Why not? Thank you, Alice." She left him in the study, and he moved to the window and looked down on the Zoo. He watched a spirited pot or crack sale conclude at the base of the steps, with the three men separating and heading in different directions very quickly.

"Hello, Tom." He turned to Marla Wingate, standing in the doorway. She was casually dressed, but neat and crisp. Next to her was a very tall, slim young woman. "This is Jennifer, Tom. She is going back to Dartmouth tomorrow but was here today for a class trip."

"Hello, Jennifer. Nice to meet you."

"Mother won't stop talking about you, Mr. Strawbridge. Why is that?"

"Sorry, Tom. I'll see you later, Dear." Jennifer left.

"She takes after her father. Too bad, really. We used to be close and were even friends for a while."

Tom thought about quoting Rodney Dangerfield's line, "Now I know why the big cats eat their young." "Does she ever stay with her father?"

"Oh, she really hates him. Lucky man."

"I see." Alice arrived with Tom's vodka and a glass of champagne for Marla Wingate.

"Before we start, I spoke to Roger, and he will not be bothering you about a ring. Poor guy. I didn't mean to mislead him. I'm not sure what happened."

"Neither is he. He's obviously very fond of you. Impossible to understand. What did you tell him?"

"That I am in love with you and can barely function."

"Now, that makes sense." They smiled and touched glasses.

Tom carefully explained what the law-enforcement agencies were trying to do, without mentioning specific people or events. He then suggested that offering Marla's brooch might not only draw out the criminal they were after but could yield a sale value well above what the piece might bring otherwise. Regardless of the sales channel. He said the insured value was excessive—he was not specific—and guaranteed, should there be any mishap. He ended by saying he doubted his idea would go anywhere, but he wanted her to know everything up front.

"You're serious?' He nodded. "Tom, I have told you to do what you think is best with my property, and I will be happy. I am worried about your safety, aren't you?"

"They are bad guys, but I am being watched and followed constantly at this point, and I don't see having to get into a risky situation. Anyway, you're OK with this?"

"Just do what you think is best, and be careful."

They finished their drinks and talked more about Marla's memories of her Aunt Dagmar. He did not mention the Van Cleef information Lily had provided.

"Stay for another?"

"I'd really like to, but I am afraid I can't. But we are still on for Thursday?"

"Of course." She walked him through the apartment to the front door. "I insist on a kiss."

He did not resist and was impressed. As she was closing the door, she said, "Please sell the damned thing quickly."

Part Eight

CHAPTER 31

Wednesday Morning

TOM SLEPT MORE DEEPLY AND SOUNDLY than he had since before the attempted robbery and shooting one week earlier. He got to the office a little later than usual. The showroom was dressed, and he was at his desk with a coffee and *The Wall Street Journal* before 8:00 a.m. He had texted David Mitchell, asking when he wanted to talk.

There was nothing in the paper on yesterday's Christie's results, which meant it would be reviewed later in the week with the Sotheby's Sale later that day. He refilled his coffee and put the paper in the salon. He pulled up the brooch details on his computer. Tom considered changing the names of everybody involved, except Arpels himself. He decided against it. There was no reason to, and there could be nothing more spectacular or impressive than the actual, extraordinary story. Discretion did not have a place, nor did it matter. And the current owner would remain anonymous. Tom realized he was the only one who knew both sides of the brooch's history. Lily had seen the brooch but did not know the details or that it was still in the original family. Marla Wingate did not know the inside history or what Pierre Arpels had organized before his death.

An evite appeared on his screen from Mitchell, requesting a call at 9:15 a.m. Tom accepted and noticed there was another request for a conference call from Monahan at 11:30 a.m. He accepted and saw Heidi come in the front door just as the office line began to ring. She answered, put the caller on hold, and rang Tom.

"Good morning."

"Morning, Tom. Mr. Roger Gillespe."

"OK. Poor sap. I'll pick up."

"Coffee?"

"I'm good, thanks. I'll call you as soon as I am done with some correspondence."

Tom was curious how this would be played.

"Good morning, Mr. Gillespe."

"Good morning. 'Roger,' please. I am afraid I misjudged my situation with Marla. And—this is a bit embarrassing—I won't be moving forward with the ring at this time."

An adult. "I understand."

"Hard to figure, really. I'm not even sure how I misinterpreted everything."

"Well, when you need me, Roger."

"Of course. May I take you to lunch to make up for your time? I'd like to learn more about your fascinating work."

"That is not at all necessary, but I would enjoy that. Can we do it after the first of the year? It's our busy time, and my schedule is jammed."

"Good. I'll be in touch in January. Goodbye." Tom felt badly for Gillespe but not badly enough to stop from hoping the lunch would never happen.

It dawned on Tom that the best way to introduce and present the brooch to Propakov and Keller would be with a brief PowerPoint presentation, given the extraordinary and complicated provenance. He would ask Heidi to start on the slides as soon as she was back from the Sotheby's Sale. He rechecked and was pleased with the history and description he'd written. He would outline the breaks for her and do the titles. Of course, this meant he would have to show her the piece and bring her in on everything. No choice.

Tom took the brooch from the safe and set it up for digital images. He got good front and back shots right away and returned to his desk with the pin. He was about to call when Heidi knocked on his door.

"An Ashley Prescott called when you were in the vault. She's calling back in five. And David Mitchell needs another half hour."

"OK. Put her through and come in as soon as I am off the phone." He could see Heidi was curious.

"Am I still going to Sotheby's?"

"Yes. And, we have a new project for the afternoon."

Tom crafted an email to Heidi and attached the provenance, description, and images of the Van Cleef & Arpels pin. He typed "CONFIDENTIAL" in the subject line.

Heidi buzzed. "She's on. And Steven Hoffer is coming in Monday morning."

"How are you?"

"Hi, Tom. Fine, thank you. My plans changed overnight, and I am going to have to get back to Texas tomorrow. I'm sorry. I'm sure there is no way you could make it tonight? I can cancel my plans."

Tom's initial reaction was relief, but he liked her.

"That's too bad. I'll tell you what. I can make myself available for cocktails, say, from 6:00 to 7:30 p.m., if that's agreeable. Unfortunately, dinner is out of the question." He had no plans.

"Oh, I'm very glad, Tom. Thank you."

"New York Athletic Club, Main Dining Room bar. Since you're such a fine lady, I'll spare you the Tap Room."

"What a gentleman. Looking forward."

Heidi sat down, and Tom explained the brooch, Marla Wingate's family involvement, and the Van Cleef inside history.

"Are you serious?"

"Hard to believe. You really can't make it up."

He hit "Send" on the email he'd crafted for her. "You have everything in an email to work on when you get back from Sotheby's." He told her how he wanted the breaks and titles to look. There would be nine slides total.

"When can I see it?"

Tom took the box from his lower drawer, opened it, and put it on his desk, turning it toward Heidi. Her eyes widened, and she put her hand to her mouth. "Oh, my God!"

"The best I've ever seen. Now, go."

He would tell her later why the PowerPoint presentation was needed.

She got up to go. "The Alexandrite will have to wait another day."

"That is so incredible."

"It is. And remember—not a word."

"Tom. Really?"

"Go." Heidi's reaction reminded Tom of the incredible nature of this jewel.

Tom emailed Mitchell and asked that he call his cell when he was ready. He wrote a draft email to Propakov, asking him to come to the office as early as possible the following morning. He wrote he had something "quite incredible" but needed to act quickly.

Mitchell called. Tom explained his plan to his lawyer, gave an abbreviated explanation of the piece and its significance, and explained the value. He would send the PowerPoint to him and Monahan when it was done.

"If you say so, Tom. I don't understand these things, you know."

"I know. Assuming the meeting tomorrow happens, what do you think about additional security?"

"You mean a guard?"

"Yes."

"Let's ask Monahan when we talk later." Tom saw movement on the public hallway security monitor. Heidi.

"David, I'm putting you on hold for a second."

He saw Heidi toss her coat on a chair and start down the hall.

"Hi!"

"What are you doing here?"

"I got downstairs and into the cab, and just felt the brooch presentation was more important than anything else. I want to get started."

"Thank you. Let me finish this call."

"Sorry, David."

"No worries. Nervous?"

"Not exactly, but given the item, players, and the circumstances—well, you know. Do you think there's a chance Yatkin, if he's even here, would show?"

"No idea."

"Right. Well, someone we don't know could show, and I'm going to push for some help."

"All right. You got the evite to dial in to them at 11:30 a.m.?"

"Yes. Speak to you then."

They hung up, and Heidi came in for Tom to approve the slide design she had created and emailed to him. He pulled it up on his computer. The headers and footers were discreet and elegant. She'd already gotten the titles done for the nine slides and made the cover slide. The slides for the pictures of the front and back of the brooch were complete. They jumped off the screen. He had momentarily forgotten what he was planning. He snapped back to reality when a text arrived from Propakov.

After Heidi left, he read the text. Propakov asked if there would be "anything to look at."

Tom texted back that he was waiting for confirmation but asked him, if possible, to keep tomorrow morning open.

"*Horosho*."

At 11:25 a.m., Tom dialed into the conference call and entered the passcode. A recorded voice asked him to say his name and to wait for others to join the meeting. A minute later, "Mr. Strawbridge?" Monahan.

"Yes, Chief Monahan."

"Mr. Mitchell?"

"I'm on with Jim Rossi."

"Good. Are you alone, Mr. Strawbridge?"

"I am."

"Good. I am putting you all on speaker with several of the fine people you met Monday. This call will be recorded. We have more information for you, some significant, but please bring us up to date first."

Tom told them about the PowerPoint presentation, and he explained he was waiting to get approval before sending the email with a definite invitation for Thursday morning.

"Send that over when you can, and go ahead and get Propakov and Keller over tomorrow. Remember: The $93,000,000 item is 'hot.' We have more information. Detective Napoli."

"Steve Napoli. Mr. Strawbridge, Mr. Mitchell."

"Detective."

"We now know Yatkin is staying in Reznikov's suite at the Sherry Netherland. The few times he's come and gone, he has been dressed as a woman. His daughter flew back to Palm Beach this morning. We got a listening device on Reznikov's coat while he was in the lobby Monday. So, depending on where the coat is, we can get a viable signal and have some conversations taped. Propakov and Keller were in the lobby at the Perrine restaurant Monday afternoon. Our man thought he'd been made and stayed behind when they left. We later got them recorded in Reznikov's suite with Yatkin. Good so far?"

"Yes."

"Apparently the Management of L.T.D. Shipping, one of the largest container carriers operating out of San Diego and Port Newark, is controlled by Yatkin. He may own it. There is a semi-temporary structure that appears very permanent, at Port

Newark, being used as their onsite office. Like the type at large construction sites. We trailed one of Reznikov's men, Viktor Donskoi, and set up cameras and listening devices after dark on Sunday. When we met Monday, nothing had come of it. Since then, we know there is a meeting to re-direct the sarin gas next Monday, and we think Yatkin himself is going there for something Saturday. They must have swept the office because they speak openly. We've been monitoring all the airports, and on the manifest at Teterboro, there's a Gulfstream G150 scheduled to take off for Palm Beach anywhere from 10:00 p.m. Saturday to 3:00 a.m. Sunday. It's leased by L.T.D."

"Questions?"

"Well, you seem close. But why is this important for me to know?"

Monahan, "It may not be. But remember, anything you hear, or overhear, might be the thing that does it. If he goes to Port Newark, we are not going to try to take him indoors, unless that's the only chance. We don't know how many men they have or if they are armed. But there are a lot of people in and out of that office. We will be prepared. Propakov and Keller will be recorded in your office, so it's just as, if not more, important to watch as it is to listen."

"OK."

"Do you have anything more for us?"

"I'll blind copy you on the email to Propakov when I send it."

"And let us know as soon as he responds."

"Now, assuming I get a meeting Thursday morning, I think the odds are low that Yatkin would come, since they won't know about the item at that point."

Monahan, "He won't come."

"But the odds are high that, besides Keller and Propakov, Reznikov will show, and maybe others. Aren't they? I can't control who they bring, and they will be seeing the item."

"What's your point?"

"What about security?"

"I'm glad you asked. Detective Napoli will be in your office posing as a computer tech working on your systems. I'll have men near the street exits to your building as soon as whoever is going up, goes up. And, I will have two more men in the service stairwell in your hall. Good?"

Mitchell, "Tom?"

"OK. Thank you." Tom hung up and sent the draft email to Propakov, adding that any time from 9:00 to 11:00 a.m. could work.

Tom noticed an email from Heidi titled "P.P. Pres," and he called her to come down.

Before Tom could open the presentation, an email from Propakov arrived.

"We will be there at 9:00 a.m."

Tom forwarded that to Monahan and Mitchell, and reviewed the PowerPoint slides with Heidi. They tweaked a few issues, and he asked her to set it up in the Salon before she left for the day. He sent the presentation to Mitchell and Monahan. He then explained to Heidi who was coming to look at the brooch and—as delicately as possible—why.

Rather than becoming anxious, Heidi seemed excited and was intrigued.

Napoli called on Tom's cell phone and said he'd be there at 8:15 a.m.

"OK, Detective."

Tom called Uli Bank and asked if there were any way he could come by in the next hour or so, instead of Thursday morning. Uli agreed and arrived 40 minutes later.

They caught up, and Tom bought a spectacular 16 carat Star Sapphire and a pair of 5.00-carat-each-gem Chrysoberyl Cat's-Eyes.

Tom then reviewed the plans for tomorrow with Heidi and headed to the A.C. for a steam before his cocktails with Ashley Prescott.

He was in a cab on Sixth avenue, headed to the A.C., when his phone rang.

Napoli.

CHAPTER 32

Wednesday Evening

Tom had just gotten his cell phone out when the driver hit a deep pothole, at speed, making the left turn on 57th Street and Sixth Avenue. Tom lost his grip on the phone and caught it with the other hand. The impact caused the driver's *taqiyah* to slide over his eyes. He skidded into the back of a double-parked car.

"For the love of God!" The phone continued ringing as Tom got out of the cab and threw a $5 through the front window. He left the back door open.

"Detective."

"Hello. We wanted to let you know that at least two people working for Donskoi and Reznikov have been casing or, at least, watching your building."

"My apartment building?"

"Your office. We are set up on the second floor, across the street from your building. We have one of them I.D.'d and are working on the other. Chief Monahan is briefing Mr. Mitchell. We have no reason to think anything more than they are just trying to get a sense of the lobby traffic for the meeting tomorrow."

"You don't think they know or suspect I have been working with you?"

"No. If they suspected that, they'd be gone. Especially after last week. We're obliged to tell you this, but don't lose any sleep over it. We are on your office 24/7 and, starting tomorrow, will have at least two men inside the building at all times until the operation is over."

"You're still coming at . . ."

"8:15 a.m. Yes. See you then."

Napoli had been flat and matter-of-fact. Tom continued walking to the Club and reminded himself to think about the meeting tomorrow as a routine sales presentation.

The main locker room at the New York Athletic Club was packed, but the steam room was almost empty. Tom finished his steam, stretched, showered, and got dressed. Walking into the Main Dining Room, he smiled at Mirko behind the bar, who smiled and gently angled his head to the left, raising his eyebrows. Ashley Prescott was sitting at the far corner of the circular bar, looking at a menu. It was 5:50 p.m.

He gave Mirko a $20 as they shook hands and went around the bar as Ashley Prescott stood up. She was stunning and immaculately dressed.

"Thank you so much, Tom. I'm sorry about the change in plans. Couldn't be helped."

"My pleasure." Mirko stood before them. "What are you having?"

"A gimlet, please."

"Mirko, Beefeater martini. How has your time here been?"

"Reasonably productive. The offices will finish on schedule. I didn't realize how much I missed the city."

"Have you found a place to live?"

"No. I spent a lot of time looking Downtown—it's so tony now, but it'll be the Upper East Side." Their drinks arrived. Mirko put down a dish of olives and a bowl of cashews.

"Well, I wish you all the continued good luck, and welcome back." They touched glasses.

They were halfway through their drinks. "Aren't you curious as to how the husband search is going?"

"Of course."

"It's been pathetic. And the men here . . ."

"Well, a tall order for someone like you. He will need to be special. I know he will appear."

"As special as you?"

"I said *special*, not *perfect*. You are going to have to manage your expectations." They both smiled.

Before she could respond, Candy, one of the Club's house drunks, sidled up to Tom. He'd had a snootful.

"Tom! It's been years." Tom stood to shake hands. Candy's eyes were glassy, and he smelled like dry booze.

"Candy, this is . . ."

"I know, your beautiful wife. I remember you as a blonde, though." Everybody smiled.

Mirko came around the bar and steered Candy to one of the communal tables by the fireplace.

Tom ordered a second round. He told Ashley Prescott he would think about suitable husband candidates.

At 7:15 p.m., he saw her into a cab. He decided to get a bite to eat in the Tap Room, and his phone buzzed as he crossed the lobby. Tom let it go to voicemail. At the Tap Room bar, Hon put a martini glass in front of Tom with a glass of water.

Tom went to the restroom to look at the message. It was from Mr. Perez, thanking him for the champagne. No mention of the Chanel pin.

Tom was halfway through his martini when he realized Hon had made him his usual—Ketel One vodka. He had forgotten to stick with gin. Tom handed Hon a $20. And the maître'd' led Tom to his favorite corner table. He was looking out at the traffic on Central Park South and considering another drink when the waiter put a fresh glass on the table and filled it from a shaker.

"With the compliments of Mr. Hon, Sir."

Tom had a lobster for dinner and was on the street walking east along Central Park South at 8:45 p.m. Turning up Park Avenue, he decided to walk for a while. The reality of his meeting tomorrow seemed more anxiety-provoking than before. He told himself it was because he had had so much to drink. And at 63rd Street, he also told himself to go to The Melrose for a nightcap.

Jack was off, and Jimmy was alone. Tom didn't have to talk to anyone. He had a vodka tonic and left. He took a cab and pocket-dialed someone, putting his wallet back in his jacket after paying the driver. The Doorman closed the cab door, and Tom stepped to the side of his building's entrance to look at his phone. Max. He dismissed the call before she answered.

She called him back immediately. He answered. "Hold on, Tom." There was boisterous party noise and music in the background. The noise lessened. "Sorry. I had to step out of our party."

"Where are you?"

"Still at Bar Wayo. Can you join us?"

"I don't think so."

"I pocket-dialed you."

"That's it?"

"I know you have to get back."

"Come on."

"Well, I had been thinking about our talk. The talk you want to have."

"Oh. Good. When can we have it?"

"I was thinking about later, but . . ."

"Perfect. It'll have to be at your place. What's the number?" He couldn't believe he'd said it. And, he'd had women to his apartment only on rare occasions in recent years.

"1165 Park." No turning back, and he would have to get some coffee.

"We have the bar until 11:00 p.m., so, I'll be there around 11:30 p.m., okay?"

"I'll tell the door my cousin is coming for a nightcap."

"Bye, Tom."

Tom got upstairs and started the coffee maker. What was he thinking? Whatever it was, Max's issues were not his problem. He put on a robe and left another one in the guest bathroom. He sat down and looked over his mail. He checked his phone.

He was watching the evening news when the house phone rang. "John, Mr. Strawbridge. Your Cousin, Miss Morehead, is on her way up."

Tom rolled his eyes. "Thank you, John."

He opened the door when he heard the elevator stop on his floor.

"I see you're all ready for our talk," glancing down at Tom's robe.

"You know, it just might be a time for non-verbal communication." He shut the door. "What can I get you?" Her fragrance hit him.

"Vodka on the rocks. Do you have an extra robe?"

"In the bathroom, third door on the right, down that hall."

"Do you mind if I have a quick shower?"

"Let me have your coat. Your drink will be ready when you return." He helped her with her coat, and she headed off down the hall, leaving one high heel and then the other behind her.

Tom was not sorry he had called. He was pouring her drink in the pantry when she appeared at the door.

"Nice place. Been here long?"

"Yes. Sorry—the robe is a bit big."

"Comfy."

"Cheers. Thank you for coming." They touched glasses, he had club soda, and he pointed her toward his office.

They sat down on the couch. "How was the party?"

"Very nice. Everyone is very happy for us . . . except Dad. He can't stand Michael."

"Michael what?"

"Michael Rubin. You don't know him."

"No, I don't think I do."

Max put her drink down on the side table and, standing up said, "Now, about our talk."

She walked around the coffee table and stood facing Tom. She eyed the low wooden table and, determining it would hold her weight, put one foot on the table and then, as she got up, the other.

"Now, let's talk." She dropped the robe off her shoulders. Tom was taken again with her natural gifts and raw sexuality.

"What would you like to discuss?"

She stepped onto the couch with one foot on one side of Tom and one on the other. She was inches from his face.

"How about this?" She pulled the belt of his robe and opened it as the knot came loose. She sat down on him and pulled herself as close as possible. They kissed intensely. And kissed, ending up in a bedroom opposite the office.

It was after 1:00 a.m. "I can't stay, you know."

"I know. Can I get you something?"

"No, thanks." She headed to the bathroom. Tom put on jeans and a sweater.

She came back into the living room and put her heels on standing up. She was the definition of erotic.

"I'll call an Uber."

"And I'll see you down. Thank you for coming."

"Thank you. When is our next talk?"

"What's going on, Max?"

"Well, let's just say I'm not sure about Michael, and you are helping me decide. Either way, we don't have this," gesturing at Tom and then herself.

She kissed him deeply, waiting for the elevator. "Let me know when you get home."

They walked through the lobby, and the night Doorman, Gerzy, opened the door. The Uber was waiting in the street in front of the awing.

"Goodnight, Cousin Tom." He smiled and closed the door.

Tom heard a car door close, up the street on the opposite corner. He looked, and the interior light of the SUV on the corner went out. Gerzy was holding the lobby door open, and Tom came in and stepped behind the screen concealing the operating board for the house phones and intercoms.

"Mr. Strawbridge?"

"Just a minute, Gerzy." As Tom looked between the two panels of the screen, the SUV passed his building and headed downtown. Two men. He stepped onto the sidewalk, but the light at the corner was green, and the SUV was already a block and a half away.

"Thank you, Gerzy. Have a good night."

Back in his apartment, Tom could not decide if the SUV sighting was unusual. It was not common for his neighborhood at that time of night.

He sat down on his bed to check his phone. There was a group WhatsApp from Monahan, Napoli, Wilson, and Mitchell. It had come in while he was downstairs. 'Mr. Strawbridge, we tried calling. Our men think some of Yatkin's men may have been watching your apartment building. We suspect they are just being cautious, but we will now have men watching you—and your office building—continuously, until further notice. Let us know when you've received this message.'

He was anxious. "Message received." Taking a shot, "Were the two men who just drove off when I was outside my building just now yours?"

"No." Napoli. "Our men will be back at 5:00 a.m. tomorrow. Did you see men you think were surveilling your building?"

"I don't know."

Part Nine

CHAPTER 33

Thursday Morning

TOM WAS IN THE OFFICE BY 7:00 A.M. In checking his phone, he noticed Max had texted him before he went to bed, saying she was home and thanking him for the visit.

He disarmed and opened the safes and took his coffee to the showroom. He began running through the PowerPoint slides for the presentation. After four run-throughs, he arranged some chairs so his guests would have a head-on view to the one blank wall for the presentation. The set-up also allowed Tom to stand behind them while presenting the slides.

He dressed the vitrines himself rather than leave it to Heidi. Employing his proven "less is more" approach to the morning's visible merchandizing display, he put one major piece in each wall vitrine. Except the largest one, where he put a parure of emerald and diamonds by Cartier from the 1950s. Necklace, bracelet, and killer ring. He put a linen tablecloth over the lean-over display case in the center of the showroom. Heidi could dust the desks, mirrors, and picture frames.

It was just before 8:00 a.m., and Tom put the brooch in the day safe in his office and sat down with the paper.

"Good morning."

"Morning, Heidi. How are you?" She had on a short leather skirt and a crimson turtleneck that matched her heels. "You're looking very smart."

"Thank you. I'm fine, but tired from Max's announcement party. You didn't tell me she'd invited you?"

"I never thought to. Good time?"

"Not really, more tedious than anything. Too trendy. I picked up the pastries from Bouchon."

"Thank you. Please use the vintage Chrysanthemum flatware and linen napkins."

"Got it. Should I have the pastries out or bring them in after the guests are in?"

"Once we are settled."

"OK. I'll be in the kitchen. Oh. Did . . ."

"I set up already, thanks. Please tell me what you think, and give a quick dust to the frames, mirrors, and surfaces."

She smiled and left.

Tom's cell phone rang. "Morning, David."

"Good luck today. And be careful."

"I'm looking at it as a sales pitch. A sales pitch to lowlifes."

"Anyway, keep me posted."

"Will do."

At 8:10 a.m., Napoli rang the bell. Tom walked down the hall and buzzed him in from Heidi's desk. He had a plainclothes man in tow.

"All set, Mr. Strawbridge?"

"Detective. I think so."

"This is Officer Menendez." He was carrying two duffle bags. They shook hands.

"Backup?"

"You could say that. Can we use that back room near the safes? I will be stationed there and live-monitoring all the surveilling devices with the team outside."

"Fine." Tom introduced Heidi to Officer Menendez and explained the plan. Menendez was staring up at Heidi in awe. "Come with me, gentlemen." Tom led them through the office back to the storage room.

Once inside, Tom offered them coffee.

"No, thank you," Napoli answering for them both. "Can Officer Menendez change in here? He's putting on coveralls from the cable company."

"There's more room in the building Restroom," gesturing toward the hall. "The code is 421."

"Good. Alberto, set up your monitor, check everything out. And then you can change. I want to have a word, Mr. Strawbridge, as soon as we are set up."

"I'll be here, Detective."

Tom found Heidi in the Salon. She had the cups and saucers, napkins, and sterling flatware laid out for six.

"Thank you. Looks good. On second thought, you can go ahead and bring the pastries in about 8:45 a.m."

"I brought extra flowers for here and the hall. Will you need me?"

"Going somewhere?"

"No, Tom."

"Maybe. Have a run-through of the PowerPoint, please, and see what you think, OK?"

Tom returned to his office, took the brooch from the day safe, and put it on his desk. Napoli came to the door and asked to talk.

"Come in. Are you planning on being seen by this group?" He motioned to a chair.

"We want them to see Menendez when they arrive. They shouldn't think it's just you and the girl. Just in case."

Tom nodded.

"About last night. What made you ask if we had men watching your residence?"

Tom relayed the story of the SUV.

"Definitely not us. As I said, until we are done, there will be two men watching your building. And we'll continue to watch your apartment now as well. We've been able to I.D. several of the men coming and going from the Sherry Netherland. They have been, almost to a man, in the longshoremen's union. They all operate, one way or another, out of the L.T.D. Shipping company building in Port Newark. Rough crowd. We have men all over the yards and live, visual surveillance on the two key buildings. Listening devices in the main part of the office. Yatkin is still here."

"Why would they be watching my apartment building?"

"The most obvious answer is that they're following you to see if you are, well, *safe to do business with*."

"Meaning?"

"Meaning, not trying to set them up with the police." Menendez knocked on the door frame.

"Where do you want it, Detective?" Officer Menendez was standing in the doorway in legitimate-looking coveralls from the cable company.

"Mr. Strawbridge. We think the likelihood of any danger is low, but I want to put a tactical shotgun where I can get to it easily."

"What!?"

"A precaution."

"Where would you suggest? And don't let Heidi see it."

"Behind the door in the office on the other side of the showroom. Menendez will be in there anyway. Leave the bag in the back room for now, Menendez."

"Sir." He left.

"Remember, everything today will be videoed and recorded. So, during the meeting, just watch and pay attention. You don't have to remember anything."

Heidi knocked. "Tom, the second history slide had one extra double space. I corrected it, and the notebook is on and ready to go. Just hit the "Enter" key, and our logo slide will come up. The presentation follows."

"Thank you."

"Anything else, Detective?"

"I'd like to have a look at the $93,000,000 item. Where is it?"

"As my dear Mother used to say, 'If it was a snake, it would have bitten you.'" Tom picked up the box from his desk and opened it. He placed it in front of Napoli.

"Please don't touch it, Detective Napoli."

Napoli's expression was flat. "What is it?"

"A brooch."

"It's big."

As Tom superficially began to explain the history and significance of the brooch, the doorbell rang. Tom buzzed Heidi to say he would let them in.

"Showtime, Detective."

"Once they are in the hall, Menendez will come out from the back so they can see him."

Tom walked to the front, and Heidi released the outside door. When the men stepped into the mantrap, Tom saw four men on the monitor. Heidi hit the release for the inside door of the mantrap. They stepped into the foyer.

Not missing a beat, "Gentlemen, welcome. May we take your coats?"

Heidi stood next to Tom as the men began removing their coats. Keller was wearing an impressive homburg.

Propakov spoke first. "You remember Matteo Keller and Mr. Reznikov. This is Mr. Donskoi, our associate." They shook hands. Heidi left with the coats.

"Gentlemen, this way." Tom was halfway to the Salon with the men behind him when Officer Menendez started down the hall from the opposite end. He was carrying one of the duffle bags. Menendez nodded to Tom as he stepped into the office they had discussed.

"Please forgive us. We are having some IT maintenance done. Our Internet signal has been spotty lately."

He turned in time to see Reznikov and Donskoi look at each other.

"In here, please," directing them into the Salon. Donskoi made a beeline for the pastry tray, picked up an immense chocolate croissant, and bit off half. Pastry flakes going everywhere. A slob. Tom just realized his clothes were ill-fitting and shabby, and his suit jacket was stained in a few places on his lapels.

Heidi came in. “Gentlemen, what may I get you to drink?”

Donskoi blurted out, “Coffee.”

The other three nodded.

“Please help yourselves to something.” Donskoi had a muffin in each hand.

“These are extraordinary things, Mr. Strawbridge.”

“Thank you, Mr. Keller. And this being Thursday, they are all for sale.”

Propakov and Keller chuckled.

Heidi returned with a tray and four cups of coffee. “Gentlemen, let Mr. Strawbridge know if you need anything else. Milk and sweeteners are there.” She smiled and turned to leave.

As they took their coffee, Tom removed a suede ring pochette from his jacket pocket. “Gentlemen, before we get started, I wanted to show you something we just completed.” He opened the pochette and took out a vivid blue Emerald Cut diamond ring. Propakov’s and Keller’s eyes widened.

“You brought us here for this?!” demanded Donskoi.

“I didn’t bring you here for anything. Please feel free to leave.”

Donskoi’s eyes narrowed. Propakov, “Please, Mr. Strawbridge, our friend does not understand these things.”

“Then why is he here? Besides the fact he likes a free meal.”

Tom had taken control of the situation and, while cool, acted annoyed.

“That blue is 15.16 carats, VS1, and has a letter from the Gemological Institute attesting to the fact that it is the finest vivid blue over 10 carats they have ever seen or graded.

“It’s magnificent! The color of a deep spring sky. How much per carat?” said Keller.

“We’ve just finished it. Before your indelicate friend opened his mouth, it was $6,900,000 per carat.”

Heidi came in, and Tom handed her the ring and pochette. “More coffee, gentlemen?”

Tom moved a fourth chair into the row of chairs he had set up. “Please find a seat, and we will get started with a brief introduction.”

Once the men sat down, Tom hit the notebook’s “Enter” key, and the corporate logo, a fantastic, stylized Art Deco bracelet, appeared with the written logo, “Live a Little,” below. One of the men chuckled.

Tom started by detailing the gemological analysis, subtly reinforcing the extreme rarity and condition of the collection of diamonds and colored stones making up the brooch. A slide showed the inventory of gemstones, by species, each stone’s weight, and the carat weight totals. Tom was indeed treating the meeting as an actual sales presentation, and did not disclose that the stated weights were his, and therefore estimates. Because he now knew the actual weights did exist, this approach was cleaner. When he was done, he used a laser pointer to emphasize the fabrication details and design elements of the piece from the back and front pictures.

Keller, “Quite something. What is the length?”

“Just under eight inches.”

"Unusual. It makes one question its practicality."

"I'll get to that in a minute."

Tom finished the visual description and brought up the first history slide. When he explained that the brooch had been commissioned just before the War, for the Queen of Yugoslavia by her husband Peter II, Keller leaned to Propakov's ear and said something.

Propakov, "And the provenance is accurate?"

"Completely. The Queen was six feet tall. All her jewels were outsized."

Tom told how the Nazi, Becker, came into possession of the brooch, leaving out the identity of the paramour and her family, only saying they were not French but Swedish aristocrats living in Paris. He ended by saying the brooch was the single most important item he had seen in his career. And that the provenance added significant value. He closed the notebook, and the projector went dark.

"Before I show you the item, assuming you are interested in seeing it, are there any questions?"

Keller and Propakov started at the same time. Propakov yielded. "Do you own the brooch, Mr. Strawbridge?"

"Let's come back to that in a moment."

"How did you come across it? It is incredible."

"We'll revisit that as well. Let me get the brooch."

"I have to use a toilet," Donskoi said.

At the reception desk, Tom gave him a key to the public Washroom, not wanting to divulge the combination. Or let him use the office bathroom. Heidi buzzed him out. On his way back, Tom looked into the office, where Officer Menendez was. He had a router and a few tools on the floor. He mouthed, "Give them another minute," and waved Tom on.

Tom walked past the Salon, without looking in, to his office. Heidi knocked, and Tom told her to wait one minute, and then offer coffee and remove the pastries. Tom took the brooch from the day safe and put the box on a black-velvet tray. He saw Heidi showing Donskoi down the hall, and Tom headed back when Heidi left the Salon.

"Gentlemen. Please step this way," gesturing toward the main desk. Tom went around behind the desk, and the four men gathered on the opposite side. He put the tray down and opened a drawer, removing a handful of white cotton gloves.

"If any of you would like to handle the pin, please put on a pair of gloves."

Keller and Propakov reached for gloves. Donskoi grunted. His hands were wet. Tom switched on the desk lamp and opened the box, turning it to the men.

Keller asked, "May I?" and Tom removed the brooch and handed it to Keller.

"No gloves?" Donskoi. Tom bit his tongue. Reznikov and Propakov took out their phones, preparing to take pictures.

"No photographs. I'll explain when you are done looking."

Keller handed the piece to Propakov and sat down. Reznikov and Donskoi showed little interest and joined Keller, who was standing away from the desk.

"What is the price, Mr. Strawbridge?" asked Keller.

"$93,000,000."

Propakov said, "One of the finest and most unusual things I have seen," handing the brooch back to Tom, who put it back in the box and buzzed for Heidi. When she left with the brooch, Tom, sat down facing the others.

"We do own the brooch," nodding to Propakov. The details of the provenance are airtight. There is something else you need to know. I am not comfortable revealing what few facts I am aware of, but there is reason to believe the brooch was stolen some years ago. I was content with breaking it up, as awful a thought as that is, but when you two," nodding at Propakov and then Keller, "approached me, I thought your resources might make a purchase of this type interesting and, more importantly, possible."

"The number—it's impossible," Donskoi.

Looking first at Reznikov, "What my associate means, Mr. Strawbridge, is there any room?" said Keller.

"Yes. We need at least half in cash. Are you interested?"

Keller said, "We are, but we need to discuss everything and get back to you. Will you hold it?"

"For how long?"

"24 hours."

"Let's say noon tomorrow, then. We have another showing tomorrow at 2:00 p.m."

"We may need to bring in another partner, and he does not like to be seen in public. If we put half the money in escrow, could we take it on memorandum? Two hours at the most."

"Look, we haven't determined if you want to buy or even arrived at a price, but the answer to that question is 'No.' Period. I have a partner, too. The piece does not leave me until it is paid for in full."

Tom stood up and, looking only at Keller and Propakov, thanked them for coming and gestured toward the door. Heidi had their coats and Keller's hat out on the settee. They collected them, thanked Tom, and left.

Napoli joined Tom in the salon. "Good job. We may have something."

CHAPTER 34

Thursday Midmorning

TOM WAS WAITING FOR DETECTIVE NAPOLI to end a phone call when a text came in from Max. It was 10:30 a.m.

"Hi. Just realized I left my ring in the bathroom last night. . . . Can you leave it with your Doorman tonight? I'll pick it up before work tomorrow. XXX"

He called his cleaning lady and asked her to find the ring and put it in the hall table drawer.

The calendar was clear for the rest of the day. There was a noon appointment for Friday with the daughter of one of Tom's oldest clients.

Napoli knocked. Officer Menendez was with him.

"Come in. Have a seat."

"Officer Menendez will be leaving now."

They shook hands, and Menendez headed down the hall. Napoli sat down, and Tom saw Menendez stop at Heidi's desk on the monitor. Tom hit the button for the silent light signal, and she stood up and let the officer out.

When Heidi came to the door, Napoli said, "Is there a chance I could get a coffee?"

"Of course. Do you want anything, Tom?"

"Club soda, please."

"I just updated Chief Monahan and Bureau Chief Wilson. They were live-monitoring everything, so it was quick. First off, no one can believe all four of them showed up. Chief Monahan feels this is a testament to your reputation and wanted me to make sure I told you that. You played it cool as well. Very cool."

Heidi came in and put the drinks down.

"Thank you. What is the 12:00 noon, Mrs. Bachman's daughter, about tomorrow?"

"S.D.R."

"You feel up to trying it?"

"Absolutely," with a big smile.

"Good." Heidi left.

"Please go ahead, Detective. Your coffee OK?"

"Yes. What's an 'S.D.R.'?"

"Solitaire diamond ring. An engagement ring."

"Oh. Anyway, just as importantly, it indicates they do not feel you are a risk. If they did, we don't think any of them would have shown. Our men outside say they had a man downstairs across from the entrance during the meeting. He left with the others in the same car. We are trying to find out if they have anyone consistently watching this building. We don't think so. It looks like they have convinced themselves that everything is safe. I sent Menendez out the back through the service area anyway."

"What about my apartment building?"

"There was someone across the street until 4:00 a.m. this morning. We don't think they'll keep that up, but we are staying, as I said. Secondly, we had excellent reception from the bugs and the cameras. You know what went on when you were there, but, when you left, it got interesting. By the way, what got your back up with Donskoi?"

"He is a crude slob. A jerk from the beginning. I took an opportunity to let them know I couldn't care less if they left or stayed. If you'd seen his expression, you'd understand my reaction. What's his role again?"

"Mostly protection—security, we think."

"So, what happened when I was out of the salon?"

"Two things. One, Keller and Propakov went crazy for the ring you showed them. They are interested. They were discussing it, and Keller mentioned Yatkin by name. We could see Propakov put his finger to his lips. And Reznikov said something in Russian. We are waiting for the translation."

"They know what they're doing. Maybe it would have been better for me to have left them alone after showing the brooch. The significance of mentioning Yatkin?"

"We think it confirms what we've been thinking. We got more from the bug in the hallway when they were waiting for the elevator. Keller said, "If Strawbridge won't either release it or memo it, how can Igor see it?" And your friend Donskoi said, "And no pictures—the snob."

"Snob? I like it."

Napoli's phone rang. He got up and stepped into the hall. Tom buzzed Heidi.

"Heidi, do you have time now?"

"Just finished. All cleaned up. Should I leave the showroom dressed?"

"Why not? And why not spend some time with the Alexandrite?"

"Great. Can we go over tomorrow's appointment?"

"Yes, later. More coffee, Detective?"

"Please."

"That was Headquarters. 'A-Hole.'"

"Excuse me?"

"What Reznikov said. It translates to 'A-Hole.'"

"Lovely."

"We'd be surprised if you didn't hear from them. Good work on the 24-hour bit, too."

"So, what now?"

"Now we wait. We are fairly confident that, even if nothing comes directly from what you've been working on, we'll have a good shot at Yatkin. We have to be vigilant and nail him whenever he leaves the hotel. Too risky and dangerous indoors. He went to dinner the other night with Keller at Cipriani—in drag, by the way. By the time our man called for backup, they were leaving. The longer this goes on, the risk of them getting wise increases. Anyway, they have interest in the jewel, so everything is active."

"If you get him without any further involvement from me, what about the reward?"

"Not my department. Ask your lawyer. That reminds me, do you want us to send him an audio file of the meeting?"

"Probably not. I'll tell him. If he listens or not, he'll charge me for the time."

"You are always concerned about money."

Tom pressed the button for the flashing light at Heidi's desk.

"OK, Mr. Strawbridge."

"Do you have everything, Detective?" Heidi.

Napoli stood up. "Keep us posted, Mr. Strawbridge."

Heidi came into Tom's office after escorting Detective Napoli out.

"Well, what's next?"

"We wait. The Alexandrite?"

"May I bring it in? I have questions."

Tom had just finished showing her the red change, in candle-light. He was schooling her on how to approach Mrs. Bachman's daughter Friday when David Mitchell called. Tom went over everything, including the debrief with Napoli.

"If I'm done, what about the reward?"

"I'm sure they'll resist, but I don't see how they can ignore your role at this point. I suppose we might have to negotiate. But you got four of Yatkin's key people in the open, and in one place."

"Wait. A text from Monahan. He's saying you did well and were 'cool as a cucumber.' And thanks us both."

"Whatever."

Tom noticed an email from Mitchell arrive while they were talking. It was an invoice.

"Are you serious about this number!?"

"I had to miss a court date Monday, Tom, and my partners aren't happy. I had to charge you for the day. Rossi is included."

"Bye, David."

It was 11:30, and Tom asked Heidi to pick up Cuban takeout from Sophie's.

Napoli emailed Tom and Mitchell to say the police were confident that Yatkin's people had stopped watching the office building.

After Heidi left to pick up lunch, Propakov called while Tom was sorting some sapphire melee. Small gemstones, usually rounds, that typically weigh less than .10 ct. or 10 points. No voicemail. Tom put the goods he had selected in parcel papers, paper-clipped those to the design they were picked for, and put everything in the safe.

"Sorry, Mr. Propakov. I couldn't take your call."

"Of course. The blue diamond. Can you send the report?"

"I'm doing it now."

"And the Monograph from G.I.A. . . . ?"

"I'm emailing that as well."

"Thank you. It's Type IIb?"

"Of course."

"We'll look at everything, and we'd like to see the stone again."

An email appeared from Napoli, asking him to try to keep Propakov on the line.

"Mr. Keller is with me. So now, the price. Will you take $85,000,000?"

"No."

"Cash."

"No, thank you. Anything else?"

"What number would you accept?"

"Goodbye, Mr. Propakov."

"Please. Let us discuss, and we will get back to you. Also, the brooch. When can we see it again? Mr. Keller and I are leaving this weekend."

"Tomorrow."

"Before 10:00 a.m., please."

"Anytime after 8:30 a.m. Who will be coming?"

"Keller and me. Please hold the blue."

"Goodbye."

Heidi. "Hi. When is lunch?"

"Now. Do you want to eat together?"

"Of course. I'll set up in the pantry."

They ate lunch and talked more about selling diamonds and jewelry. He explained that diamond sales, especially event-based sales were, for the most part, all about education. He told Heidi always to determine what the client knew, or did not know, first. Whatever the knowledge level, walk her through the Four Cs. He explained, when a woman is shopping on her own, interests and motives could range from very specific and technical, to as general as, "It has to be bigger than my sister-in-law's." Tom told Heidi to reach out during tomorrow's presentation at any time if she got stuck. He would stop in after 20 or 30 minutes, anyway. He started to explain some of the high-level differences between selling diamonds and colored stones. "We'll be spending a lot of time there."

As she was clearing their plates, "Oh, Marco called. He held 14 carats on the sapphire. 14.07 carats, to be exact. He says it turned out incredibly well. Cornflower blue. He's pleased with himself."

"Excellent. Are you going out later?"

"FedEx. I'll pick it up?"

"I'm having dinner with the owner of the brooch tonight, so can you put the deck you made on a jump drive? In case she wants to have a look. Two of the men from today, Propakov and

Keller, are coming back tomorrow between 8:30 and 10:00 a.m. Listen, I want to thank you for everything you do around here. You're an incredible asset and really growing and developing quickly. Not to mention, you bring every man to their knees just by smiling."

She blushed. "That means everything, Tom. Thank you. And thank you again for the added responsibility and training."

"My pleasure. Now, I want to look at the numbers for the 15 carat blue Emerald Cut we have on memo. We could make some serious money this week."

Tom went back to his office and began calculating how far he would allow himself to be chiseled on the blue diamond. He had a lot of room.

Tom had forgotten to update the police and David Mitchell. He crafted a bullet-point summary of the call he'd had with Propakov. A minute later, Napoli called.

"Mr. Strawbridge. I need to be there, this time unseen. Menendez and I will both be in the back. How early will you be in?"

"No later than 7:15 a.m."

"We'll be there at 8:00 a.m. Was there anything else to the call?"

"Like I said, Propakov was with Keller, but there were more than two other voices in the background."

"Good. We've lost the bug from the coat. It's on the street somewhere. See you in the morning. Oh, by the way, we are not listening to or watching you, unless you have our guests."

"Goodbye, Detective."

Heidi returned from her errands and brought the recut sapphire to Tom's office. The winter light was low, but the sapphire was a changed stone. For the better. By removing some material from the pavilion of the stone, the color had strengthened and become more even, and much more saturated.

"Excellent. Good buy, Heidi. We can ask at least $12,500 per carat in the trade, and $19,000 or $20,000 at retail."

Heidi came in with her coat on to leave for the day and asked if she should get pastries again.

"Not necessary. Have a good night."

Tom worked until just before 6:00 p.m., armed the safes, and locked the office. He decided to walk for at least a while on his way to Sistina to meet Marla Wingate.

Passing The Sherry Netherland, walking up Fifth Avenue, he kept an eye out for any of the men who had visited his office. Pedestrian traffic was light, and the weather was very similar to the night of the attempted robbery. He stayed on Fifth and resisted the urge to stop in at The Melrose, crossing 63rd Street.

It was 6:50 p.m. when he turned down 81st Street. Sistina is closer to Madison Avenue than Fifth. He climbed the stairs of the townhouse, went in, and checked his coat.

"Your guest is at the table, Mr. Strawbridge. Please follow me."

Tom had requested and been given the best table, in the better room, in front of the fireplace. Marla Wingate was talking to the maître'd' as they approached. Tom thanked the greeter and sat down as the maître'd' adjusted Tom's chair and placed his napkin.

"Hello, Tom."

"Hello. What are you having?"

"Cosmo."

Tom ordered a martini.

"You look stunning."

"So do you, Tom."

"Please. A long day."

His drink arrived, and he told Marla the meeting about the brooch had taken place and that there appeared to be interest. She asked if he felt he was in danger at any point, and he explained about the two officers.

They looked at the menus, ordered dinner, and had another round. Tom took the jump drive out of his pocket. He had left the history slides out of her presentation.

"We made you a copy of the deck we prepared for the showing if you'd like to take a look when you get home."

"What's a deck?"

"Basically a slide show. Images and data used for marketing, selling, pitches, and so on."

"Maybe you can show me sometime. I hate to say it, but I am just not that interested. I do care about selling the brooch. And I'd like it to be quick. You know why, don't you, Tom?

"Maybe you'd better remind me," putting the jump drive back into his pocket.

She smiled, took a drink, and raised her eyebrows.

"Well." Their drinks arrived. "Thank you for allowing me to repay you for the other night." They touched glasses.

"Don't be silly. And you are sure my—shall we say, my very *forward* behavior—was not offensive? Very few men get my attention, but you sure have."

"I'm flattered. You know how extraordinarily beautiful and sexy you are. I appreciate your understanding on the timing here. Your item is exceptionally fine, and I must be laser focused on getting the right outcome. Then we can discuss all things lavender."

Their food arrived. Tom explained the fine details of the auction process during dinner. He told her auction would most likely be the best route, if he could not identify a serious buyer or collector.

When they had collected their coats and were on the sidewalk, Tom asked, "How did you come down?"

She had walked, and Tom walked her downtown a few blocks to her apartment on Fifth Avenue. She did not ask him up for a nightcap, and they said goodbye under the awning to her apartment building.

Tom walked the rest of the way home. Once in his apartment, he put Max's ring in some tissue paper and put it in a large envelope. He wrote her name on it and went downstairs and gave it to the Doorman. He texted Max that it was waiting.

It was 10:30 p.m., and Tom poured a nightcap and sat down. Max texted, "Great, in a car headed uptown, I'll swing by now. Would you like company?"

He texted back he could not tonight. And added, "How's the decision-making coming along?"

"We'll talk."

Part Ten

CHAPTER 35

Friday Morning

Tom was inside his offices and disarming the security system when Heidi put her key in the outside door. It was 7:50 a.m.

"You're early."

"Morning, Tom. I have a lot to do. Do you want the meeting today in the Salon or somewhere else?"

"The Salon—I don't want them in my office. Do you mind dressing the vitrines? Please—not anything we had out yesterday. One piece per case, except for the large one. You can put that South Sea pearl-and-diamond necklace and earring set, and whatever diamond ring you think in there. A big one. And leave it that way for Mrs. Bachman's daughter. Who knows? What's her name, anyway?"

"Good. Wendy. Coffee?"

"Thanks. I'll get the safe room."

Tom disarmed the safes and opened the main one. He took the vivid blue Emerald Cut diamond and the brooch to his office and put the boxes on his desk. Checking his tie and hair in the mirror, he saw Heidi come in behind him and put a coaster and coffee down on his desk.

"Can I have a quick look?"

"Inspiration? Sure. Tom noticed she was wearing jeans, black boots, a button-down white oxford shirt and a camel-colored blazer.

"Different look."

"Do you approve?" she said, looking up from the brooch box she was holding.

"You look great."

Tom was going over the ring and the brooch with a cleaning cloth just after 8:00 a.m. when Heidi walked by his office door with a tray of jewelry for the Salon. The doorbell rang. Napoli and Menendez.

"I'll get it. Go ahead with the jewelry."

Tom got to the front door when he saw a third man coming from the elevators. Henry Stacks. The cops were staring down at him.

Tom buzzed everyone into the mantrap and then into the office.

"Good morning, gentlemen. Henry. What a surprise. Please wait in the kitchen for a minute, will you?"

Henry trundled down the hall, holding a leaky brown bag in two hands. "Please leave your coats on the bench."

"We'll head to the back and get set up, okay?"

Heidi stepped in front of them, coming out of the Salon as they were passing.

"Oh. Good morning, gentlemen," smiling broadly. "Coffee?"

"Thank you. Once we set up."

She walked down the hall across from the Salon toward the kitchen. Menendez was rubbernecking in the extreme.

"Take a picture, Officer. It will last longer. This way."

Tom left them in the small room next to the vault. He looked into the Salon on his way to the kitchen. Henry was standing next to Heidi, laughing and smiling, when Tom walked into the kitchen. His expression leveled, and his eyes widened when he saw Tom.

"Good to see you, Henry. Not a good morning."

"Shua, Tom," grasping Tom's arm. "It's been more than a week, and I brought coffee and Danish. Danish is from Fienberg's in Brooklyn." Pulling Tom in and whispering, "Who are those guys? They look like cops."

Looking past Henry Stacks, Tom could see Heidi smile as she worked.

"Never mind. Look, I owe you lunch. How's Monday?"

"Cops. Bye, Heidi."

"Henry, thank you for breakfast. I'll see you next week." He showed Henry out.

He looked in on the police. They both had on headphones and were plugged into a small device. Napoli put his hand up, and Tom left, noticing a short, black tactical pump shotgun leaning against the wall behind the door.

Heidi was leaning over Tom's desk as he continued to review how to explain the diamond "language" to a private client when Napoli knocked.

Heidi stood up. "I'll get your coffee. One black, one milk and sugar—yes?"

They nodded. It was 8:20 am. "You were early today."

"We wanted to double-check all the systems. Who was that guy?"

"An old-time dealer and old friend. What is your plan?"

"Can we wait in the office I worked in yesterday?" Tom nodded. "We'll be there until they come and then head to the back. Same drill as yesterday. And leave them alone again after they've looked at the items."

"For how long?"

"A few minutes."

Heidi came with their coffee.

"Please leave the coffee next door." After she left, Tom asked, "Is there anything new?"

"There are two men at L.T.D. in Newark who have been talking about 'his visit' tomorrow. All we have heard so far is 'him.' They are quieter than they had been, and the weather has been dry, so they move around. Everyone is still at The Sherry Netherland, as of now. And we think Yatkin is still there, too. The rest are enjoying the city. Propakov and Keller spent some time at Sotheby's yesterday. Know anyone there?"

"The Head of the Jewelry Department and I are good friends."

"We may ask you to speak with him. Anything for us?"

"No."

"Oh. There was no one watching your apartment last night. We'll be next door. Let us know when they get here."

Tom got his supplies and continued sorting sapphires for two bespoke designs. He finished picking stones for a necklace when Napoli knocked on the door. It was 9:15 a.m.

"What do you think?"

"Do you want me to call Propakov?"

"Text him. Let me know." Napoli went back to the office.

Tom texted.

Almost immediately, "We'll be there around 9:30 a.m."

Tom got up and told Napoli. He went to Heidi's desk and asked if she had any questions about her presentation.

"I'm good. Anything else you want to tell me?"

"Always try to get a budget after the 'education.' Delicately. Stress color and proportions, and 'make,' above all else. The things that might be obvious to a layperson when two women are holding their rings next to each other's."

Propakov and Keller rang the doorbell as Tom was going back down the hall. He turned to Heidi. She looked up from her monitor and nodded to Tom. 9:40 a.m.

"Go time. When can we let them in?"

"As soon as you see our backs."

Tom looked at Heidi on his way to the kitchen with the cops' coffee cups. Heidi buzzed them in and took their coats. No homburg today.

"Good morning." Tom motioned them to the Salon.

They shook hands. Keller seemed uncharacteristically stiff.

"Please be seated, gentlemen. I will get the items. Is there anything else I may show you today?"

"Just the ring and the brooch, if you please."

Tom returned with a tray and sat down. He opened the box and handed the ring to Keller.

"May I?" nodding at the window.

Tom waved his hand. The Salon windows faced west, and the City's Winter light was still low, but enough was reflecting off the building across Fifth Avenue to bring out most of the best of the stone.

"Seeing any orange or red?" referring to the warmest, and rarest, colors caused by dispersion in diamonds. The warm colors are particularly desirable and dramatic when present in fancy-color diamonds. Especially in blues.

"Ah, yes. The fire is magnificent," Propakov said. And the blue fire is like a Kashmir. They sat down at the desk.

Before they could speak, "To be clear, I am not interested in any 'package deal.' Any transaction with these two items will be separate. Buy one, buy both, buy neither—anything is okay. But one's price will have nothing to do the other." Cost averaging is common in the gem and jewelry trade for both buyers and the sellers.

"On comprend, pas de problème," Keller.

"Bien. Êtes-vous intéressé par ces articles?"

Smiling, Keller said, "That will depend on the prices, of course, and other things. You indicated the brooch was most likely, shall we say, *appropriated*? Was it?"

"As far as I know. We know nothing more than that. Supposedly it was a long time ago."

"Nevertheless, my partner and I—we mentioned him yesterday—are interested. For our private collection. And because of the 'issue,' we are willing to pay cash. In full, if you like, assuming we can arrive at a price."

"That is helpful. But the volume is impractical."

"Gold, then."

"And the blue?"

"Yuri and I are interested in the blue. But not for cash. If we come to an understanding, can you organize and manage delivery? Taxes and duties, you know."

"Where?"

"Geneva or Gstaad."

"Of course."

Keller shrugged his shoulders.

Tom got up and closed the Salon door. "What are you thinking?"

"$96,900,000."

"A $7,000,000 haircut. Actually, a $7,704,000 haircut, about $508,000 per carat, no?" Keller and Propakov looked at each other. "Math is not a strong point, gentlemen. It takes me a minute to work things out. Forgive me." They smiled. "$11.9 million more than yesterday. Terms?"

Keller, "We are prepared to wire you $20,000,000 today. You hold the ring, and we wire the difference within 14 business days. You see to the delivery of the ring within three days after full payment."

"We will not be declaring for importation? There is no buyer?"

"Correct. You understand, of course."

"Oh, I understand. You know, should Customs get lucky and discover it at entry, I will have no choice but to quickly produce a memorandum. If the paperwork is solid and ready, they will accept *'It slipped my mind.'* If one pays the penalty on the spot. As you know, even if I then sold the stone, it would still have to come back out of Switzerland because of the Carnet Regulations."

A carnet is an international customs and temporary export-import document. They are commonly used by international salespeople to clear customs in many countries, without paying duties and import taxes on merchandise that will be re-exported within twelve months.

"What is Plan B?" Tom wondered if Interpol and the F.B.I. would have enough on Keller for knowingly avoiding import duties and V.A.T.

"There is no Plan B, Mr. Strawbridge. See that they do not find the diamond." Keller leaned back and crossed his legs.

Since none of this was ever going to happen, Tom moved on. "Very well. How about this? Let's call it an even $95,000,000 and you wire $50,000,000 today. "Balance within 14 days. If you default, we keep $2.500,000. Think of it as an 'opportunity cost.' I'll even throw in the mounting," which was, of course, understood. Tom extended his hand over the middle of the desk, smiling.

"Very well, Mr. Strawbridge." Keller and Propakov shook hands with Tom. They wanted the diamond.

"Shall we say, *Mazal* and *Bracha*?" smiling, the traditional Hebrew phrase said with a handshake when closing a diamond transaction. "Fortune and blessing." Tom put his finger under the desk and pressed the button signaling for Heidi.

"Only Mr. Propakov understands these things," Matteo Keller said with a dramatic wave of his hand.

"Well, I wish you both luck and thank you for the business. You could make money at that number in the spring sales." If this deal came together as outlined, Tom's profit was almost $8,000,000 at just the first 50 million.

"We always hope to make a profit, Mr. Strawbridge," said Propakov. "That reminds me. I neglected to ask yesterday. Is this a new stone?"

Tom took a chance. "Yes."

The dealer Tom had bought it from recently acquired the diamond in the '70's for next to nothing. It had come out of India long before. A terrible cut, it had started life as an Oval, which did not reveal the stone's overall potential, or the vivid blue color. The owner decided to recut within the last ten months because the prices for fancy-colored diamonds had gone mad. And he was ready to retire. It lost almost 11.00 carats. A huge percentage, but it was well worth the weight loss. Tom reckoned that even if Propakov and Keller had seen it, they might not have put it together. The dealer told Tom there were only two people who knew about it besides himself. But these two were so strong and connected, it was always possible they could have heard something.

"This diamond may be presented in any way you like, any provenance, with confidence."

"Incredible."

"Funny," looking at Propakov, "I have a colored stone that just came in that I feel the same way about." Propakov stared at Tom.

Heidi knocked and came into the Salon. Tom waved her over.

"Gentlemen?"

"Some sparkling water please," said Keller. "And an espresso," Propakov.

Tom jotted down the terms of the deal for Heidi. "We will write up a memorandum of understanding, reflecting what we discussed. Once signed, we will seal the ring, if necessary, and you may sign the envelope. What bank will be wiring the funds today?"

"That won't be necessary. We know you are honorable. UBP," Keller said. "Union Bancaire Privee. I'd best get on the phone, as a matter of fact." Keller now seemed invigorated.

"Would you like a hard line?" Tom said, handing Keller a card. "Our bank information is there, as is the name of our Personal Banker if your man needs him. Would you like privacy?"

Keller, already dialing his cell phone, waved his hand. Tom got up and walked Heidi and the ring to the door.

"When you finish, bring it in. Let me know if you have any questions." Heidi flashed her eyes at Tom and smiled. "Anything from the back?"

"Nothing."

"Anything else? Henry Stacks called."

"Please."

She chuckled as Tom went back into the Salon.

"I'll receive a confirmation text when the money has been wired. It is a large amount. He says it may show 'processing' in your account until tomorrow."

Tom took out cotton gloves from the drawer, opened the brooch box, and turned it toward Keller and Propakov.

"Absolutely unique, one of a kind," Keller.

"Truly fabulous. Just to think of that collection of colored stones," Propakov added.

They were more effusive today. Heidi returned with the Perrier and espresso, and left.

"What are you thinking?"

"Well, our friend must see the piece."

"Is he in New York? Can he come now?"

"We don't know."

"You don't know? Well, if he is, wouldn't it be easiest to have him come here? I cannot let this piece go out of the office unless it goes with me. Aren't you leaving town?"

"If we can come to terms, there may be a way," Propakov.

"What are you thinking?"

"Well, as the item is . . ."

"Please, Mr. Propakov. Remember what I've already agreed to do for you."

"Yes. We feel $93,000,000 is insurance value. Retail."

"It could not be duplicated today. The provenance is legitimate."

"Yes. Well, $45,000,000. All Swiss bullion. As you said, the volume for paper is impossible. For us and you. 21 kilos at today's price, more or less, per million."

These guys are really strong, Tom thought. "You're saying 2,000 pounds of gold? Basically 73 bars? When? Where?"

"Yes. Within 24 hours, 48 at the most. This is up to you. But there can be no risks. We can arrange for 'delivery' to your bank from our people in London. No actual gold is moved, and nothing is traceable."

"Our account in the Cayman Islands?"

Nodding, "Within a day. We 'pay' them, and they assign existing gold to your account. You can then draw down paper as you see fit."

"Are we wasting each other's time here? We go nowhere without your partner, no?"

"Please. If you agree to the price, and the arrangement, we will work something out."

"Let me call my partner. Will you excuse me, please?"

Tom stood up, waved at the brooch, indicating they were free to handle it, and left, closing the door behind him. Tom walked back to the storage room.

"Okay so far. Keep it going."

"That's it?"

"You got a lot. Get the meeting now."

Tom left and met Heidi in the hall. She was holding the memorandum of understanding.

"I think we are wrapping up. I'll ping you as soon as we're done."

Tom went into the Salon and sat down. Propakov and Keller were at the window with the brooch. Tom walked over to them.

"My partner wants me to confirm the brooch will not be released until the gold has been received in our account. We are considering your offer."

"May we make another call?"

Tom moved for the door, but Propakov put his hand up. He began speaking Russian. Tom knew they would get a translation.

"We will find a way. Let us sit down. Our partner does not like the public places. Can you see us and show him the brooch at a company he invests in tomorrow afternoon?"

"Where?"

"New Jersey. Newark."

CHAPTER 36

Friday Midmorning

Tom told Propakov and Keller that it would be impossible for him to commit to an offsite meeting without consulting his own partner. He mentioned, matter-of-factly, that his partner was now not available again until after 12:00 noon. Both Propakov and Keller seemed anxious. Tom picked up a pen and asked for an address. Propakov said he'd get Tom an address if the meeting could definitely be arranged. Tom asked again why their partner could not come to the office, but they didn't offer an answer.

"We can do it here in my office any time of the day or night, you know."

"Impossible. Our partner is private and takes security very seriously."

After signing the memorandum of understanding for the 15.16 carat vivid blue diamond ring, Propakov asked what Tom thought of their offer for the brooch.

"Honestly? Not much. But my partner is much more motivated to sell than I am. We'll see."

Tom showed them out. He told Heidi to prep the Salon for her appointment and went back to the storage room. Napoli was on the phone. Menendez stepped into the hall to tell Tom the Detective was debriefing with headquarters.

"You're in some business. Oh. The men outside your building called in at their shift change. There was no one outside your apartment building last night."

Tom was on the phone with Marco, the lapidary, when Napoli came to the door. Tom motioned the two men to the chairs in front of his desk. Menendez surveyed the room carefully. Napoli was staring at his phone.

Hanging up, "How'd I do?"

"OK."

Nonplused, Tom said, "Really? What didn't I do, and what else could I have done?"

"Not the point. You made progress. We have what we need on Keller and Propakov. Knowingly buying stolen property and seeking to avoid import duties and tax evasion. Does a lot of that, you know, illegal importation, go on in your business?"

"I wouldn't know."

"Obviously, we wait to pick them up. I'm waiting to hear back from Chief Monahan. He's talking with the F.B.I. now. Unless something changes, we will want you to agree to the meeting. When you left them the first time, it was clear they wanted the brooch. You should know: they took some pictures."

Tom saw Heidi buzz in Wendy Bachman. Menendez absent-mindedly reached out for the fluorite specimen on Tom's desk.

"Please, Officer. That's really annoying. About the pictures. But not surprising."

"I wouldn't worry about it. As of now, all the players are still at The Sherry Netherland. And the L.T.D. people are preparing for a visit and meeting tomorrow. No names, but the 'Boss' is expected."

Napoli's phone rang. Tom excused himself and left the office.

Heidi had been with Wendy Bachman for about 15 minutes when Tom walked into the Salon and introduced himself.

"Very pleased to meet you. Mother adores you."

"Well, she is one of our favorites. Remember us to her please."

Wendy Bachman's head was almost the size of a basketball, and her hairline seemed to start in the center of the top of her head. Her eyes were small, round, and black. Like a mouse.

"Who's the lucky man?"

"Oh, we've known each other forever. He'll be joining us in a few minutes."

"Wonderful. Everything going well?" looking at Heidi. She smiled and was very relaxed.

"Well, have fun, ladies."

Detective Napoli and Officer Menendez were laughing when Tom got back to his office.

"So?"

"So, we need you to accept the meeting and then come to the Midtown North Precinct on East 67th Street at 2:00 p.m . . . Okay? 153, between Lexington and Third Avenue."

"I know it. That's in an hour and a half. Any idea how long this will take?"

"Think two hours. They are already planning, so there shouldn't be too much down time. David Mitchell will be there."

"I'll be there."

"Chief Monahan and Bureau Chief Wilson wanted me to thank you and to say that you exceeded their expectations."

Tom stood up. "I assume I'll see you later. Who do I ask for?"

"Don't worry about that. Just announce yourself to the Duty Officer at the desk."

Tom noticed Wendy Bachman's fiancé had arrived as he walked the policemen past the Salon to the front door.

Tom tried Propakov, but the call went straight to voicemail.

He returned to the Salon and introduced himself to the fiancé. There were four 3.00 and 4.00 carat Round Brilliant Cut loose diamonds on a display tray in front of the couple.

Heidi was still with her clients when Tom walked by and motioned for her to come out. He noticed that champagne had been broken out. Heidi was on a roll. Tom quickly explained what was going on and told her that he would be back as soon as possible. It was 1:45 p.m. when Tom got to the street and started walking.

The weather was gray, raw, and drizzling. Tom got on the Madison Avenue bus. The traffic was light. The bus got to 66th Street in less than ten minutes, and he got off. The rain picked up as Tom climbed the stairs to the precinct house. He had always admired the 19th-century red sandstone façade. Tom went through the metal detector. He was unarmed. An Officer pointed to the main desk. There was a lot of activity, uniformed and plainclothes, and there were heavy wooden chairs bolted to the floor along the right wall. There was a disheveled, filthy young man handcuffed to the last chair. He had only one sneaker.

The Officer at the desk motioned to the chairs and made a call. Rather than sit down, Tom stood off to the side and checked his phone. "Congratulate me! 4.06 carat RBC, F/VS1, triple x. Can we choose the baguettes together? Full price!"

He texted, "Well done, Heidi."

"Mr. Strawbridge?"

Tom turned and had to look up at an immense plainclothesman. At least six feet nine.

"This way, please." He led Tom past the desk and down a hall to an elevator. They got off on the fifth floor and walked to the back of the building. The cop knocked on a set of double doors.

Napoli opened the door. "Thanks, Tiny. Come in. You remember Chief Monahan of Special Operations, Bureau Chief Wilson, and Assistant Director Sprang of the F.B.I., New York."

Tom nodded and took off his coat, putting it on a chair against the wall. "Where's Mitchell?"

"On his way. Sit down, please. We want to thank you for your help to this point. Detective Napoli has told you that we now have enough on Matteo Keller and Yuri Propakov to convict." Napoli was leaning against a windowsill with a condescending expression. Monahan continued, "We have a team assembled, and they've been briefed initially, for the operation designed to recapture Igor Yatkin. Have you been able to reach Propakov?"

Tom explained.

"Okay. We have to know one thing first. You are definitely willing to go forward with a meeting?" Adding, "If we don't get a shot at him before."

"I said I was."

Someone knocked at the door, and David Mitchell and Jim Rossi walked in past the huge policeman. They were soaking wet. "Sorry, gentlemen. We had to walk the last three blocks."

Monahan repeated what he had told Tom.

"Can David and I have a private word?"

Monahan nodded and motioned at the door to the hall.

Once outside, "They are really pleased with what you've done."

"Yeah?"

"Napoli doesn't trust you. He told Monahan and Wilson he's not sure they can count on your performance if there is a meeting. From what I can gather, Officer Menendez has been a real balance."

"Screw him. He's smug and arrogant."

"How do you feel?"

"Okay. I haven't felt threatened or in danger. But it's all been on my turf so far."

"I heard from one of their attorneys last evening. They've started grousing about paying you the reward. Or at least started to make a case."

"At this point? Or even after the Yatkin meeting, if it happens?"

"At this point."

"Honestly, I don't care about it one way or the other. I guess let's hear what they have to say, but I am ready to walk."

They went back in.

"What's the plan, Chief Monahan?"

Monahan explained that if the meeting took place, it would undoubtedly be at the L.T.D. Shipping building in Port Newark. They would send Tom with a team of two. Someone posing as his partner, and a security man as driver.

"Okay. What if it's not in Newark? I tried to get them to come to my office."

"We heard. Then we reevaluate. What do you say?"

"We've come this far."

Monahan told Tom to text Propakov, agreeing to a meeting. He was to decline transportation if it was offered. He also said to tell Propakov up front that Tom's partner and a security person and driver would be coming.

Tom texted Propakov. He ended by saying that he and his partner had not yet agreed to their offer. Monahan asked Tom to forward the text to Detective Napoli.

Propakov texted right back, saying he would be in touch as soon as possible.

"The sooner we have confirmation on the location, the better." Monahan confirmed to Tom and the lawyers that the whole crew was still at The Sherry Netherland.

Tom's phone began to ring. Propakov. He let it go to voicemail. He played the message on speaker. Propakov had asked Tom to call him back.

Monahan asked Tom to return the call. "Detective Napoli, take our friend into an empty office. And wait with him."

"Please come with me, David. Okay, Chief Monahan?" He nodded.

The three of them went into a small, windowless office down the hall. It was painted in institutional bilious green. Tom did not make eye contact with Napoli before he sat down and dialed Propakov.

Propakov confirmed a 5:30 p.m. meeting for Saturday evening at the L.T.D. office in the Port Newark complex. "Our partner is not enthusiastic about the piece at this point. Too expensive. Rather than negotiate further, let's see if he likes it, and we can take it from there. Payment arrangements and so on."

Tom wanted to make a comment about the pictures they'd taken but held his tongue.

"Your name will be at the security gate."

Tom hung up, and they went back to the conference room.

"Good," said Monahan. "Now, Yatkin just needs to be there."

Monahan described possible scenarios regarding the meeting. The F.B.I. and the N.Y.P.D. Special Operations Division would have men stationed at various locations around the Port Newark facility. He explained that, with extra surveillance and manpower, it would be hard for Yatkin not to be identified when he left the hotel before the meeting. So, the meeting would most likely not take place. Monahan was hoping to grab Yatkin exiting The Sherry Netherland. And only if they did not spot and pick him up, would they go ahead with the meeting in Newark. The likelihood of Yatkin getting to the Port Newark facility without being seen was low. "If he gets to a vehicle before we can get him, we are prepared to and will stop the car."

"Are you sure he is still in the City?"

"We are. And the plane is still on the manifest for Palm Beach from Teterboro Saturday night. We'd like you to join us with other members of the team, in case the meeting does take place."

Tom agreed, and they all followed Chief Monahan down the hall to a large room with two rows of chairs arranged in semi-circles. There was a slightly raised platform in the front of the room and a video screen. Seven or eight people were scattered around the room, talking. All of them made for chairs as soon as they saw the brass.

"Have a seat, gentlemen," to the attorneys and Tom. "We're just waiting on a few more."

David Mitchell again asked Tom how he was feeling.

"Okay. This should be interesting. If they get him before the meeting, what . . ."

Mitchell cut him off. "We will have a fight. If they get him at or after the meeting? We should be golden."

A few minutes later, Chief Monahan stood up and nodded to the back of the room.

"Good afternoon, everyone. Mr. Strawbridge, the good people you see around you are the best of the best. Some are N.Y.P.D., and some are F.B.I. Please stand up so everyone can get a look at you."

Tom rolled his eyes to Mitchell, stood up, and turned around. He looked each of them in the eyes. Thirteen people, three women, all plainclothes, all expressionless.

"Thank you, Mr. Strawbridge." Monahan called for the lights and started what amounted to a virtual tour of the Port Newark Container Terminal. It included still shots, maps, diagrams, and drone footage. Tom was surprised by the quality. He recognized many of the major features of the complex, from looking down on it from the Casciano Memorial Bridge crossing Newark Bay to New Jersey. Monahan outlined and described the positions of various personnel to be stationed around the L.T.D. building. Including one sniper position in the cab of one of the tall container cranes that are idle on weekends. "If he goes in, he can't get out."

"If we haven't picked Yatkin up by 3:00 p.m. on Saturday, the meeting is on. We're almost done for today, Mr. Strawbridge. Agent Moss will be your driver. He'll be in a business suit. One of our best. You'll be using an armored Lincoln Town Car."

Monahan motioned to Moss, and he stood up, nodding to Tom. Flat expression, flat dark eyes.

F.B.I. Director Sprang, "You'll find Agent Moss to be extremely well versed. He works regularly with the Department."

Monahan, "We'll leave from your apartment around 4:00 p.m. Once we get to L.T.D., if you see him"—Yatkin's mug shot appeared on the screen—"and we have not, press the button on this key fob. We will give you this tomorrow."

"What about the third person?"

"Your partner? That will be Detective Napoli."

"Impossible."

Mitchell stiffened.

"Excuse me?" Monahan looked like he was ready to blow.

"Chief Monahan, whatever kind of criminals these men are, they are smart, well educated, and sophisticated. They would know Detective Napoli was 'on the job' before he got out of the car. You have been lucky so far. It would be a shame to blow it at this point."

Sprang, Monahan, and Wilson looked at each other. Clearly agitated, Monahan said, "Please be back here at 11:00 a.m. tomorrow. We'll finalize everything then."

Tom leaned to David Mitchell. "Can you make it?"

"Yes."

"We'll be here." The atmosphere in the room was thick with tension. Rossi, Mitchell, and Tom got up, and Officer Menendez held the door. He led them back to the original meeting room. They got their coats, and Menendez put them on the elevator to the Ground Floor.

Outside, the rain had stopped, and a sharp wind was gusting.

"Seriously?" said Tom. Mitchell. Rossi was smiling.

"What? Look, I don't like the guy, but I'm telling you he won't do. They can figure it out."

Rossi sent for an Uber. They shook hands, and Tom headed west to Lexington.

Tom walked down to 64th Street and went into Donahue's. A Manhattan old-school bar and restaurant. One of the last. Tom hung his coat on a hook, sat down at the bar, and shook hands with Tommy, the bartender. He waved to Madge, the owner, who was taking an order from a couple in the back.

"Handsome as ever, Tommy. Ketel martini."

"Right away, Tom."

Propakov had texted during the meeting, asking for the full names of anyone coming to the L.T.D. meeting. Tom forwarded it to Mitchell and asked him to get it to Monahan. It was just past 4:30 p.m., but Tom didn't want to go back to the office. He called Heidi, congratulated her, and asked her to close the office for the day. She said there were no important messages.

"What are you doing tomorrow?"

"Not sure. Why?"

"It looks like I have to come into the office. I'll let you know."

"I'll come in if you need me. Oh, I checked the bank. $30,000,000 is showing as 'processing.'"

"Thanks, and good job today."

Tom's drink arrived. He took a sip and continued cleaning up his texts and emails. Tom decided to eat at the bar and ordered a strip steak and a Caesar salad. He had just finished his dinner and was watching the news on the bar's TV when he became aware of someone at the end of the bar. Napoli and another cop from the meeting. Tom had just ordered a nightcap and wished he hadn't. They looked at each other with no acknowledgment. Tom paid his bill. When his drink was done, he put on his coat, shook hands with Tommy, and put a $100 bill in his palm. Tom left without looking in Napoli's direction.

Tom got a cab and was home by 7:30 p.m. He looked through the mail. There was a hand-delivered invitation from Marla Wingate for cocktails on Sunday. Across the front was written "10 people, please come." He would think about it.

He was reading when a text from Max came in. "Hi. Can we talk tomorrow? I need decision-making advice." He smiled.

David Mitchell texted, and said to copy and paste the contents of an email sent to Mitchell by Monahan into a text to Propakov. There were three names. False identifications that would appear legitimate if researched. Tom did it.

Part Eleven

CHAPTER 37

Saturday Morning

TOM WAS UP EARLY. He wondered if the meeting would take place. He also wondered why Propakov and Keller still wanted to show the brooch if the partner was cool. He finished dressing and sat down with a coffee.

A text from Detective Napoli had come in late the night before: "We need to clear the air."

"Not necessary, Detective. I know how you feel. What I said yesterday has nothing to do with your opinions."

Tom decided to go to the office before the 11:00 a.m. briefing at the precinct house. He dressed in jeans and a blazer, figuring if the meeting did happen, he'd change later.

It was raw and drizzling. Tom got into a cab and breezed down Fifth Avenue. Napoli had phoned on the way. No message.

Tom disarmed the alarm system, started the coffee maker, and opened the main safe. He brought the box containing the brooch to his office and threw his coat on a chair. Heidi had uncharacteristically left champagne glasses in the sink. Tom was putting them in the dishwasher when his phone rang again.

Napoli. No message. And then a text, "Please call me. Confirm with Propakov."

Tom sat down and waited for the coffee. He texted David Mitchell. "Morning. Anything new?"

Back at his desk, Tom checked his account on the U.S. Trust App. The $30,000,000 was still "processing."

"Nothing new. I'll see you at 11:00 a.m. Do you want me to pick you up?" Tom texted that he'd see Mitchell at the precinct.

Tom texted Propakov. "Good morning. Are we still on for this afternoon? You're leaving town. What about the Alexandrite?" He cut and pasted the first two sentences to David Mitchell and asked him to get it to Napoli.

Tom prepared his briefcase for the meeting. He packed cotton gloves, various light sources, two velvet pads, and cleaning clothes. He would carry the brooch separately in a small nylon gym bag.

Heidi called. "Good morning. Well done, yesterday."

"Tom, I forgot to clean the kitchen and . . ."

"All taken care of."

"Oh. Sorry. Do you need me today?"

"I don't think so. It's, let's see, after 9:00 a.m. already. By the time you get here. . . . I'm going to leave around 10:30 a.m."

"Okay. Let me know if you need anything. I'll be home all morning."

He was reading the paper when David Mitchell called. "Tom, please call Napoli. He's pissy and saying you ignored him at a bar last night?"

"I must not have seen him."

"Look, just call. They are all worked up about this operation. Do what you need to, OK?"

"Okay. See you later."

Propakov had returned Tom's text while he was on with Mitchell. "I'll leave as soon as I can. We will confirm by 1:00 p.m. Please work with the Alexandrite as long as you want."

Tom was forwarding the text to Mitchell and Napoli when the phone rang. Napoli.

"Detective. Just sent you a text from Propakov. Anything new?"

"Thank you for taking the call. Nothing new that we know of. We believe everyone is still at the hotel. We haven't gotten eyes on Yatkin again, but, based on the chatter from L.T.D., he should still be in New York. There has been more activity at the Newark site. The last shift change of our men before tonight will be at 2:00 p.m. We'll go over everything later."

Tom said nothing.

"Mr. Strawbridge, your lawyer shouldn't have told you what Chief Monahan had told him in confidence. You understand the importance of this operation. We need to have confidence that you understand your role."

Tom thought, *Right. My lawyer.*

Tom thought of Mark Twain's saying: "Never argue with stupid people; they will drag you down to their level and then beat you with experience." Tom knew there was no point in engaging.

"You're not sure I can manage it?"

"Well. You can be a little slick at times."

"Slick?"

"You know—glib."

"What exactly *should* I be doing?"

Tom was half listening as Napoli explained the importance of concentration and the importance of protocol. "We don't expect it, but there is always the possibility of trouble. Especially if our element of surprise is diminished."

Tom assumed Napoli did not like his occasional patronizing attitude.

"I'll try, Detective. But my whole life, I've felt like a man trapped in a man's body."

Sensing victory and control, and not getting Tom's crack, "You are very successful, Mr. Strawbridge, but the investigation of criminal activities is very complicated and specialized."

"Yes, Detective. I will see you later." Tom hung up.

Tom finished the paper and emailed his insurance broker, asking him to secure an extra twenty-four-hour supplemental insurance rider for $10,000,000. Tom's basic jewelers block insurance covered him to carry $50,000,000, and, even though the police were responsible, the exercise was good business practice. His phone rang instantly.

"Eddie, how are you?"

"Dammit, Tom. How can I reach Lloyd's with this amount? On a Saturday?"

"This is why you are the best. Do what you can. I have to go."

"You know it won't be cheap."

"Do what you can. Bye."

Tom got his coat and bags, locked up, alarmed the office, and took the elevator to the lobby. It had stopped raining, and he decided to walk. It was 10:40 a.m.

The holiday shopping crowds were just starting to get thick on Madison Avenue. Tom thought about how the nature of the shoppers, the types of people, had changed since he'd started in the business. Where would the international luxury brands be in ten years?

He walked to Park Avenue, which was deserted by comparison, and got to the Precinct on 67th Street at 10:55 a.m. The cop at the metal detector smiled, recognizing Tom from yesterday. Tom went to the Desk Officer, who pointed to the chairs against the wall. Tom stood off to the side. There was a bald, older man with an immense red beard, handcuffed to the last chair on the right, a Bible beside him on the floor. He had no shirt and was muttering.

"The Desk Officer said, "Same room as yesterday. The big one at the end of the hall on Five. Can you find it?"

"Thank you."

Tom was about to knock on the door when it opened, and an older, uniformed sergeant stood aside and waved Tom past him. He nodded and saw David Mitchell talking to F.B.I. Assistant Director Sprang, Chief Wilson, and another man. Chief Monahan was at the podium, looking down at a stack of papers.

Tom walked over, and Sprang smiled and extended his hand, "Thank you for coming. Mr. Strawbridge." As Tom was shaking Chief Wilson's hand, Sprang said, "Mr. Strawbridge, this is the New York Director of the F.B.I., Clark Floyd." Sprang's boss. He looked like an accountant.

"How do you do?" Tom said, shaking hands.

"Nice to meet you, Mr. Strawbridge." Monahan came over and said hello to Tom and David Mitchell. He looked preoccupied and serious.

"We'll be just a few more minutes."

Tom noticed the waiting group was bigger than yesterday. Probably 25. And there were more video screens set up.

"Tell me," said Director Floyd, "what is it about gemstones, diamonds?"

"Do you mean why are they valuable, or why do people like them?"

"Both, I guess."

"Some people find them interesting for several reasons beyond their beauty. And, simply put, their rarity accounts for their value. Early in my career, I was evaluating the jeweled cover of the Lindau Gospels in the collection of the Morgan Library. My little group was talking about the history of the ecclesiastical use of gemstones. We speculated that some people might consider them a reflection of the mystery and beauty of creation."

Floyd raised his eyebrows and walked off.

Monahan stood up. "Please find a seat, everyone."

Monahan got behind the lectern. "Good morning. As of right now, the whereabouts of all our friends is unchanged. Propakov and Keller ate at Cipriani last night. Reznikov and several others went to Gallagher's. We finally got confirmation from the hotel that everyone is scheduled to check out today. Still no more signs of Yatkin coming or going. We interviewed the housekeeping staff who services their suites, but they could not confirm anyone stays in the rooms while they work. Having said that, we still believe Yatkin has not left the hotel. Checkout is at 1:00 p.m. We are in position now and have cars on Fifth Avenue ready to block 60th Street if they come out the side. There is an old service hall out to 59th

Street. It is locked, and one of our men is at the door anyway. Detective Philips?"

"What if they exit and Yatkin isn't with them? Do we grab the others?"

"No. There is always the possibility Yatkin could slip by, and we still assume Propakov and Keller are going to Newark. So, we wait."

Monahan put up a drone photo of the Port Newark container facility and reviewed the positions of all the men.

"Mr. Strawbridge, you and your 'partner' are to go to the door and ask if your driver can join you. I'd be surprised if you're not frisked. Either way, go in, and get down to business. If you can I.D. Yatkin, hit the fob we are going to give you. Your 'partner' will have ways to signal as well. We thought about what you said yesterday, which is why we sent you three I.D.'s for Propakov. You will be a team of three. Agent Moss will drive. Your 'partner' will be Detective Napoli. Period, the end."

"My 'partner' and driver will not be armed?"

"We are leaning toward no."

It was 11:45 a.m. Monahan, "Let's take a 10-minute break."

"Where's Rossi?"

"Today is on the house. You good?"

"Fine. Coffee?"

"I'll bring you one."

Tom checked his phone. Propakov had emailed confirming the meeting for 5:30 p.m. and gave the address for L.T.D. Shipping in Port Newark. He walked over to Monahan, who was talking to several men.

"Just a minute, Mr. Strawbridge."

Tom sat down with David Mitchell and told him about the email. Monahan came over. Tom showed him the email. He told Tom to confirm with Propakov.

A uniformed policeman walked up to Monahan. They walked to the front of the room. He waved over Chief Wilson, Assistant Director Sprang, and Clark Floyd. They huddled for a few seconds, abruptly walked to the back of the room, and left.

It was close to 12:15 p.m. when they came back. Monahan was red-faced, walked right to the lectern, and rapped on it with his fist.

"Unbelievably, Propakov, Keller, Reznikov, Donskoi, and three others checked out of the hotel. They got in two cars and got on the F.D.R., headed north. At least we don't think any of our people were spotted. They hit the George Washington Bridge just as we started the meeting. We'll pick them up on the other side in Fort Lee. What is it, Philips!?"

"So, we are a go?"

Tom leaned over to David Mitchell. "Do you think now would be a good time for me to object to Napoli again?" Mitchell chuckled.

The same uniformed policeman came up to Monahan and leaned in.

"God damn it!" He walked out again with Wilson, Sprang, and Floyd in tow.

"What do you think?"

"I think Yatkin got by them, and they are panicked. Especially with the F.B.I. involved. And I think you are going to Newark later."

"I think you're right." Ten minutes later, Monahan stormed back in and got behind the lectern. He was even more red. Silence in the room.

Taking a deep breath, "We thought our entourage was heading to Teterboro, but they got on 95 South. Apparently heading to Port Newark. They got off and are having lunch at the Segovia Steakhouse in Little Ferry. We have no idea where he came from, but Igor Yatkin was just identified by our man in the security booth at the Port Newark Container Terminal. Our people at The Sherry Netherland are positive he didn't leave there today. We may not find out what happened. Operation Double Take is on."

Monahan put a live drone feed on the main screen in time to see the car that brought Yatkin pull around behind the L.T.D. building. "If no one has any questions, let's break. We will work from this room, starting at 1500 hours for everyone on that shift. Mr. Strawbridge, please stay behind."

Everyone but Monahan, Wilson, Sprang, and Floyd left the room. Agent Moss and Detective Napoli moved into two chairs next to David Mitchell. Tom had not noticed Napoli.

"You will be picked up at 1600 hours, 4:00 p.m. Do you need to stop at your office?"

"No. I have everything," nodding to the gym bag on the chair next to him.

"Good. When you go to the door, you ask if your driver can come in. If not, Agent Moss will wait outside. Follow their lead, but get at it as quickly as you can. Your fob—please attach it to your briefcase or keys—is also a listening device. Agent Moss and Detective Napoli have listening devices in two of their jacket buttons. Detective Napoli, known as 'Mr. Thomas' for today, has been instructed to speak only when spoken to. There are six main rooms in the building. The conference room, where we expect you to meet, is here." He used a laser pointer to outline the corner of the building to the left of the front door. "The front offices appear to be quite comfortable. There is no inside access to the warehouse behind the offices. Once we have confirmation that Yatkin is there, we will wait for you to finish and leave the building. We do not need you to do anything, except to be convincing. And cool. Feel no pressure to do anything, including identifying Yatkin. Understood?"

"Yes. Are Agent Moss and Detective Napoli going to be armed?"

"Moss, yes. Napoli, no. We don't expect any trouble, but we will be prepared. Once you are inside, we'll have several men within steps of the building. Including two on the opposite side of the front parking area behind some containers. What else?"

"I don't think anything. David?"

"Nothing."

"Okay. Detective Napoli is your sole contact for the rest of the operation. Understood?"

"Yes."

"Good luck."

Everyone shook hands, and Detective Napoli and Agent Moss took David Mitchell and Tom to the elevator.

Once on the street, Tom said, "I won't be surprised if we never get in front of him after they see Napoli. Did you see his hair?"

"God awful. Was that meant to be a civilian disguise?"

"Who knows?"

"Well, good luck, be careful, and give me a call after, as soon as you can."

Tom walked to Third Avenue and caught a cab home. The streets were dry, and the sun was trying to come out. Tom walked into his apartment at 1:30 p.m. He heated some soup and sat down.

He took a few minutes in his study to take some pictures of the brooch. He would write something about the piece for the industry journals eventually, and he wanted some less-technical images. He was reading when Heidi called.

"How'd it go?"

"OK. We're on. I'll tell you everything Monday. What's up?"

"Nothing. I felt badly about the kitchen, so I came in anyway. And, I had paperwork. Oh—the $30,000,000 cleared."

"Good. I didn't notice the alert that the office was disarmed until just now. How long are you staying?"

"Max was supposed to call me from the street an hour ago. We planned to go to L'Avenue for lunch. I'll give her a few more minutes and then head home."

"OK. A lot of good work this week."

"Thanks, Tom."

It was 3:00 p.m., and Tom had cleaned up and dressed in a black double-breasted suit, white shirt, and a silver-and-black striped tie.

Napoli called. "Just as an FYI, everyone else has arrived at L.T.D. There's been a procession of various visitors in and out. Yatkin has not left. The 2:00 p.m. shift changed out, and we're ready to go. Anything?"

"No. Still 4:00 p.m.?"

"Yes."

Tom sat down. On the table in front of him was his briefcase and the gym bag. Next to the bag was his Sig Sauer .380.

CHAPTER 38

Saturday Afternoon

THE HOUSE PHONE RANG AT 3:50 P.M. The Doorman, "Mr. Thomas is here, Mr. Strawbridge."

"Thank you, John." Tom put on his suit jacket and overcoat.

They were just entering the Lincoln Tunnel before anyone said anything.

"Do you have any questions, Mr. Strawbridge?"

"Not really. Well, is there any chance you and Agent Moss . . ."

"Mr. Reneke."

"Whatever—*Mr. Reneke*—will arrest Yatkin while we are inside? Assuming he's there."

"There's a chance. We've been briefed and discussed what could trigger that possibility. But those are not our orders. Safety first."

"If you know he's there, why go ahead with the meeting?"

"He's skilled and slippery. We have to be sure. Our team will be inside L.T.D.'s offices the minute we leave."

It was drizzling when they came out of the Tunnel. The sky was choppy, dark-gray, and low.

"We've got plenty of time. Bob, let's avoid the Turnpike."

They headed South on Route 9 from Weehawken. They picked up Route 440 at Jersey City. They could see the Hackensack River off to the right.

"We're still going to be early, Steve. I'll pull into that little park up here for 10 minutes, OK?"

"Good. I'll call Richie and text the Chief." Napoli made a call, and Tom realized for the first time that there was another car behind them.

They parked. Another Lincoln pulled in behind them a minute later. Tom wanted to get out of the car, but the rain had picked up. He was bored and mildly anxious at the same time. His phone rang.

"May I get this? Heidi."

Napoli nodded.

"Hi. Hold on a second." Tom got out and walked over to a small picnic table pavilion out of the rain.

"What's up?"

"Hi, sorry. Is it all right if I am a little late Monday? My parents want me at their house for a brunch tomorrow. You have Peter Hopper at 11:00 a.m., but I'll be in by then, anyway."

"Of course. Last minute?"

"Yes. Dad wants me for support. Mother's cronies."

"Have fun."

"By the way, Max's fiancé' just called. He can't find her. And she never showed for lunch or got in touch."

Tom smiled. "You know her, Heidi."

"Well, I thought you might have heard from her. She's been talking about you and asking a lot of questions lately. Is anything going on?"

"Seriously? I would forget it. I've got to go."

"Bye."

Tom was reading an email when Moss flashed the headlights. He walked back to the car.

Agent Moss pulled out of the parking lot and turned back onto Route 440 South.

Napoli unfolded an overhead schematic view of the Port Newark Container Terminal. "Here's the latest, just so you know. There will be six men, besides us, inside the Terminal. One of the two guards in the security gate at the entrance, a watchman at the Morton Salt warehouse across the parking lot from L.T.D., three maintenance workers positioned around the dock area, and one man in the closest container crane. South of the parking lot, on the river. He'll be in the cab, 120 feet up, looking down on L.T.D. Two more vehicles, four men in each, will pull in one minute after us, and will wait just behind the L.T.D. office, next to their warehouse. The car behind us now will wait on the street in front. The three closest men will move in as soon as we come out."

"Okay. How many people will be in their offices?"

"As far as we can tell, there have been six or seven on average. Based on the latest intel on the comings and goings, we are expecting six or eight. Keller, Propakov, Reznikov, Donskoi, plus Yatkin and one or two others. Like you heard this morning, there's been a lot of traffic today. By the way, the container with the sarin gas was loaded yesterday and shipped out overnight. There's a dedicated team working on that."

Agent Moss directed the car onto the approach ramp for the Casciano Memorial Bridge, which goes over Newark Bay. Even though Tom was on the far side of the car, he had a clear view of the Bay and Port Newark on the far bank. The Container Terminal sat on a square man-made peninsula, with the Port Newark Channel on the north side and the Elizabeth Channel on the south edge. There was a container ship anchored some distance away in the middle of the bay. The immense red and white container cranes were clearly visible. Tom imagined the man inside the one closest to L.T.D. Shipping. The facility was brightly lit. He could see ancient pilings on the east side of the Bay, sticking out of the water. The current was coming in, as there were long depressions on the near side of the pilings. It was almost completely dark.

Agent Moss said, "Right on time."

As they started down the west side of the Bridge, an Air China 767 glided by silently from right to left on its way to Newark International Airport. It was at eye level, and remarkably close.

They got off at the first exit and onto Port Street, and then turned south on Corbin Street. That brought them to Tyler Street, the entrance to the Port Newark Container Terminal. They stopped next to the Security Kiosk. The gate in front of them was heavy and operated electronically. The rain picked up. It was 5:20 p.m.

"There are three men in the booth, Steve. Is that Butler?"

"Can't tell."

The door to the Kiosk slid open, and a man in a heavy, black rubber raincoat with a big silver metal shield on the outside came to the car. Agent Moss lowered the window.

"Identification, gentlemen." Agent Moss handed out two I.D.s and Tom's driver's license. The guard went back to the security booth and shut the door.

"Well, that wasn't Butler."

"What do you think, Steve?"

"The third guy is probably a union requirement."

The door to the booth slid open, and the guard walked to the driver's window. He had a flashlight and motioned to lower the window. He put the light on the faces of Tom and Detective Napoli in the back seat and looked again at Agent Moss's face. The rain was beating hard on the roof of the Town Car. He handed the I.D.s through the window.

"You're expected at L.T.D. Shipping. Straight ahead as far as you can go, take a right on Export Street, and your first left on to Calcutta. L.T.D. is the last complex on the left."

"Thank you." The guard touched his cap with the flashlight as Moss put up the window.

The gate jerked into motion and slid open on a track behind the Kiosk. Agent Moss drove straight ahead about a quarter of a mile and turned onto Export Street. Tom looked up at the container cranes lined up along the dock. Brightly lit, they looked hazy in the steady rain. They stopped to let a straddle carrier rumble across the road, with a shipping container held tightly at the four bottom corners.

They turned left on Calcutta and into the L.T.D. Shipping Company parking lot, close to the end of the street. A guard stepped out of a small booth and waved them past with his flashlight, directing them to park in front of the stairs to the office.

"Look at the number of stairs. The offices look like they are ten feet above the ground. Did you know that, Steve?"

"I knew it was elevated, but the pictures didn't make it clear how much. All set, Mr. Strawbridge?"

Tom nodded and picked up his bags. Agent Moss got out, trotted over to Tom's side of the car, and opened the door. Moss held an umbrella for Tom and closed the car door after him. Tom noticed Moss was very sharply dressed. The car's locking mechanism beeped as they jogged up the steps. Detective Napoli was waiting for them under the canopy over the entrance.

There was an intercom to the left of the steel door. Tom was about to push the button when the speaker quickly crackled, "One minute, Mr. Strawbridge," Propakov. A few seconds later, the door opened to a stark entry hall. A stocky, expressionless man with an open shirt and a cap with the L.T.D. logo motioned in the three men. The man led them to an empty room on the left of the hall. He pointed to a coat tree in the corner and then to some chairs and went back to the hall without saying a word.

Tom had been told that the rooms would undoubtedly be mic'd. He wanted to say the interior of the facility seemed much bigger than he had expected. The room was clean and comfortable. There were photographs of L.T.D. facilities in different parts of the world and photos of their ships at sea, laden with logoed containers. The three men stood in a circle and made small talk about the weather.

The door on the opposite wall from the hall opened, and Yuri Propakov walked in, closing the door behind him. Propakov looked at the briefcase and the nylon gym bag on the conference table as he walked over to Tom.

They shook hands. "Mr. Propakov, this is Mr. William Thomas. A venture capitalist and my partner in the brooch. And please meet Mr. Francis Reneke, my driver and sometime security provider." Nobody smiled or said anything.

"Unfortunately, our associate will be unable to make our meeting, but he's sent another colleague on his behalf."

Moss, Napoli, and Tom said nothing.

"He sends his apologies and is disappointed not to be here."

Tom asked, "What is his name, Mr. Propakov?"

"It is not important. Before we begin, are any of you gentlemen carrying firearms?"

Tom looked at Detective Napoli, who shook his head and said, "No."

Agent Moss said, "I am."

"Mr. Strawbridge, Mr. Reneke can either leave his weapon with Josh and join us," nodding to a man in a cheap suit who was entering from the hall, "or remain here while we meet."

"What do you think, Bill?"

"I think he can wait here. Is there any reason Mr. Reneke cannot wait in the car?"

"No. But it is a miserable evening."

"What do you prefer, Frank?"

"I'll be in the car. Call me when you are ready, and I'll be up with the umbrella." The man near the hall led Agent Moss to the door. From where Tom was standing, he could see Moss through the curtain wall walk quickly down the stairs and get into the car.

"I hope you don't mind, but we must frisk you, as you say in America."

Tom shrugged his shoulders, and the man patted him down and then grunted at the two bags on the table. Tom opened the gym bag. "That is a piece of jewelry."

"Open," a heavy Eastern European accent.

Tom opened and closed the brooch's box. He opened his briefcase, and the man put his hand in and moved the cotton gloves from one end to the other. Satisfied, he patted down Detective Napoli.

Propakov said, "Please follow me" and led them through the door opposite the hall.

A rectangular conference table with eight chairs sat in the center of the room. The man with the cheap suit closed the door behind them and stood against it. There was a large window running almost the entire length of the room on the parking-lot side.

"Please be seated, gentlemen. May we offer something to drink?"

"No, thank you."

"Not for me."

"I will be back directly." Propakov left the room.

Tom asked Detective Napoli how he saw the markets preforming for the balance of the year.

"About the same as now." He took out his phone and began scrolling through messages.

A minute later, the door opened, and Propakov entered. Three men followed him in. Matteo Keller, Viktor Donskoi, and Igor Yatkin!

CHAPTER 39

Saturday Evening

YATKIN WAS DRESSED in a navy Armani suit and a black open-collared shirt. Tom had come across men like Yatkin before. Powerful and ruthless.

As they stood up, Napoli said to Tom, "I sent that text."

Tom wasn't sure if that meant he'd alerted the team that Yatkin was there—or something else. While Propakov was introducing Napoli to the others, Tom reached into his left pants pocket, and hit the fob button on his keys. He brought his hand out, holding his loupe.

Tom shook hands with Keller and Donskoi. Yatkin was introduced as Vasili Aldeberg, a shipping magnate and serious collector of fine art and world-class gemstones. Everyone sat down. Napoli and Tom were sitting with their backs to the large window. They were offered drinks by Yatkin, who poured himself a glass of water from a pitcher in the center of the table.

"I am sorry my colleague could not be here." He spoke good English.

"Well, we understand from Mr. Propakov there wasn't much interest in the end. But because of the uniqueness of the item, and the unusual circumstances, we felt your associate should see it anyway. There are not many customers for a piece like this. And even fewer who could fully appreciate the remarkable provenance. Let alone manage the payment requirements. Perhaps this will lead to further business, if nothing else." Tom was his usual smooth self. He looked at Detective Napoli, who smiled awkwardly and nodded at the men across the table.

Tom opened his briefcase and took several pairs of cotton gloves, a black-velvet display pad, and penlights, white and ultraviolet fluorescent, and put everything on the table. Tom reached into the nylon bag, picked up the brooch's box, and put it on the velvet pad in front of him. Yatkin never took his eyes off Tom's. Tom handed a pair of gloves to Yatkin.

"Do you need a loupe?"

"That won't be necessary." Keller put a loupe on the table.

Another man in a brown suit came in from the back office door and stood in front of it, bookending the man on the opposite door.

Tom opened the box and turned it away from him. He stood up and placed the tray in front of Yatkin. Yatkin surprised Tom by smiling broadly as he put on the cotton gloves. "As advertised. A picture could not do justice."

Tom leveled a stare at Propakov and Keller. Donskoi's phone rang, and he got up and went out the door.

"You've seen a picture?" Napoli tapped Tom's shoe with his.

Yatkin, unapologetically and still smiling, "Of course."

Yatkin picked up the brooch and turned it over to examine the back. He knew what he was doing. He louped the setting carefully. He then louped every stone on the front of the piece. When he was done, he carefully put the brooch back in the box. He gestured at it, looking to Keller and Propakov. When they shook their heads, Yatkin closed the top of the box.

As Yatkin was taking off the gloves, he said, "You know, of course, $63,000,000 is out of the question."

"I see. Well, you are interested?"

"Maybe. Do you mind giving us a minute?"

Tom nodded, "Of course."

The man at the door closed it behind Yatkin, Keller, and Propakov. The first man with the cheap suit remained at the opposite door. Tom stood up and put his briefcase on the table. He put back and arranged the unused gloves, display pad, and penlights.

"What do you think?"

"I wish you could have left the picture bit alone."

The man at the inner door was staring blankly. Tom wondered how much the task-force team for Operation Double Take was hearing. And what, if anything, they were seeing. Tom's job was done. He stood up and walked to the window. The rain had turned to a drizzle. Tom nodded down at Agent Moss, who sat motionless behind the wheel of the Lincoln. The whole of Port Newark Terminal was brightly lit, as was the L.T.D. office complex. The streetlamps had hazy halos surrounding them. He looked up at the cab of the closest container crane. A large window closest to the office was open. Napoli came and stood next to Tom. He held his phone so Tom could see "Everyone is in position. Out as soon as you can."

As the door opened into the meeting room, they watched a car drive from behind the west end of the office, across the parking lot, and turn right out the gate. Yatkin came back and sat down. The same man closed the door behind him and stood in front of it, clasping his wrist over his belt buckle. Tom and Napoli took their chairs.

"Unfortunately, my colleagues have another meeting and had to leave." He sat back in his chair and stared at Tom and Detective Napoli. The atmosphere had completely changed.

Starting to stand, "Well, Mr. Thomas and I will be on our way then. Thank you for your time."

"Sit down, Mr. Strawbridge," aggressively, actually commanding him.

"Here is what is going to happen. You will put the jewel on the table and walk out of here immediately. We have paid you handsomely for the blue diamond, which is not yet in our possession. I feel that amount will cover the brooch as well." Napoli stiffened instinctively.

"You have paid me part of what you owe me for the diamond."

Tom could see and feel that Yatkin's move reflected the way he was wired and, therefore, his default operating approach. Tom was ready to comply, hopeful, if not confident, that the brooch would be returned safely once Yatkin was taken into custody. But he felt the dance had to go on for legitimacy's sake.

Smiling, with an air of condescension, "And why would I do that?"

"Let's just go, Tom." Detective Napoli's knee closest to Tom was bouncing.

"Stay seated! If you don't mind."

The man at the inner door to their left let go of his wrist and rolled his shoulders down and up.

"You'll do it because I say so."

"We may do it, but you'll never see the diamond, and there will be consequences."

"OK. Enough. Let's go, Tom."

"Quiet! Mr. Thomas!"

Turning to Tom, "You'll do it because I say so. And because of this," waving his hand to the inner office door.

The man to their left knocked twice on the door. It opened, revealing a man standing behind a woman sitting in a chair in front of him. Her hands were on her lap in front of her, wrists held together by zip ties. There was some kind of gag over her mouth and around her head. Her eyes went straight to Tom's. It was Max.

"Who is that!?"

Before the door was closed, the man in the meeting room produced a short-barreled pump shotgun that must have been leaning against the inside wall.

Flat and cool, "That, Bill, is a friend."

Napoli stood up so quickly his chair fell over backwards. The man pumped a shell into the chamber and pointed it at the floor in front of Detective Napoli. Yatkin stood up. The man in the cheap suit to their right pulled out a large caliber semi-automatic handgun and chambered a round. He held the gun to his side.

Walking toward the man with the shotgun, Yatkin said, "Now put the jewel on the table, and get out." Tom heard what he thought was the Town Car's door close. "As soon as you leave, your friend will be returned home. Get out. Now!"

The man with the pistol reached behind himself to open the door.

Tom bent down to pick up his bags. As he stood up, he heard a pop in the window glass behind him and splintered glass tinkle to the floor. A hole appeared below the right eye of the man with the shotgun. Simultaneously, the wall and part of the door behind his head were covered by a cloud of blood and matter. As the man slid down the wall, the shotgun discharged, hitting Detective Napoli in the left arm. The rest of the load blew out the majority of the window behind them.

Yatkin recoiled and burst through the door into the back office.

The man with the pistol yelled something unintelligible. Detective Napoli looked at him and jumped over the body and through the door. The man fired at and missed Napoli.

Tom dropped to the floor behind the chairs to his right. He got his hand in the outside flap of his briefcase and took out his Sig .380. The man with the pistol was on the opposite side of the table, heading toward the door after Napoli. Tom fired twice before he hit the man's ankle. The man went down. Tom ran around the table as the man raised his gun in Tom's direction. Tom fired three quick rounds at the man's wrist, almost severing the hand from his arm. Another shot from behind Tom put a bullet between the man's eyes. Agent Moss was standing in the doorway, lowering his weapon.

"This way, Strawbridge! Outside. Leave your things!"

Tom followed Agent Moss down the hall and out the door. There were two unmarked cars with interior and grill lights flashing blocking the gate. Three or four men were moving fast around both sides of the office. At the bottom of the stairs, they heard two shots from behind the office.

Agent Moss took Tom to one of the cars by the gate and left him with a plainclothesman. Tom recognized the officer from the second meeting at the precinct. The officer's Kevlar vest seemed to be for a much larger man. Tom released the clip and cycled the round in the chamber out of the Sig and put it in his suit pocket. He loosened his tie. An N.Y.P.D. ambulance came down Tyler Street and turned in the gate. The officer with Tom moved one of the cars, and the ambulance drove in and up to the front of the office.

Ten minutes later, six men in single file, agents and police on either side, walked from behind the west side of the office. The six men's hands were behind them, held together with zip ties. A minute later, an officer walked Max around the side of the office and over to the other police vehicle near Tom.

Finally, Chief Monahan appeared holding Yatkin's elbow. Another officer walked behind, with his handgun at his side. Yatkin had been shot in the arm.

A man dressed in black from head to toe emerged out of the mist from the street and walked quickly between the two unmarked vehicles. The skin around his eyes was visible. A white oval. The man picked up his pace and moved quickly toward the stairs to the office. He had a long, black sniper rifle with a long, thick silencer slung over his shoulder. He was ignored by everyone, as he took the stairs two at a time.

Tom noticed Detective Napoli standing at the back of the open ambulance. Napoli put his right hand up. Tom returned the gesture.

Agent Moss was walking toward Tom with his coat, the nylon bag, and his briefcase.

"I shouldn't be doing this, but there isn't much doubt about what went down. Let's not discuss it, anyway."

"Thanks. How's Bill?"

Moss laughed. "You are cool, Strawbridge. He'll be fine. Three or four double or triple O buckshot in the upper arm. One probably hit the bone. Lucky. Go over."

"OK."

"I'll put your things in the back seat of this car. It'll be 15 minutes or so before I can let someone take you home."

Tom saw Max sitting in the back of the other car, talking to two officers through the window.

"Can I see my friend?"

"Go see Steve, and I'll let you know when you come back. They are doing the preliminary interview."

Tom thanked Agent Moss and started across the parking lot. Four more N.Y.P.D. vehicles with lights flashing pulled up to the gate as Tom got to the ambulance. For the first time, Tom noticed the noise from a helicopter hovering over Newark Bay just off the dock. Detective Napoli was sitting on the back of the ambulance, with his feet on the ground. Two paramedics were working on his arm.

"Hi, Bill. Congratulations."

"We got him. The Chief is beside himself."

"How are you doing?"

"Lucky. You?"

"Probably heading into shock."

"What about the gun? I know you didn't answer when Propakov asked us."

"Would you believe me if I told you I forgot it was there?"

"No."

"I couldn't decide at home. So, I stuck it in the outside flap of my briefcase, fully planning on disclosing it if asked. When he didn't find it. . . . well, I don't know."

"Good work, anyway. There are a lot of things that need explanations and a few surprises to review."

"Can I do anything?"

"Go home. We'll be in touch."

Agent Moss met Tom halfway across the parking lot and walked back to the car with him.

"That officer standing by the car will drive you home. Do you think you need to see a doctor? Do you feel all right?"

"I do."

"Here's my direct cell number. Call anytime if you think you need help or want to talk."

Tom took his card. "Thank you. And thanks again for everything."

"You have one sentence to say goodnight to your friend."

Tom walked over to the car Max was in. The two officers nodded and moved a few feet away, toward the back of the car.

Tom leaned down to the open window.

"Hi, Tom. I think I've made my decision."

Epilogue

CHAPTER 40

Later Saturday Night

It was 11:15 p.m. before Tom got to his apartment. The officer who drove him back into the City left the police scanner band loud enough so Tom could hear most of the follow-up communications regarding Operation Double Take.

Matteo Keller, Yuri Propakov, and Viktor Donskoi had been in the car that Detective Napoli and Tom had watched leave the L.T.D. facility just before Igor Yatkin had returned to the office. The car was followed by one of the mobile units all the way to Teterboro Airport. Two other teams were already in position at Teterboro, and they were taken into custody without incident.

Keller and Propakov were eventually convicted on violations of the National Stolen Property act. The Act prohibits the interstate or international transportation of proceeds of theft and forged securities, as well as the receipt or fencing of stolen property, forged securities, or tools for forging securities.

The investigation led to proof of several other crimes committed by Keller that had been under investigation. He was convicted on four counts of the National Stolen Property Act and received a sentence of thirty years.

Yuri Propakov was convicted on two counts of the National Stolen Property Act. Further investigations led to a conviction of one count of Utility Fraud relating to natural-gas price gouging in Eastern Europe. He received a sentence of twenty-five years.

Viktor Donskoi caved immediately. He turned state's witness and copped a plea. His testimony and information led to the arrest of Boris Reznikov and nine others in Palm Beach and the New York and New Jersey areas. He received a sentence of four years, with ten years of probation upon his release.

In the Weeks That Followed

The N.Y.P.D. had played hardball regarding the reward. They based their position on Tom potentially endangering the welfare of N.Y.P.D. Officers and F.B.I. Agents because he'd used his weapon. David Mitchell argued that Tom had never been told not to carry his handgun. Further, by disabling the second gunman, Tom probably saved Detective Napoli's life. Tom had received extensive positive notoriety in the press because of his involvement in the recapture of Igor Yatkin. After six weeks and threatening to go public with the potential reneging of the reward, the team of N.Y.P.D. and F.B.I. attorneys settled on a reward of $20,000,000. Tax free.

Because of the ongoing negotiations, Tom had heard from no one in the department after his full day of interviews and debriefings the Sunday after the operation. The day after the reward was settled, Tom received an email from Chief Monahan's office, asking him to come downtown for a meeting.

In the meeting room with the spectacular view of the Brooklyn Bridge, Tom was joined by Chief Monahan, Detective Napoli, and Special Agent Moss. He was greeted warmly. The Chief told Tom that Robert Moss had gone through an internal investigation because of his shooting of the second gunman. After the inquiry concluded, Moss received a promotion and became Special F.B.I. Liaison to the N.Y.P.D. A newly created position. Detective Napoli had recovered from his injuries quickly and was promoted to Detective First Grade for his contributions to Operation Double Take.

Max had been picked up outside her apartment on her way to lunch with Heidi. Two of Yatkin's men each took an arm and put her in the back of a van. She was taken to the L.T.D. Shipping facility in Port Newark. She was not harmed or mistreated, and she had been told she was part of an elaborate practical joke at the expense of her "boyfriend." The men were identified, as a result of Viktor Donskoi's information. Each man was sentenced to a minimum of twenty years, without parole, on kidnapping charges.

Tom had indeed seen men watching his apartment. He asked Monahan if it was surprising that the Yatkin crew had taken this tack. He was told it was Boris Reznikov's plan. Monahan told Tom that the men apparently thought Tom would collapse as soon as Yatkin got tough, and they would not even have to reveal Max's presence.

Monahan went on to say Igor Yatkin had a very particular and deviant psychological profile. A severe form of something known as "Conduct Disorder." The N.Y.P.D. psychiatrists noted that the theft of the brooch, specifically the money side, was of much less importance than the bullying and the thrill of kidnapping. In other words, Yatkin was largely motivated by power fantasies.

When she got home Saturday night, Max told Heidi everything. Including her friendship with Tom. Her confession caused an immediate rift between the two old friends, and Heidi had moved to an apartment of her own within the month.

Tom told the cops about the Alexandrite Propakov had left with him on memorandum. When Tom was done, Monahan said Propakov had told his interrogators about the gemstone. He had said, "Mr. Strawbridge will know what to do." Tom asked if that meant he should tell the police if and when it was sold, and turn over the proceeds to the N.Y.P.D. Monahan shrugged his shoulders.

Chief Monahan openly expressed his relief at the recapturing of Igor Yatkin. The well-orchestrated escape had been the singular blemish on his entire career. Monahan told him that Tom had been proposed for and would be given New York City's Bronze Medallion, the City's highest civilian honor. Tom accepted the award at a special City Hall ceremony the following January. The Mayor and the Governor were in attendance, and the event was well attended.

Six Months Later

Christie's had created a separate catalog for the brooch's sale in the May Magnificent Jewel Auction. The catalog detailed the brooch's extraordinary history and had extensive personal biographies of everyone involved. It featured the original designs, gemstone counts, and the original ledgers from the Paris Van Cleef & Arpels shop. Full-page pictures of everyone, including the former King and Queen of Yugoslavia. The current owner had asked for anonymity. Tom's role was glorified in the catalog. Having been dubbed early in his career as "The Indiana Jones of the Gem World" by *The Philadelphia Inquirer Magazine*, Tom's legend and brand were further strengthened. The trade was green with envy. The April *Wall Street Journal Magazine* had featured the brooch and Tom in an article. The Christie's marketing department had christened the brooch *The Queen Rose.*

The Head of Christie's Jewelry Department told Tom that they had never seen more interest for any item ever put up at auction. Every major dealer, all the great museums, countless private buyers, collectors and, of course, Van Cleef themselves.

They agreed to Tom's usual seller's commission arrangement—0% between the reserve and low estimate, and 3% of the hammer price above the low estimate. They wanted to set the reserve at $50,000,000 and the estimate at $55,000,000 to $60,000,000. Tom insisted on a reserve of $55,000,000 with an estimated range of $55,000,000 to $65,000,000.

Marla Wingate insisted that she and Tom split anything over $40,000,000 based on Tom's work. He did not argue. They had grown close since Operation Double Take, and she was anxious for the sale to take place without her status as owner being discovered.

Christie's had connected two major galleries to allow for as many guests and bidders as possible. There was a lottery system set up for people who were not bidding but wanted to attend. The last time these exhibition rooms had been configured similarly was for the Elizabeth Taylor estate jewelry sale.

The sale room was wide enough to allow for three sections of chairs, to reduce the amount of climbing over each other for the attendees. To the right of the auction podium, there were fifteen people lined up, manning telephones. Next to them were nine people to ensure all Internet bidding was correctly received and acknowledged. Four spotters walked the aisles, making sure no raised paddles were overlooked. The digital screen showing each lot and the currency conversion key column was immense. To the left was an equally immense picture of "*The Queen Rose*."

Tom and Marla Wingate were in the center section, second row on the left aisle. As the last lots came up in the regular Sale, Tom was calculating his potential profit on his one purchase of the day. An 8.00 carat Sugarloaf Kashmir sapphire that was heavily worn and needed re-polishing.

Francois Puriel hammered the last lot, and the room fell quiet. He thanked everyone and announced there would be a 10-minute recess before the sale of *The Queen Rose*.

Tom and Marla Wingate, like several other VIPs, had reserved seats. They had arrived halfway through the regular sale. Puriel stepped off the podium, and the screen showing the last lot changed to *The Queen Rose*. There were now two huge images of the brooch on the front wall.

The silence instantly transformed into a din. A small crowd formed around Tom, and he stood up, looking down on everyone, and began shaking hands. He did not introduce Marla Wingate to anyone. Tom did not know half of the people in the small crowd, and several just watched or listened as others asked Tom questions.

As Francois Puriel was taking his position behind the podium, Lily appeared and took Tom's arm. They walked to the front of the sale room, just in front of and below Puriel. The camera shutters sounded like a swarm of insects. As she thanked him for all the positive comments he had made in the press about Van Cleef & Arpels, he realized this was a photo opportunity. For Lily. He smiled and returned to his seat.

Puriel looked at Tom. "Attention, everyone. The moment is upon us."

Marla Wingate, who was wearing a stunning tailored black Celine suit, took a lavender scarf out of her purse. She tucked it into Tom's breast pocket.

"Good evening. Welcome to the sale of *The Queen Rose.* We all know the extraordinary history and provenance of this remarkable jewel. But I remind you all: the successful buyer will agree to a six-month loan of the brooch for a special exhibition at the Louvre, before taking possession."

A murmur swelled across the sale room.

"We have nine bids already. We start the bidding at $60 million. Do I have $60 million $500 thousand?"

All the telephones were engaged. A man on the opposite aisle in the front row put up his hand.

"$60 million $500 hundred thousand to the gentleman in front."

Tom did not know him.

"$61 million. Do we have $61 million?" His singsong cadence was in good form.

A young woman on one of the landlines put up her hand excitedly.

"61 million with Jennifer on the phone."

Looking down at the last bidder, "$61 million $500 thousand?"

The bidding slowed down, and Puriel was in no rush. A grandstander by nature, he was in his element.

Ten minutes later, "$67 million $500 thousand to the lady against the wall. $68 million? Do we have $68 million? Last chance for anyone. We are selling it now. $67 million $500 thousand, with me. In the room. $67 million $500 thousand. $67 million $500 thousand." He brought the gavel down hard on the podium. The room erupted in applause.

Tom looked at Marla Wingate. "Congratulations."

"Thank you, Tom. A long road. Let's get out of here."

On their way out, Tom saw Lily surrounded by a crowd of people. She was shaking hands.

About the Author

Flawless is P.C. Schneirla's debut novel. Peter is a well-known presence in the diamond, gemstone, and luxury goods industries, having built his career in those arenas over the course of the last four decades. A recognized jewelry and gemstone expert, he can often be seen striding from one meeting to the next in New York City's famed Diamond District. He is a unique bon vivant, a charismatic and charming personality, and a true Renaissance Man in terms of his abilities, interests, and pursuits.

Peter has spent half of his career in the jewelry industry as an entrepreneur and half at international luxury brands. He has owned and operated his own business, P.C Schneirla, Inc. (schneirla.com) for over 30 years, and he has also held notable corporate positions, serving most recently as the Vice Chairman of Harry Winston and the Chief Gemologist of Tiffany & Co.

Peter holds a Graduate Gemologist Degree from the Gemological Institute of America and has achieved the status of Fellow of the prestigious Gemological Association of Great Britain. He has taught at The New School for Social Research and was a faculty member of the Jewelry Design Department of the Fashion Institute of Technology. In addition to appearing on CNN, Good Morning America, the Charlie Rose Show, and The Curse of Oak Island, he was dubbed "the Indiana Jones of the gem world" by the Philadelphia Inquirer Magazine. Peter wrote and published "Tiffany: 150 Years of Gems and Jewelry," and curated their sesquicentennial exhibition at The Field Museum of Chicago and The American Museum of Natural History in New York City.

Peter has traveled extensively to most of the important worldwide gemstone and diamond mining locations. He is an accomplished competitive international fly-fisherman, outdoor photographer, painter, musician, and now published fiction author.

P.C. Schneirla resides in Key West, Florida with his beautiful wife and his spirited German Shepherd, and he is currently hard at work on his second novel.